# REBELS & REJECTS

## R.A. SMYTH

Rebels & Rejects

Rebels & Rejects Copyright © 2022 R.A. Smyth

ISBN: 978-1-915456-00-7

Cover by Pretty in Ink Creations
Interior Design by Nikki Epperson.
Editing by Lunar Rose Editing.
Formatting by Rachel Smyth.

*Blood will be shed.*

*Lives will be lost.*

*Retribution will be dealt.*

I work in the darkness that is Black Creek. If there's a secret to uncover, a package to deliver, or a story to be told, I'm your girl. I'll do whatever it takes to provide for my little brother.

Once upon a time, The Feral Beasts ruled Black Creek with an iron fist, but they're long gone now. The Antonelli family stepped in, only caring about their family and their money. I've heard the whispers... The Reaper Rejects are growing and they want control of Black Creek. But this town isn't big enough for the both of them.

When the leaders of the Rejects ask for my help, I'm reluctant. Trouble follows gang life. I shouldn't want to get involved, but Oliver knows just how to tempt me, and the pain in Cain's eyes calls to my need for vengeance.

**A war is coming and this town has never been more deadly.**

This will be your only warning. If you're looking for a sweet romance, this book is not that. This is a story of vengeance; of justice; of righting wrongs and standing up for yourself. For not settling in life, and instead fighting for what you rightly deserve. It's about opening your heart and mind to new possibilities and seeing your enemies in a new light. This book is about fighting for what might feel impossible. It's dark and gritty. It's violent and masochistic. It's everything you love and hate in dark romance. So continue at your own risk, and remember...this is only the start.

Black Creek will be a 4 book series that will ultimately end in an HEA—after one hell of a rollercoaster. So buckle up and enjoy the ride.

# *Black Creek Playlist*

DEVIL – Shinedown
Closer – Nine Inch Nails
S&M – Rihanna
I Get Off – Halestorm
Addicted – Saving Abel
Pavement – SayWeCanFly
Cold – Crossfade
Move Your Body – My Darkest Days
Riot – Three Days Grace
Breakdown – Seether
Live Like Legends – Ruelle
Infamous – The Faim
Always – Saliva
Down And Out – Tantric
Lowlife – Theory of a Deadman
Up All Night – Hinder
Monsters – Shinedown
Start A War – Klergy, Valerie Broussard
...And many more

Check out my Facebook Group for the list
– Rachel's Rebel Rehab

## Prologue

*Eight years ago*

"P-p-please," the pathetic sack of shit at my feet pleads. "I told you everything I k-know."

I tilt my head as I stare down at him impassively, noting every shake and tremble of his body as I press the muzzle of my gun against the center of his forehead. Why do they always beg? They know who I am, who I represent. They know we don't offer mercy. Who would want to die groveling on their fucking knees? When my time comes, I wanna go out staring death straight in the face, giving it a final *fuck you*.

*Bang*. There's minimal kickback from the revolver as the loud sound ricochets off the stone walls, echoing around the dark alley. The bullet makes a perfect circle in the front of the scumbag's forehead, and I watch as he crumples into a heap on the ground, feeling absolutely nothing—no remorse, no guilt. Not even happiness or satisfaction at a job well done. There's something fundamentally wrong with me. My father knows it too. Apparently, the fact that I'm incapable of feeling emotions is a good thing. It's why I'll be the most ruthless leader the Antonellis have ever had. Because it means I can make the hard decisions, do what needs to be done—like kill this sorry fucker who thought he could spy on us—and still sleep like a baby tonight.

Staring down at the sorry sack of shit, I take in the pool of blood around his head that's growing progressively larger and his saggy, sallow skin that looks yellow in the dim light from the flickering street lamp down the block. Something sparks within me. It's small, and it disappears before I can place it. Hunger maybe? It definitely has a heady feel to it.

"Hey!" a voice barks from behind me. The deep bellow is followed by the sounds of a scuffle that draws my attention away from the corpse at my feet, and turning around, I find Lor wrestling to contain a scrawny little street urchin in his arms. The kid is writhing and kicking out as he grunts and groans with exertion, attempting to escape the bands of steel wrapped around his waist. He's so busy fighting against Lor that he is oblivious to the real threat observing him closely—me.

Whoever the fuck this kid is, he's just seen me commit a crime. Not that I'm worried he'll go to the police. *Ha, that's a laugh*. Every police officer in this city is in someone's pocket. If it's not ours, it's The Feral Beasts or one of the other smaller gangs running around in this rat-infested city. Regardless of

2

whose pocket they're in, none of them would dare pull any of us in.

No, what I can't have is this bag of bones running off and telling The Feral Beasts that I've just taken out one of their moles. They'll find out in a few days when they don't hear from him, only it will be too late. By then, we will have fished out the other fuckers they've planted within our organization.

"Let me go!" the little thing snarls out, surprising me. It's not just the angry tone and defiant boldness that catches me off guard, but the high pitch of the voice.

He's not a he, but a *she*—a girl.

I cast my eyes over her squirming frame once again, but it's impossible to see any curves or tits in those baggy clothes that hang off her scrawny frame. By the looks of things, she's too fucking skinny to have any anyway.

"Why would he do that?" I bark out in a deep, menacing growl that thunders through the narrow alley. She instantly freezes in Lor's arms, her head snapping up to meet my steely gaze as I slowly close the distance between us. My heavy boots boom with every step I take until I loom over her, casting her in shadow.

She peers up at me with wide, fearful eyes as I silently take her in. There's nothing special about her. Coated in dirt and grime, with her dark hair like a bird's nest, filled with knots and split ends, she looks like some sort of feral animal; a wildcat—similar to every other street urchin... except for those eyes. Even in the poor lighting, those endless pools of blue hold me captive. They're a brilliant cerulean, like how I imagine the Caribbean Sea looks. Not that I've ever seen it in real life, but I've caught a glimpse of it on TV. It's one of those scenes you can't tear your eyes from. You're convinced you can see right to the seabed at the bottom, read all of the secrets hidden in its dark depths, but it's a lie. While it draws you in, making you think you can see more than you can; in reality, it holds all of its mysteries close, unwilling to give any of them up.

The girl's eyebrows draw together, and her chin lifts in defiance, probably thinking my silence is a scare tactic and not that she just rendered me mute. I shake off the weird feeling she's evoked and give a slight jerk of my head, silently telling Lor to let the girl go. Before she can scamper away, I grab ahold of her arm with my free hand. My gun is still clasped in my other, and I bring it up to aim at her head, watching as the fight instantly drains out of her and she goes stock-still in my grip. Her eyes widen, making her look like a deer caught in headlights, but unlike the sorry sack of shit behind me, she doesn't collapse to her knees at the realization she's about to die. Instead, she surprises me by setting her jaw into a hard line and pushing back her shoulders. Straightening her spine, she stares brazenly back at me. *Hell, she's got bigger balls than most of the men who find themselves on the wrong end of my revolver.*

However, despite her bravado, I can see the terror in her eyes. It's the same fear everyone seems to experience when they realize their time is up. Seeing it doesn't bother me, though. If anything, it just makes me more curious about human nature. I don't understand the notion of fear. It seems pointless. Yet, looking into her captivating eyes as she blinks rapidly—as if hoping she can just blink the scene in front of her away—for the first time in my life, it makes me pause. I don't want to have to kill her. *What the fuck is happening to me?* It must be because she's a kid. I've never killed anyone so young before. That's gotta be it.

We both continue to stare at one another, and I recognize the flicker of warmth that ignites in my chest. I've felt

4

it only a handful of times in my life and it always seems to extinguish before I can place it. But not today. Instead, it sits there in my chest, simmering at a low heat, like the dying embers of a fire. It's still too small for me to identify, but it's present all the same.

*What is this? Who is she?* Questions arise to the forefront of my mind as my gaze bores into hers, hungrily seeking answers. She returns my stare unbidden, and I have no idea what she sees when she looks into my soulless eyes. Can she glimpse the monster I am? Or am I nothing more than a cold, hard, unreadable shell?

The whole time, she spears me with her incensed glare. Fearful but defiant 'til the very end. It's impressive.

Keeping the barrel pointed at her forehead, I lift my thumb and pull back on the hammer, cocking the gun. She startles at the sound of the loud click before hardening her features again, refusing to let me peer any deeper into her psyche. I press my finger against the trigger, knowing what I need to do. It's easy. Merely the flexing of a finger, and yet...

A lifetime seems to pass in a single moment as her life hangs in the balance, while I find myself struggling for the first time in my life with knowing what needs to be done. Her death was written in the stars as soon as Lor caught her. And yet something I can't quite put my finger on is urging me to go against the rules of the Family, rules that are ingrained into the very fabric of my being.

Time ticks on, one long second after another, as my finger repeatedly tenses against the trigger before hesitation hits, and I relax it again.

She needs to die.

But...

She's a witness.

Still...

Without giving the action any conscious thought, I ease my finger off the trigger and drop my arm down to my side, ignoring the flash of confusion that darkens her irises. Using my tight grip on her arm, I yank her into me so I can hiss in her ear, "If you mention this to anyone, I'll fucking gut you," before flinging her backward, away from me. The distance between us allows me to take a much-needed breath that thankfully douses the confusing heat in my chest.

She stumbles before quickly righting herself, gaping at me in astonishment, most likely unable to comprehend how she's still alive; how she's about to walk away with her life. Trust me, it's something I'm still struggling to understand.

"Get the fuck out of here before I change my mind," I bark when she makes no move to run. "Don't show your face here again!"

Without a second's hesitation, she sprints for the end of the alleyway and ducks out of sight. In her absence, I can feel the heavy weight of Lor's gaze on me, and when I finally look away from the spot where the baffling girl disappeared, I find him watching me with a mixture of surprise and confusion.

"Boss?" he questions. I don't fucking blame him. For the first time in my life, I just showed someone mercy, and a witness, no less. One of our cardinal rules is that witnesses can't be allowed to live. Witnesses who walk, talk. It's as simple as that. Only the dead can keep secrets.

"Follow her," I order. "Make sure she doesn't talk to anyone."

His gaze lingers on me for a second longer before he nods, following after the kid who has somehow managed to fuck with my head. I stand and watch the darkness swallow him up as he disappears down the alley, still trying to wrap my head

6

around what just happened. I've never disobeyed an order. Never put our Family at risk by letting someone who I know needs to die, live. Whatever that girl did to me, it's a weakness I can't afford. A shortcoming I can't let my father know about.

Pretending like my interaction with the street urchin never occurred, I turn on my heel and stride out of the alley toward my awaiting car and climb in. On the outside, I'm the epitome of calm and control. No one else would be aware of the inner turmoil currently whipping up a storm within me. Whatever that spark of warmth was that that girl ignited, as much as I want to pretend I never felt its electrifying heat, there's a more prominent part of me that wants to feel its soft caress again.

# SAWYER

## Chapter 1

With a final shove and a grunt, the package rolls over the side of the dock, splashing into the black ocean below. It bobs on the surface for a moment before the water drags it under, welcoming the tarp-wrapped shitstain into her murky depths where he can forever rot amongst the fishes and algae.

*So long, motherfucker. May you forever burn in hell.*

Turning my back on the water, I pull the burner phone out of my pocket and fire off a quick text to confirm the job is done. While I wait for a response, I pull up my contacts, find the number I'm looking for, and call it.

Arnie answers on the first ring. "Yup?"

"Got a delivery for you down by the docks."

"A good one?"

I smirk. "I think you'll be pretty happy. Brand new Camaro."

He lets out an appreciative whistle. "Alright, kid. I'll get someone down to pick her up now. It's late, get yourself home."

As I'm hanging up the phone, I receive an alert that payment for tonight's job has been received. Finished here, I pull out a Henley and black leather jacket out of my duffel bag, pulling the top on over my bralette and slipping into the jacket before slinging the bag over my back. I lift my helmet off the seat and push it on over my head as I lift a leg to straddle Raven, my black Ducati Streetfighter. She was payment for making sure Arnie's daughter's abusive boyfriend didn't keep coming around to harass her... that, and thanks for the regular work I send his way. Arnie is a balding, brick wall of a man in his mid-fifties. Covered in tattoos and with a RAP sheet the length of his arm, he's not someone you wanna mess with, although what he doesn't let most people see is that he's a fucking softie underneath his hard exterior. He runs the chop shop in Black Creek, so he's someone most people want to keep on their good side, and *man*, does he get some of the sweetest rides. Sometimes, on nights like tonight, I get to send him an expensive car that he can make some decent money from, even though his warehouse is full of cars that are already worth a fucking fortune. I have no idea how he accrued so many, but hey, who was I to complain, especially when he told me to pick any ride I wanted. I'm telling you, it was a hard choice. Most of the cars he had were models I would never be able to afford, but when I saw this beauty hiding at the back of his shop, I knew I had to have her.

Starting the ignition, I rev the engine, loving the deep rumble and resounding roar as I peel out of the docks onto the street. People stop to stare as I pass by, but no one can see who I am with my full-face helmet and black-tinted visor on. I prefer it that way, to be a faceless person in the crowd. It's the only way to survive in Black Creek. If anyone knows your name here, it's because they have some sort of beef with you.

I ride through the derelict city, and even though it's late, the streets here are never quiet. There are always homeless people trying to carve out a safe corner for themselves, gang members patrolling their territory, and hookers shaking their tits in the hopes of earning themselves enough to buy a solid meal the next day. It never used to be so bad. Black Creek has always been home to vagrants and outlaws, but there was some sort of order before—when The Feral Beasts ruled the town. Sure, they instilled fear in the hearts of residents, and the streets ran red with just as much blood as they do now, but there was order to the chaos. Now, it's just complete and utter mayhem.

Broadly speaking, you could divide the city into three main territories based on who they belong to. The Antonellis own the docks, Grim Bastards have laid claim to most of the East District, and the Reaper Rejects are quickly accruing land in the Downtown area. The problem is, any part of the city that isn't owned by one of these three has been snatched up by small, disorganized street gangs, evidently breaking the city up into a multitude of different pieces. It's impossible to keep track of who owns what, and each gang is just as dimwitted as the last. Boys with guns and absolutely zero common sense. Idiots who will shoot first and ask questions later, and then think they're big shit because they strut around with a gun that's bigger than their dicks. It's just asking for trouble, and with each passing day, tensions rise. Rival gangs are at each other's throats, and all of them are dissatisfied with the tiny bit of land they occupy.

It's hitting two a.m. when I slow down, pulling into a small garage hidden behind an abandoned building. I'm a block away from my apartment, but I don't dare park Raven on the street—she'd be stripped and sold for parts before sunrise. I also don't need people questioning how I came about owning her. She's all pretty and new looking, with her shiny black fairing—not something that just anyone in Black Creek can afford. Don't get me wrong, there's the odd, brand spanking new Benz or SUV that's obviously stolen, but for the most part, gangsters drive around in souped-up Buicks or Lincolns, with their arms hanging out the window, thinking they look like hot shit. The point is, everyone knows it's only gang members who can get their hands on that sort of thing. And anyone who knows me knows I have absolutely zero fucking affiliations with any gangs. They bring nothing but trouble and heartache to the everyday residents of Black Creek, those who are just trying to carve out some sort of existence for themselves.

Anyone who had the means or opportunity to leave Black Creek left years ago, back when I was barely more than a baby. It was apparent back then—as soon as The Feral Beasts started making a name for themselves—that things were only going to go from bad to worse. Whoever is left has stayed because they crave the life of being an outlaw, with all its bloodshed and violence, or because they couldn't leave. They didn't have the money, they couldn't risk the livelihood they had here, or some other reason kept them trapped. I, unfortunately, fall into category B—I can't leave. I grew up here. I work my fucking ass off to make a living here for myself. I don't even know what the fuck I'd do if I moved to another town. My skill

12

set is not exactly transferable nor is it one that can be applied to most legal occupations. So, I guess, for now, I'm stuck here. And on days like today, when I rid the city of one more piece of trash, I'm okay with that. Ask me again tomorrow, though. I'll most likely have a different answer.

Turning off the engine, I remove my helmet and shake out my waist-length, copper-colored hair, and climb off the bike. Patting the seat in farewell, my chunky-heeled boots tap against the concrete floor as I walk out of the garage, closing and securing the door behind me.

Once I'm sure that she's safely tucked away for the night, I make the short walk to my apartment at a brisk pace, keeping my senses on high alert. You can never let your guard down in Black Creek, especially not at this time of night. No matter who you are, no one is safe in this town.

I've just rounded the corner onto my street when I hear a gunshot go off, but it sounds like it's several blocks away, so it's nothing to worry about. I pick up my pace nonetheless and quickly reach my dilapidated apartment building that is covered in graffiti and looks like it's one minor earth-rumbling tremor away from collapsing. Heading inside, I stride past the elevator that has been out of service since I moved in here five years ago, and hike up the dimly lit stairwell to the top floor, hurrying past bland, paint-peeling doorways until I reach number twenty-three. My apartment.

Sticking my key in the lock, I have to jiggle it before the mechanism gives and the door opens into a gloomy interior. The only light is the faint glow of the TV, bathing the small apartment in an array of colors as images flicker across the screen, which has been left on. I scowl. *Seriously? Every night. How difficult is it to turn the TV off after yourself?*

My apartment is tiny—barely enough space for two people to co-exist. A narrow kitchen with chipped cabinet doors and a linoleum floor that, no matter what I do, always bubbles up, has a view into the living room through a window cut in the separating wall. The living room isn't much bigger. It just about fits a television set, a side table, and a small sofa wedged under a grimy window that constantly lets cold air in during the winter. Off the living room are two bedrooms and a small bathroom, containing the main reason why I chose *this* apartment over the other shitholes I looked at... the tub. It's nothing special or fancy, but it's a tub all the same, and I am all for soaking in a hot bubble bath after a long day like today.

I drop the duffle bag on the floor and kick my boots off by the door, hanging my leather jacket on the wall hook before I cross the shaggy, discolored carpet. I flick on the kitchen light as I pass by, snatching the remote off the sofa to turn off the TV, bathing the room in silence. Pausing, I take a second to listen for any movement coming from the bedroom. When all I hear is the noise of the always-bustling city coming up from the street, the sound of our neighbors arguing through the thin walls, and the always present hum of our old refrigerator, I move to the bathroom.

Turning the rusty taps, I run the water for the bath and light a few candles. Adding a lavender-scented bath bomb—one of the few extravagances I allow myself—I let it disperse while I head back into the kitchen. I open the fridge and grab a bottle of white wine from the door, fetch a glass from the cupboard, and pour myself a large serving. Alcohol and Black Creek go hand in hand. We're all borderline alcoholics at best. I'm not sure if it's a poverty thing, a despair thing, or a need-to-forget thing for most people. For me, it's a *you successfully dealt with shitheads all day and didn't drag their brains out through their nostrils, so you deserve a glass of wine* thing.

I sip on the drink, the tension slowly dropping from my shoulders as the cold, dry, fruity flavor slides down my throat, taking with it the last of today's problems as I let out a long, low, "ahhh," before carrying the glass with me back to the bathroom. I ignore the blackened grout lines that never seem to stay clean for long and the chipped tiles along the wall as I set it on the cheap, plastic bath caddy before stripping out of my leather pants, black Henley, and bralette.

When the water is piping hot, and bubbles are threatening to overflow the side of the tub, I step into it and lower myself into the warmth with a sigh. Tilting my head back, I close my eyes, inhaling the soft lavender scent and allowing it to calm me.

My thoughts drift to the asshole back on the dock. He'd been way too fucking easy to lure there, but then again I'd been watching him for a while, and I knew precisely what to say and do to get him all alone.

The fucker had been beating on his wife for the last ten years of their marriage. I guess the wife finally had enough. A quick phone call and explanation of my price, and that shithead was all mine to do with as I pleased.

I've spent the last week stalking him, and tonight, I made a point of bumping into him at a club on the outskirts of town. Most people avoid Black Creek like the plague, but you get plenty of middle and upper-class men—and women—who come here for the thrill; who think it'll be fun to hang with the ruffians for a night. Our whores are dirtier than the high-class prostitutes, and there are plenty of bored middle-aged housewives who find some excitement in fucking a thug covered in tats.

It wasn't difficult to coax him into taking a drive with me. Dressed in skin-tight leather pants that hug my ample curves and enhance my ass, along with a bralette that draws men's eyes to my D cups, it was practically a sure thing. Add in a hushed whisper about how I wanted to choke on his cock, and he was almost coming in his pants as he escorted me out of the club.

I directed him to the docks, where I'd left my bike earlier. It was a piece of cake, distracting him with my tits and pussy as I ground against his dick until I could slip my gun out of my clutch and bash him over the head with it—I couldn't very well blow his brains out all over the gorgeous leather interior and ruin a perfectly good car for Arnie.

The hardest part was dragging his heavy ass out of the car and over to the edge of the dock where I'd stashed my duffel bag, equipped with everything I needed to wipe the sorry sack of shit off the face of the earth for good. But once I'd finally managed it, getting him all wrapped up and into the water was a cinch. I didn't even give him the courtesy of killing him first. The dark, sadistic part of me hopes the cold water startled him to consciousness, just in time for him to drown.

A sick sense of achievement warms me at that thought. It would be nothing less than he deserves. I'll never understand a man's need to inflict violence on the very people they claim to love and should instinctively feel the need to protect. Does it honestly make them feel more manly to beat on people smaller and weaker than them? It's the same pattern I've witnessed every day of my life. I grew up with it, and I've watched women and children around me be subjected to it, so there has to be some reasoning behind it. Just not one I'll ever understand.

My thoughts move on to my to-do list for tomorrow. I have my regular meeting with Enzo and then work tomorrow night because, in this town, a girl needs to have multiple sources of income in order to get by.

The water is lukewarm by the time I drag myself out of it, wrapping a towel around me as I pull the plug before heading to my bedroom—which is really more of a box room. Suddenly feeling exhausted, I throw on some sleep shorts and an oversized t-shirt and climb under the covers. I fall asleep to the satisfying thought that tonight there is one less abusive shitstain on the planet.

\*\*\*

Strands of my still-damp hair whip around my face as I jog across the street. My electric cut out this morning, so I couldn't blow dry my hair, which also meant the coffee machine wouldn't work, and to top it all off, I forgot to set my alarm. So I'm running late, and all-in-all, I'm in a crabby mood by the time I arrive at G&T that afternoon for my monthly meeting with Enzo.

Beyond the paycheck, I never look forward to these meetings. They're awkward and extremely uncomfortable. I always feel like I'm under a microscope with my every action and inaction being analyzed and cataloged for future examination. Something about Enzo just doesn't sit right with me. Besides, I do not enjoy spending my free time in dingy bars with drunken assholes. I get enough of that at work.

The rickety door of the bar squeaks on its hinges as I pull it open and step into the dark interior. I'm immediately assaulted by the smell of stale cigarette smoke, sweat, and beer. It's midday, but every seat at the bar is occupied with patrons talking in hushed whispers, staring absently into their drinks, or watching this afternoon's entertainment—an aged stripper dancing on the small stage at the side of the room.

I glance around the small, stuffy space, faintly aware of some song from the nineties playing from the ancient jukebox as I locate Enzo through the haze of smoke, sitting at a table for two at the back of the room. I make sure my resting bitch face is in place before striding towards him while ignoring the way the soles of my boots stick to the floor with every step.

"Where's my money?" I demand once I've reached the table. The legs of the barstool scrape against the wooden floor as I pull it back, sliding onto the hard seat and fixing Enzo with a stony-faced expression.

"What, no *hello, how ya doing?*" Enzo asks, one side of his lip hooking up in a small grin that I think is supposed to be friendly, yet it doesn't quite hit the mark. He's a strange guy and probably not much older than me. He's attractive with his dirty blond hair and striking green eyes, but there's something about him I can't quite put my finger on. I don't know if it's his too clean appearance, the lack of desperation in his eyes, or the fact that he doesn't leer at me the way everyone else does. I'm not big-headed. However in a town where everyone is stick and bones, my wide hips, round ass, and big tits definitely make a splash, regardless of how much I try to hide them. I gave up even trying a long time ago and learned to embrace my femininity, using it for my own gain. Whatever it is about him, though, he just stands out from everyone else in the bar, and everyone in Black Creek, for that matter. But he's never made a wrong move toward me, and he does pay me handsomely for the tidbits of information I slide his way. "At least let me get you a drink."

"No, thanks," I reply bluntly. He's always trying to get me to stay and have a drink with him, but this is nothing more than business to me, and it will remain that way.

He ignores me as he waves over a waitress, ordering two glasses of whiskey before focusing his apple-green eyes on me. Getting down to business, I pull an envelope out of the inner pocket of my leather jacket and hold it out for him to take.

He gives me one of his placating smiles, not making any move to take it from me. "How have you been?"

I sigh, dropping the envelope on the sticky bar table in front of him. It's the same song and dance every time. Has been for the last seven years. I first met Enzo when I tried to steal his wallet. I was pretty damn good at it, so I've got no idea how he even knew I'd done it. I barely made it two steps before he grabbed me by the back of my shirt and threw me against a wall.

He looked absolutely furious, but after a second, some of the anger bled out of his expression, and he offered me an opportunity to earn the money instead. All I had to do was tell him anything I knew about a small street gang making moves on the old, abandoned docks at the time. I think they called themselves the Mad Dogz. Something stupid like that. They're long gone now—no surprise there. Anyway, I didn't know much. I'd overheard one of their members discussing their plans outside a bar down the road from the shelter I was staying at one night, and I relayed the information to Enzo. He seemed satisfied with what I knew and asked if I wanted the opportunity to earn more money. My shoulders slumped when he offered me that, assuming he was after a quick fuck or a blow job. It wasn't the first time I'd been offered money for such an exchange. Nor would it have been the first time I'd accepted, but he shocked me when he told me I just had to keep my ear to the ground, and there'd be more money if I could tell him anything useful.

Since then, we have been meeting once a month, and I hand over any information I have. He no longer bothers to go

19

through what's in the envelope. He just hands over a wad of cash, asks a fuckton of personal questions, and goes on his merry way. I have no clue what he uses the information for—whether it's for his own gain or sells it—nor do I give a shit. His money made it possible for me to get off the streets. It helped me survive when I had no other prospects and before I was old enough to get a job at one of the strip clubs—apparently, there is a very gray moral line even in Black Creek. The point is, the money he gave me every month prevented me from having to resort to less than savory actions just to get by, and for a fifteen-year-old girl, that meant everything.

"Fine," I snap in answer to his question. I learned a long time ago it's just easier to give him something small about my life.

He nods his head at my response. "Good. You're being smart?"

"Always."

"And no one's giving you any trouble?"

I smirk. "Why? You gonna handle them for me if they are?"

He frowns, and something that makes him look ten times more deadly than half the thugs walking the street with their big-ass guns, flashes across his eyes before he blinks and it's gone.

Ignoring whatever that was, I shake my head. "No, they aren't. And even if they were, I can deal with them myself."

Living on the streets for most of your childhood makes you scrappy in a fight, and after I watched a girl no older than myself kill a man with a single punch to his throat, I sought her out and made a deal for her to teach me a few things. The moves she showed me... were insane, and I get the impression what she did teach me had only been a very small part of her repertoire.

Although we had built a tentative relationship, she was always reluctant to talk about how she became so proficient in the art of killing. Unfortunately, she rarely comes around to Black Creek now. Still, our shared pain—and the fact that we were both young females trying to survive in a male-dominated world—bonded us in a way that will last a lifetime.

The waitress returns with our drinks, and while I make no move to take mine, Enzo lifts it right out of her hands, frowning at the glass before lifting it to his lips. He stifles a grimace as the liquid burns its way down his throat. Just another red flag that—if I ever had the inclination to open up to him—he can't be trusted. No one, and I mean *no one* in Black Creek, would screw up their nose at the taste of cheap whiskey. We grow up on the shit. We can down it like water, yet the bitter taste seemingly doesn't appeal to this guy's more refined palate.

Feeling annoyed and frustrated now, I snap out, "Money," repeating the word with more force.

"You know, a man could get his feelings hurt. Is my company really that bad?"

I purse my lips, trying to keep my cool as I let out a long, suffering exhale. The last thing I want to do is piss him off. While I have other, more lucrative means of income now, his money means I don't have to get on my knees for some asshole if I don't want to.

"I'm sorry," I grit out with a tight smile. "I just have a lot to do today."

He nods, downing the rest of his whiskey with an unimpressed frown. It's the same expression every time. You'd think he'd stop ordering the damn drink if he truly didn't like it. It's as if he's trying too hard to fit in, to appear like one of us. When you put all of his minor abnormal behaviors together, he stands out worse than a polar bear in the desert. Even though I file all of the weird mannerisms away for future analysis, I don't let myself dwell on who he really is for long. I don't give a shit, and it's better not to ask; not to get involved. If I know jack shit, then I don't have to worry about some gangster showing up at my door in the middle of the night, waving a gun in my face, and demanding answers.

So instead of overthinking it all, I let it go and hold out my hand in a silent gesture for him to give me my payment. Fucking finally, he slaps the bills into my palm, but when I go to tug them out of his grip, he tightens his hold around the pile of notes until I look up at him in confusion.

"Same time and place next month?"

"Isn't it always?"

He grins brightly, finally letting go and getting to his feet. "Looking forward to it."

With that, he turns and strides out of the pub. I don't relax until the squeaky door swings shut behind him. If push came to shove, I'm not sure if he'd be an ally or a foe. If he's not from Black Creek, who knows what sort of people he has backing him or how much money lines their pockets. I just hope I never have to find out.

# CAIN

## Chapter 2

Standing in the doorframe with my arms crossed, I watch my men hard at work as they rip off wallpaper, tear out kitchen cabinets, and drag worn mattresses along with rotten furniture from the bedrooms of the long-abandoned apartment complex I've claimed as home to the Reaper Rejects. Our numbers have grown considerably in the last few months, and it was past time I found a base of operations for all of us. Not to mention, many of these men deserve a place to call home, somewhere they can rest their heads at night and feel protected. Given the harrowing past of many of my newest—and youngest—members, I want them, more than anything, to know they are safe here. That their lives are theirs, and they are free to come and go as they please.

I might need every able body for my war, but these men are more than just soldiers to me. They are my responsibility and under my protection, but more than anything, they are my family.

Pride and hope swell in my chest as I watch them all hard at work, turning this shell of a building into a home for us all. It will take some time, but I know we will get there. And, in the meantime, I plan on continuing to take over the southern part of the city. With every passing day, more and more people recognize our name, and with every block we claim as ours, they'll come to realize we are an indomitable force not to be messed with.

It's all just killing time as I wait to go after my actual target. The source of everything that has gone wrong in my life. The cause of all my pain and suffering. The Antonellis—the Italian Famiglia who hover like a dark cloud over this city for as long as anyone can remember. Always present, always watching, yet rarely ever seen.

Anger burns through my body as I think of them. Vengeance sears a path through my veins, increasing the pounding of my heart so it pulses in my ears, and my vision blurs as the scene before me is replaced with the image of a girl with a rueful grin and long, black, untameable hair. *Evie*. My sole reason for existing; the purpose behind everything I do.

*I'm getting closer, Evie. I'm almost there. One day soon, revenge will be mine. Their blood will run beneath my boots, and they will rue the day they took you from me. From us. Your death will not be in vain.*

This promise has been my driving force since that fateful day. The one I recite over and over in my head. I was only a boy when they stole my sister from me, but the horrors of that day molded me into the man I am now. I'm no longer the

26

helpless kid who hid when bullets started flying, unable to help my sister as she screamed and cried for me. I may be too late to save her from her fate, but I refuse to let her death pass without consequence. What the Antonellis did to my family, they have done to countless others; to anyone who gets in their way. Of course, I've managed to recruit many of the aggrieved family members—brothers, fathers, sons—to my cause, and one day, we will rise up against them.

Unfortunately, though, going after the Antonellis isn't as easy as storming some street gangs' territory and gunning them down. The Antonellis have resources, money, and men on their side, all of which makes them an enemy no sane man should try to conquer. *Thankfully, no one has ever claimed I was right in the head.*

If I want to go up against them and win, I need to play it smart, and that starts with building a secure home for us. One that will protect us from any backlash from the many unorganized gangs that run rampant in this city, or the Grim Bastards. I need to ensure we have adequate resources and a reliable income. I can't hope to face the Antonellis on equal footing; however, I need to give us the best possible chance at success.

"Things are coming along well," Oliver says, coming to stand beside me. "Most of the bedrooms have been gutted and are ready to be painted and furnished, and security cameras have been installed all along the perimeter. Once everyone has suitable accommodations, I'll get them to start on the lobby."

"Good." I eye the insubstantial fencing along the sidewalk, still tempted to build a thick, cement wall in its place. Except, many here have spent their entire lives imprisoned behind concrete walls, and I refuse to make them feel trapped ever again. So instead, I've built a new, ten-foot-tall iron fence, topped with electrified barbed wire, and ensured every inch of the property is under surveillance. We've set up a room filled with monitors which will be manned twenty-four seven. I've also hooked up an alarm system to all of our phones, so we'll be notified no matter where we are, if someone dares to breach our property line.

All in all, I'm confident in our defense mechanisms, although I'm hopeful we won't need them. I don't think many of the lesser gangs would dare darken our doorway, and while the Grim Bastards are an ever-growing thorn in my side, I don't think they will start a war with us any time soon either. The main reason I'm so intent on establishing such a high level of security is in case the Antonellis catch wind of our plan, and inevitably make a counterattack.

Oliver claps me on the shoulder, giving it a quick squeeze. Looking in his direction, I find him scanning our surroundings, taking in the men hard at work, and the gradual coming together of the apartment complex before he turns to meet my eye. There is the same determined resolve in his eyes that he no doubt sees in mine. Oliver is my closest ally, the one person who I trust whole-heartedly. We're together in this fight, unified in our hunger for justice, and it feels good to have him at my side in this. To see the same war waging in his eyes and the shadows darkening his features. He craves this vengeance just as fiercely as I do. We were all friends once—before everything fell apart. Before our lives were destroyed. Before Evie was taken.

"Evie would be proud of all you've achieved," he says in a soft voice before quickly glancing away, hiding his pain from me. Not that he needs to. It's an all-consuming ache I'm far too familiar with.

28

I give him a sharp nod, unable to respond to his statement with words. Would Evie be proud? I'm not so sure. She never believed in an eye for an eye. She was always asking me to take the high road. Evie was my moral compass, my guiding star when I was lost. I always felt like she was an angel, filled with an ethereal purity that shone so bright it should protect her from the violence of men. Of course, I know now that's total bullshit.

I swallow roughly, clearing my voice before tilting my head toward the interior of the apartment complex. "Come on. We need to discuss our next moves."

I hear the light scuff of his boots against the hardwood floor behind me as we make our way toward my office, stepping inside. The room isn't much bigger than my old office, in what used to be my mother's house—mine, now that she's gone. As a gang, we've vastly outgrown the small terrace house, but I still own it. I'm not sure I'll ever be able to bring myself to part with it. Although, I have to admit, it's like a weight off my chest no longer living under the same roof I shared with my sister. I swear her ghost haunts the place, taunting me, whispering in my ear, and pursuing me into my dreams.

I hear the door close behind Oliver as he follows me into the room, and I skirt around the desk, sitting down behind it as he collapses into a seat on the opposite side.

"We have firm control over Joker territory, and I've sent men to help rebuild and aid the residents in whatever way they need," Oliver begins, getting straight down to business. I simply nod my head, already expecting as much. The Unfazed Jokers owned the part of town we're currently residing in. We had easily destroyed them and took control several months ago. So far, we've had minimal resistance, but we always have to remain alert.

29

"The fighting pit has proven to be very popular." A grin flashes across Oliver's face, similar to my own.

"Excellent." I'd been hoping the fights would be lucrative and provide us with another viable source of income.

He grabs a file off my desk, holding it out to me. "Marcus showed me last month's figures this morning. We doubled the previous month's income, and have already out-earned last month."

My grin widens at the news as I take the file and flick through it. "Fantastic. We'll have to scout locations for an expansion soon." Oliver gives a nod of agreement, and I know the task is in capable hands.

Having updated me, he leans back in his chair, the smile slipping off his face as it's replaced with a more intense expression. "How are things coming along on your end?"

While Oliver has been getting the apartment block up to scratch for my men and ensuring no one thwarts our rule, I've been busy looking into our sworn enemies, learning everything I can about them—not that I've been able to learn a whole hell of a lot. The Antonellis have more people in their organization than we could ever hope to obtain, and they're immensely more organized. Still, ultimately, my beef is with one man in particular—the head of the Antonelli family. The Don himself. The man who made the final call when it came to kidnapping my sister and destroying my family. His entire empire needs to come crumbling down, though his death will be at *my* hands.

My lips flatten as I release a long sigh. "Not so well," I admit, running a hand through my thick coal-black hair in frustration. I've employed some men to spy on the Antonellis, but unfortunately, it hasn't been an easy task. The Antonelli family is well protected. The Don has an extensive security team who escort him every time he's in the city, making it impossible for any of my men to get close to him, even to gather information. The men I've planted—a croupier in their casino and a bouncer at one of their sex clubs—are at the bottom of the food chain within the organization, meaning they have to gain the trust of the caporegime and prove their loyalty to the Antonellis before they can work their way up, which is a time-consuming process.

"We're going to be waiting a while until they are in a position to undermine them or provide us with the intel we need to make any drastic moves."

Oliver pinches his lips as he mulls over what I'm saying. "I don't see that we have much choice for now. At least we have eyes and ears inside their operation. Let's see what they come back with while we get ourselves established here, then we can go from there."

With a reluctant nod of agreement, I reach down to open the bottom drawer of my desk and pull out two tumblers and a bottle of the whiskey I know Oliver likes. I have to admit, he's got me hooked on this expensive shit ever since he came back from Crescentwood. You'd think prison would have knocked that refined taste out of him, but evidently not. Pouring the amber liquid into the glasses, I hold one out to him. He takes it from my outstretched hand, and we both knock the drink back, swallowing our frustrations as the alcohol burns a path down our throats.

...

Hours later, my head is just this side of fuzzy as I sag against a couch in the half-completed bar, where a party rages around me. The surrounding noise and alcohol coursing through my system are enough to quiet the incessant voice in the back of my head telling me to move faster, fight harder, be better, and every time the voice starts up again, I just down another glass of whiskey.

I refocus my gaze on the skinny blonde grinding her ass against my dick as she moves to the music. *Fuck, yes.* This is exactly the stress reliever I needed. My head falls back against the sofa, my eyes drifting shut as she moves to crouch between my legs, her nimble hands making quick work of my belt, and I groan as she sucks me into her mouth.

In a blissed-out daze, I tilt my head to the side, watching as another girl rubs herself all over Oliver. He's staring at his phone with a ridiculous amount of intensity, making a very clear point of ignoring the girl without downright telling her to fuck off.

"Dude." The word isn't much more than a grunt as the blonde sucks me deeper into her mouth. "Chill the fuck out. Let her blow you. You'll feel so much better for it."

He lifts his head to scowl at me before casting a quick glance at the girl between my legs. His scowl shifts to a frown before he focuses back on his phone.

*Whatever, his loss.* Shaking my head, I look away from him, choosing to watch the hottie as she sucks and slurps at my dick like it's her favorite flavor of ice cream. If Oliver wants to walk around with all that tension, then so be it. Personally, I prefer to offload it whenever I can.

Later that night, I'm lying in my bed with my arm bent, my hand behind my head as I stare up at the ceiling. My buzz from earlier has worn off, and the sniping voices have returned, preventing me from getting a restful night's sleep.

I run my hand down the front of my face, groaning. With every passing day, I'm getting increasingly agitated as next to no progress is made. It's become impossible for me to think about

32

anything other than my goal. It's become an obsession, one that haunts me and refuses to let me have one single moment to myself. Fighting, drinking, and fucking no longer hold the same appeal they once did. No matter how hard I try to drown out the thoughts, guilt gnaws on my insides, mixed with anger, and the memory of deep green eyes that assault me as I slip into the past.

*"Cain! CAIN!" The sound of my sister's screams reaches me in the silence between rounds of gunfire. The fear in her voice has me looking out from where I'm hiding in a ditch underneath the side of the house as she is hoisted into some asshole's arms.*

*Another round of gunshots go off, and wooden fragments spray down around me as the bullets imbed themselves somewhere in the boards above my hiding place. I look around our small yard frantically searching for help. But no one is around. Everyone disappeared as soon as the sound of the first gun going off echoed around our usually quiet street. I can't even see any signs of Beck or Oliver, but they must be hiding nearby. The four of us were hanging out on the front porch steps when we heard the squeal of tires that preceded whatever's happening right now.*

*My sister emits another terrified scream, and I whip my head back to look at her. She's writhing and squirming in the asshole's arms, but he doesn't let her go as he drags her toward the pavement and the cars abandoned in the middle of the street. Digging my toes into the dirt beneath me, I wriggle out from beneath the house to go to her aid. The other men, all of whom are dressed sharply in black suits that seem in complete contrast to the devastation they are leaving in their wake, have*

33

lowered their automatic rifles to their sides and turned to follow the man carrying my sister back to the car.

The second I'm free, I jump to my feet and rush toward her. She sees me and struggles more frantically to get free, clawing the man's arm and screaming bloody murder. Tears stream down her face as she kicks and twists in his hold, but if anything, he only grips her tighter as she thrashes against him. None of them pay her any attention, but one of them must spot me running their way out of the corner of his eye as he turns to face me, lifting his gun. I don't even register the significance of the action, or maybe I just don't care. I'd happily die if it saved my sister from these monsters.

I barely spare the man pointing the gun at me any attention, my focus too intent on my sister as I push myself faster across the dried grass in an attempt to reach her. Her glassy eyes, sheening with tears, widen as the scene unfolds, and she freezes in the man's arms as his comrade's gun comes level with my chest. I hear the pow-pow-pow of bullets firing rapidly within seconds after someone tackles me from behind, taking me to the ground and knocking the air out of my lungs. Whoever it is probably just saved my life, except I can't find it in me to even look at them—never mind, thank them—as my sister is thrown into the back of one of the cars.

Shaking off whoever it is, I push to my feet once again as the car door is slammed shut, blocking my view of her tear-stained face as her screams for help are cut off. Before I can even reach the sidewalk, the car speeds off down the street. I can't do anything aside from watch as it disappears around a corner, and my heart crumbles to dust in my chest. The other cars parked in the street take off, and in slow motion, still not able to comprehend the reality of what is happening, I turn my stunned gaze to the last one as the man who just tried to kill me climbs

*into the front passenger seat. He turns at the last second, and I
see the details I missed earlier—the tattoos on his fingers and
the row of X's running like a line of tears down one cheek. His
neatly trimmed russet-brown hair is styled back, and the corner
of his lip hooks up in a malicious grin when he catches me
watching him.*

*"Payment for your daddy's sins, kid. Next time tell him
not to fuck with the Antonellis."*

*The car door closes behind him, and I watch helplessly
as the car speeds down the road and out of sight. The street
appears abnormally quiet in the aftermath of the chaos, and I'm
not sure how long I stand there for, watching the spot where the
cars disappeared as if the one carrying my sister might turn
around and come back, deliver her back to me safe and sound.*

*I'm faintly aware of two people moving to stand beside
me, their shoulders brushing against mine. My best friends. I can
feel their devastation as potently as my own, but I can't tear my
eyes away from the end of the street. All the while I stand there,
I can feel that newly vacated space in my chest where my heart
once resided, filling with something dark and menacing. It floods
into my bloodstream and whispers sweet promises of revenge
in my ears until the only reason my heart still beats; my lungs
still expand; my legs still hold me upright, is to save Evie and gut
the motherfucking assholes who took her.*

A snort of disgust rips from between my lips as I shake
off memories of that day. What a foolish, naive child I was then,
making promises I could never keep. I could make my sister all
the promises in the world, but I had no means by which to follow
through with them.

I'm eleven years too late, and Evie is long gone by now,
but revenge still beats a rhythm in my chest. It's ingrained in my

every move, every action, every thought. It's the sole reason for my continued existence.

*I might be too late to save you, Evie, but I will not let your kidnappers go unpunished.*

## Chapter 3

"Evening, Kenny."

"Red." The bouncer by the staff entrance nods his head, opening the door for me to enter. The pounding of the club's music—*Closer* by Nine Inch Nails—thuds through the walls as I make my way along the narrow hallway, passing the manager's office and staff toilets before reaching the changing rooms.

"Hey, girl!" Bee greets as I walk in.

"Hey, Bee." I smile as I pass by her, not really paying attention as she pushes her tits into a bikini that barely has enough material to cover her nipples before plonking my bag down at my own dressing table and lifting up the outfit that's been laid out for me—a black g-string with matching lace suspenders and thigh-high stockings, a bra that doesn't appear to have much more material than Bee's does, and a pair of clear-colored platform heels.

"You're up in five, Red," a gruff voice barks through the door while I'm in the process of changing, belonging to Drew, the floor manager here at Strip Tease.

Sighing, I quickly slather my face in excessive makeup and my body in glitter, then stuff my bag in a locker and head out of the dressing room, ready to put on a show for the horny-ass men of this town.

I slip through the staff entrance door into the front area of the club as the dancer before me on the main stage finishes up. The club is dimly lit, with spotlights directed at the three stages, where different dancers are performing. I can just make out enough outlines of men in the audience to know we have a full house tonight.

The tables around the stages are all occupied, and most of the booths are full, too, by the looks of things. Scantily clad waitresses skirt around tables and crowds of people on their way to deliver drinks, and I can just about make out a few men receiving lap dances or being escorted to private stalls for some more *intimate* attention.

The song comes to an end, and the dancer—a relatively new girl I haven't had the chance to get to know yet—steps down from the stage, giving me a soft smile before she moves toward the bar, ready to work the floor.

I run my hands over my outfit, flattening the lace strap of my g-string before I climb the steps onto the stage. The music switches, the fast-paced beat of *I Get Off* by Halestorm starting up as I wrap my hand around the pole. The overhead spotlight flashes down on me, blinding my view of the rest of the darkened room as I shift my weight and swing my body around the pole in time to the music. I've been perfecting these moves for over five years now. I can work the pole like a goddamn pro. It helps that I've got an ass that men seem to enjoy digging their fingers into and hips they can picture themselves grabbing ahold of. Not to mention my long auburn-colored hair that they all want to wrap around their fists and tug on.

The next thirty minutes pass in a blur of swaying hips, shaking my tits, and grinding my ass, so when the last song in my set comes to an end, Drew meets me at the side of the stage.

"You're on the floor the rest of the night."

Nodding, I stride past him to the bar. Drew's all business. He keeps it professional, never allowing his eyes to stray or linger where they shouldn't. The same can't be said for some of the other staff here.

"Damn, Sugar, you're looking hot tonight," Mike, one of the bartenders, greets as he pours a shot of something—vodka, maybe—into a glass and slides it across the counter to a customer. Mike is in his mid-twenties, probably only a year or two older than me, and he's an absolute flirt. The thing is, he knows he's hot shit. The other girls here drool all over him, only boosting his ego further, and I've seen more than a few of them leave with him at the end of a shift. But he's a one-time-only kinda guy, and I'm sure a couple of the girls have been left with broken hearts after spending the night with him.

I'm all for a good time, and I've no doubt he would have some pretty decent bedroom skills, but I don't mix business with pleasure. And honestly, overinflated egos aren't really my thing. Sure, I like a guy with confidence, but Mike is just too much. That cocky, flirty personality just doesn't do it for me, even if his good looks are on point—and with his muscular biceps, high

41

cheekbones, and the dark dusting on his chin, his looks are *definitely* on point.

Giving him a flirtatious wink, which has become our usual banter—I think by now he's figured out I'm not interested in him, not that that stops him from trying—I grab a tray already loaded with drinks and move to distribute them around the lively room.

Without the bright lights blinding my view, I scan my eyes over tonight's crowd—which seems to consist of the usual mixture of rowdy drunkards—as I sashay around the room, dropping off drinks and taking orders while ignoring the occasional hand brushing along the side of my breast or over my ass.

The largest throng of people are gathered around the stages, wanting an up-close and personal view of the dancers. Still, plenty of others are sitting at the small circular tables, with some of the wealthier out-of-towners occupying the velvet booths that line the walls. You can tell they don't live in Black Creek. It's obvious—from their crisp white shirts, fitted black pants, and polished shoes to their expensive haircuts and the way they cast their eyes over the rowdy Black Creekians with a look of casual disgust. They think they're so much better than us, yet here they are, in our town, in our club, with their hard-ons and sleazy leers, so how much better can they actually be?

As much as most of us want to escape the daily grind, violence, and bloodshed that occurs here, the appeal of it also draws men like them to our chaotic neck of the woods. Men with money who come to Black Creek to revel in debauchery and bathe in sin. This city is a far cry from their daily lives. It's a place they can come to escape their boring marriages, relieve the stress of their busy workday, and avoid whatever other nonsense privileged, rich people have to endure.

42

For the most part, customers who live in Black Creek are pretty easy to handle. They're mostly here for the stage show and maybe a lap dance, but if they do want *extras*, they're usually pretty good when I say no. However, men with money... they're not so easy to turn down—hence why we have bouncers on the doors and security dotted along the perimeter of the room.

As I work my way across the floor, my gaze swivels to the biggest threat in the room. A crowd even more relentless than the wealthy assholes in their cushy booths. Satan's Advocates.

Satan's Advocates is the street gang that currently occupies this part of the city. They usually stop by a couple of nights a week to cause havoc and remind us all of their dominion over this area. They're easy to spot, all of them wearing their Satan's insignia like a badge of honor, either sewn onto their leather jackets or tattooed onto their skin. The atmosphere in the room changes the instant they walk in, and one by one, people get up and move away from their large group, not wanting to inadvertently gain their attention or incur their wrath. Those who are brave enough to remain nearby frequently flick their gaze in their direction, watching them warily and ready to make a run for it if shit hits the fan.

"Hey, baby, give us a lap dance," one of them calls out as I pass by.

Plastering a fake, coy expression on my face, I turn to look at him. "Sure thing, handsome. Let me just offload this round of drinks, and I'll be over, yeah?"

I hate this part of my job, especially when it's with an arrogant, self-entitled shitstain like this idiot appears to be, but it's a job requirement if you're working the floor, and even if it wasn't, I can't say no to a Satan. None of us can.

43

He gives me a cocky smirk, biting on his lower lip as his gaze roams over every inch of my exposed skin. I'm more than used to it, so I don't feel any of the revulsion or sudden need to cover up that most people would probably experience. It's just part of the job, and I've been doing it for long enough. The nervousness that comes with strutting around half-naked and on display for everyone to see quickly dissipates in this line of work. Within a month, I learned to walk with my head held high, confidence brimming with every step. Not only does it help with the tips, but I quickly realized I have nothing to be ashamed of. So I use my body to make money? Everyone in this fucking town does that. Men use their bodies to intimidate other gangsters, to threaten and coerce whoever they need to. Just because they do it with their clothes on, that somehow makes it better?

"Yeah, okay," he pouts. "But I might need more than just a lap dance if you keep me waiting too long."

I smile tightly at him, ducking my head and moving on through the crowd to disperse the last of my drinks. Being up on stage is one thing. It's actually something I enjoy. With the bright lights beaming down on the stage, it's next to impossible to pick anyone out of the crowd. It makes it easy to pretend no one is watching, and I can just fall into the music and escape into my own world. Lap dances, not so much. It's impossible to forget what you are to the men in this room when they're trying to shove their face in your tits and grab a handful of your ass.

The great thing about Strip Tease is that *extras* are at the discretion of the girls. If we don't want to partake, then that's fine. I personally choose not to. I've made a point of ensuring I earn enough money from various sources to no longer have to. I wasn't always so fortunate, though I have come a long way from the teenage girl struggling to survive from one day to the next.

The only challenge comes when it's a Satan's Advocate asking for that *extra*. The club pays its protection tithe, but we can't afford to have them pull that protection, or worse, decide to get rid of us altogether just because we piss them off. It sounds crazy, but businesses have been destroyed over less. The gangs here run our lives. We live and breathe on their say so. Last week, the pawnshop on 8th and Hudson was set on fire because the owner fucked some girl the leader of the Black Spiders had apparently claimed. The Spiders didn't even own that territory, but they got their hands on it, and next thing, a Molotov cocktail was being thrown through the shop owner's front window—with the owner still inside.

Too many hard-working men and women, just trying to get by, rely on Strip Tease. As such, we all do whatever we can to keep the Satan's Advocates happy, and you can bet your ass we will do exactly the same with whatever gang takes control after them. That's just the way it is now. The Satan's seized control of our little part of Black Creek when The Feral Beasts collapsed, and the whole city was suddenly up for grabs. At first, they weren't too bad. They mainly kept to themselves and were too busy making sure they held onto the five-block radius they'd seized control over to hassle us too much. However, as time has gone on, they've gotten cocky, showing their true colors and demanding anything they want from us.

Dropping off the last of my drinks, I return the tray to the bar and make my way over to the rowdy table of Satan's Advocates. The guy jumps to his feet as I approach, once again taking the time to skim his eyes over my body.

"Don't you want a lap dance?" I question, eyeing the table of burly men, many of whom are watching me with eager eyes. They're all rough-looking, with scruffy beards and stained teeth.

It's very evident hygiene doesn't factor in all that high on their daily routines.

The man smirks. "I was thinking we'd go somewhere more private."

I nod my head, painting on a seductive smile while smothering my groan. "Of course, follow me."

"Baby, I'd follow you anywhere when you sway your hips like that."

It's the same sort of shit every guy says, and it evokes zero response from me as I lead him toward a line of private booths at the side of the room, intended for precisely this purpose. A couple of back rooms have been repurposed solely to accommodate *extras,* but I deliberately don't take him there, hoping I can still get by with just a private dance.

He's grinning like a fucking idiot as he plunks himself into the chair. I take the time to look over his scrawny frame. He's young and arrogant looking, with a short, wiry, dark-haired beard that looks like it hasn't fully grown in some places.

I pull across the heavy purple curtain, blocking people's views of the booth and giving us some privacy before turning back to face him. The stall is darker now, making it harder to read his expression, although his wide eyes and the way he rubs his hand over his crotch are telling enough.

"Money." I hold out my hand for the fee, and he happily slaps the small pile of one-dollar bills into my palm. I tuck them into the tiny strip of fabric covering my tits, and as a new song starts up—*Addicted* by Saving Abel—I step between his spread thighs and sway my hips. Leaning in, I stroke my hands down the front of his top before thrusting my chest out, practically shoving my tits in his face.

He groans and squeezes his dick. I spin, mentally counting down the seconds as I jut my ass out. When he smacks his hand against my skin, grabbing hold of my ass, I spin round and glower at him. "No touching."

"Oh, come on, baby. I'll pay you extra."

"No."

The muscle in the back of his jaw works as he grinds his teeth, anger flashing across his face. I mentally chastise myself, working to soften my naturally brash personality as I move to straddle him, grinding down on his erection.

The anger quickly melts off his face as he takes my continued performance to mean free rein to touch what he wants, sliding his palms up my thighs and groping my tits in a painfully firm grip. I keep my mouth shut, biting the skin along my inner cheek as I hold back each snarky retort I want to spew out. When the song finally comes to an end, I move to get off his lap, but his hands clamp tightly on my upper thighs, holding me in place as his finger trails along the strap of my g-string.

"Come on, baby. It was just getting good." I try again to get off him, but then he digs his fingers into my skin, no doubt marking it, and that flash of anger from before re-emerges. "You got me all worked up. You can't just leave me hanging."

I have to swallow back the reminder that *he's* the one that asked for a fucking lap dance. He starts using his grip on my legs to pull me in against him, so the bulge in his jeans bumps against my scantily clad pussy, and all I can think about is wiping the arrogant as fuck look off his face. The one that says he *knows* he's going to get his way and he *knows* I can't stop him.

Except, I definitely could. He might think he's the most dangerous one in the room, but in reality, it's me. I've killed many men like him—self-centered assholes who don't give a shit about anything or anyone but themselves. But I can't. That would only get all of us in deep shit. This type of behavior from a Satan isn't unusual. It's just something I have to grin and bear, so taking a steadying breath, I do just that. I have to work really hard to fix a tantalizing smile onto my lips and trail my fingers down the front of his shirt instead of wrapping them around his neck like I want to.

"That'll be another fifteen." I grind my pussy against his hard cock, distracting him so he can't begin to haggle with me. If I'm going to have to give the asshole a blow job, the least he can do is fucking pay me.

"Fine," he grits out, hissing between his teeth as I grind down on him again.

Now that negotiations are done, he slaps a few more bills into my hand, and I don't waste any time getting it over with. I quickly lower myself to the ground between his legs as he unzips his pants and pulls himself out, giving his dick a few tugs before eyeing me up expectantly. I give him a pretty mediocre blow job, refusing to do anything but the bare minimum to get him off. As he swells in my mouth, his hand slams down on the back of my head, forcing me further down on him as he comes down my throat. *Fucking asshole.* I curse him out in my head while keeping my face impassive as I release him with a pop and get to my feet.

He tucks himself away with a smile on his face, and I open the curtains in a silent indication for him to get the fuck out. With one final squeeze of my ass, he murmurs, "I'll be back for more real soon, baby," as he steps out and moves to rejoin his buddies.

With a roll of my eyes, I readjust my bra and g-string before getting back to work. The rest of my shift goes by without incident. Thankfully, the Satan's left not long after, and the regulars are usually pretty easy to handle.

It's the early hours of the morning when I finally leave the club, showered and dressed in black jeans and my kickass black, chunky-heeled boots. I'm walking back to the apartment when my phone goes off in my pocket. Checking the caller ID, I immediately know what this is about and that I won't be getting any sleep for a while yet.

"Yeah?" I say into the receiver, bringing it to my ear.

"She's back."

I sigh. *Yup, exactly what I thought.*

"What shape is she in?"

"A black eye. I'd guess a few broken ribs too. She's got the kid with her." The woman hesitates before blurting out, "She's got bruises on her, too."

*Goddammit.* I told her this would happen. I fucking knew it would. It's the same fucking pattern every time with these assholes.

"I'll be right there."

Hanging up the phone, I stuff it in my pocket and pick up my pace. At the next block, rather than heading in the direction of my apartment building, I turn the opposite way down the street toward the *New Beginnings Women's Shelter.*

The shelter is in a repurposed community hall, and the place is quiet when I push open the door. Beatrice, a gray-haired woman in her sixties with balls of steel—making her tougher than any man I've ever met—is sitting behind the check-in desk. She looks up as I walk in, giving me a sad smile. Beatrice and I go way back. I've spent more than my fair share of nights here, under her watchful eye. She's good people, and even most of the men in this town know not to mess with her. She's got herself a reputation, although I guess that's what happens when you bludgeon your deadbeat husband and cut off his cheating dick.

49

At least, those are the rumors. No one knows for certain since his body was never found.

"Where is she?"

She jerks her head toward the back of the building. "I put her in one of our private rooms. Last door on the right."

With a nod, I move to head down the hall, but as I'm walking past the counter, she leans across it and hisses in a low voice, "Don't let her go back to him. If she can't make the decision for herself, then make it for her."

I press my lips together, glancing at her out of the corner of my eye, before walking on and passing the doorway to a large, cafeteria-style dining hall that, during the day, is normally filled with residents and volunteers. However, at this late hour, it's dimly lit, with only a few women sitting around, nursing hot drinks or consoling one another. Moving on, I pass another, smaller hall which has been set up as a communal sleeping area, with bunk beds filling up the room. No doubt every one of them is already occupied with women and children in need of a safe space for the night. Unfortunately, come morning, many of them will go back home to their abusive, cheating, scumbag partners, with apologies pouring from their lips, only to end up right back here in a week or month.

Every single one of their worthless partners should be shoved off the side of the dock and left to drown. It's the only fitting fate for any asshole who uses his larger size and greater strength to beat on someone weaker than them. I just don't have the time or resources to do it all myself. Getting rid of them all would be a full-time job, and most of these women can't afford to retain my services—which is why I have to be so selective with the cases I take on.

As I pass by several more communal sleeping rooms, I can hear the faint sounds of women whispering, children crying, and the crinkle of plastic sleeping mats as someone rolls over in their bed. It brings back memories of my own time living in shelters like this. I was only a child, and thankfully, many of the volunteers took pity on me, but it still wasn't an easy life. I had to fend for myself, scavenge my own food and clothing, and move from shelter to shelter when I'd stayed for as long as I could.

I preferred staying in a women's shelter since being with just women and children was generally safer. I had a few incidents in homeless shelters, instances where men would try to corner me or sneak into my bed at night, which resulted in me sleeping with a stolen kitchen knife under my pillow and learning never to let myself be alone in a room with someone of the opposite sex. It's one thing for men to proposition a thirteen-year-old girl, but to try and just take what doesn't belong to them—that's a whole different level of fucked up.

I push thoughts of the past aside as I reach the last door at the end of the corridor, where Beatrice said she'd put Sheryl, and knock on the door.

A weak sob comes in response. "Y-yeah?"

Opening the door, I slip into the room and take in the pitiful state of my oldest—and only—friend as she sits on the bottom bunk, sobbing. Her eyes widen as I close the door behind me, and she awkwardly gets to her feet, coming to hug me.

"Sheryl," I sigh into her embrace, careful not to hold her too tightly. Beatrice said she thought she had broken ribs, and based on the way she's favoring her right side and wincing with every deep inhale, I'd say she's right.

I pull back, running my gaze over her face. She's skinny—far too skinny—and her right eye is already swollen shut and turning a horrific shade of black. Her one good eye is red and puffy, glistening with fresh tears, and blood is crusted around her nose. There's another red smear on her chin where blood has trickled from her split lip.

Once I've taken in all I can bear to look at of her face, I glance behind her to where there's a small lump sleeping in the top bunk.

"How's Grace?"

Sheryl's shoulders drop, and a fresh set of tears build in her eyes before she dabs them away, "H-he hurt her." She chokes on a sob, burying her face in her hands as I rub soothing circles along her back and usher her over to the bed. Once I've got her settled, I rifle through the duffle bag she most likely hastily packed before escaping, digging out some baby wipes and tucking my hand under her chin. I gently lift her face, dabbing around her nose and chin to clean her up.

This isn't the first time Sheryl has turned up here with Grace. Hell, it isn't even the third time this month. Sheryl and I grew up together. Black Creek is filled with street kids, but Sheryl was one of the first people I met when I first joined them. See, I wasn't always homeless, though I barely remember that time of my life, and the only memories I do have are coated in violence and drenched in blood. Not ones I care to think about most days. When I was first trying to figure out this new life I'd been upended into, she showed me the ropes. She was the one who pointed out the best homeless shelters and taught me how to survive from one day to the next. I owe her my life.

As we grew older, our lives took very different paths. Sheryl fell into gang life, enticed by the adrenaline rush of booze, drugs, and partying. When we were fifteen, she started hanging around with the Crystal Takers—I'm sure you can guess how they made their money. They were nothing more than drug users who thought they should be more. Back then, Python—the leader of the Satan's—was a runner for them, but he took a special interest in Sheryl and didn't waste any time claiming her as his and knocking her up. And at first, I think things were going okay for them, but Python had bigger ambitions than simply working for some drug-taking idiot, and when The Feral Beasts left, he saw the opportunity to form his own little ruthless gang. Over the last couple of years, the power—or maybe it was the drugs—has gone to his head and he's begun to unravel.

Sheryl was seven months pregnant with baby number two when she first showed up at the shelter down the road from me, so beaten and bloody I was worried she wouldn't make it through the night.

Thankfully, she did, but the baby didn't. That was nearly two years ago, and I still remember the unadulterated fury that pumped through me when I saw her. I wanted to murder Python there and then, but she begged and pleaded for me to leave it alone. Ever since then, she shows up here every few months with Grace clinging to her, covered in new bruises and injuries— although never as bad as that first time. She always stays a few nights, allowing the worst of the injuries to heal while she rests before going back to him, even when I've pleaded with her to let me deal with him.

"What happened?" I ask her softly.

She ducks her head, lowering her gaze. I sit and wait patiently as she fidgets, gathering her thoughts and building her courage.

"He... " The emotion is thick in her voice, and she trails off, gathering herself before continuing, "Sometimes he makes me... perform for the others, and... d-do things."

Her hands are shaking, and her eyes remain glued to her lap as she struggles to get the words out. I'm already close to blowing a fuse, picturing the asshole's death, and I'm pretty sure I haven't even heard the worst of it yet.

"Usually, I put Grace to bed before any of them get too drunk or rowdy, but she's been having trouble sleeping recently. S-she's been wetting the bed." She shakes her head, her chin wobbling. "She got up when I was... " Unable to put words to whatever he was making her do—based on what she has said already, I think I can work it out—she trails off as fresh tears stream down her face, and she sniffs, wiping at her nose. "I tried to explain to him I just needed to sort her out, but he'd had too much snow. There was no reasoning with him." She shakes her head again. "He's never hit me like that in front of her. And when she started crying, he screamed at her and shoved her backward. She... she crashed into the table behind her."

She falls apart then, her voice breaking as she buries her face in her hands. Her shoulders quake as she cries, and I rub soothing circles along her back. We stay like that for a long time until she cries herself out, sagging against me as I wrap an arm around her shoulders.

As her sobs quieten, a hush falls over the room until she whispers in a small voice, "I've found bruises on her recently. Along her arms. When I asked her about it, she said she tripped."

I sigh, pushing past my anger so I can provide the comfort Sheryl needs right now. But hearing that determines one thing for me—Python must die. Whether or not Sheryl agrees or wants me to act, I *have* to. It's no longer acceptable for me to just sit back and take her word for it, hoping she will come to her senses and leave him on her own. Sometimes we need someone to give us a push in life, to overcome the things we are afraid to face, and that's exactly what I'm going to do for Sheryl.

"You know this can't continue, right?"

She nods but doesn't lift her head to look at me.

"It's not a safe environment for her," I push. "If he's already hurting her, just think about what he might do in the future."

She nods again. "I know. I know. But I'm scared."

I squeeze her shoulder and nudge her, so she looks up at me. Her eyes are wet and clouded with fear. "Let me take care of it." My words are pleading, yet there's an insistence behind them that I'm hoping she will heed. Even though I'm expecting her to tell me to leave it, the way she hesitates, gnawing on her bottom lip as she mulls over the idea, gives me hope. I mean, I'm killing him either way, but I'd feel a hell of a lot better about it if Sheryl was on board.

I push harder. "You can't take her back there, Sheryl. She deserves better. Do you want her to end up trapped in this town, just like us?"

She frowns, and it takes a long moment before she responds, "O-okay... do whatever it is you do."

Sheryl doesn't know much about the late-night activities I get up to when I'm not at the club, nevertheless I've offered to permanently remove Python from her life enough times that she knows I'm not just saying it for the sake of it. The first time I brought it up, she laughed me off, but when I mentioned it again, I knew she could see how serious I was. I wasn't half as experienced back then as I am now, but I'd have done it for Sheryl. For Grace.

I run my eyes over her face, giving her a chance to change her mind. I can see the resolve in her eyes, though. Tonight—him hurting Grace—has crossed a line for her. She might finally be starting to accept the toxic relationship she's in.

We don't say much else as I pull her down onto the bed and lie down beside her. It takes a while, but eventually I hear her soft snores. As I lie there, I stare up at the bottom of the top bunk, where Grace is sleeping soundly, and mull over various plans. It won't be the easiest job I've had—getting to Python—but it's definitely doable. Being the leader of a gang, he will have a certain level of protection around him at all times, despite that I'm hopeful their arrogance is a weakness I can use to my advantage.

Regardless of the obstacles in my way, my blood hums at the challenge and the knowledge that one more scumbag will soon meet his fate. I live for this. It gives me a sense of purpose and allows me to sleep easier at night. It's not enough for me to just struggle from one day to the next, doing a job I hate and abandoning any principles I might otherwise have if I had a choice in this life. At least, this way, I'm contributing something to this fucked-up world.

## Chapter 4

My thighs burn, and my body is stiff from crouching for so long. I'm hidden in the shadows of an empty lot across the way from the dilapidated house that the Satan's have claimed as their main base. They seem to have taken over most of the street, but the place I'm watching is Python's, and it's where they currently have a rager of a party underway. I've spent the last couple of days watching them from afar, learning their movements. I already knew the basic things about them—that they drink too much and do too many drugs, that they usually spend their days harassing citizens, and that they like to hang out at Toxic on a Friday night, but I don't know anything about *them.*

In order to figure out the best way of getting to Python, I need to learn what security measures they have, pinpoint their weaknesses, and identify my window of opportunity where I'm least likely to be seen or caught. So far, it appears the Satan's are more concerned with getting high than with delegating anyone to the task of security. Even as I watch their house now, people are coming and going freely like it's any other house party. It seems ridiculous to me, but it works in my favor.

Leaning down, I unzip my duffle bag and shimmy out of my black skinny jeans, switching them out for a short skirt that matches the skin-tight crop top I'm wearing. I shrug out of my leather jacket and stuff it along with my pants into the bag before lifting out a blonde wig. Ensuring my unique, red strands are carefully hidden beneath it, I get to my feet and slip through a hole in the chain-link fence onto the sidewalk.

With slow, unhurried steps and an exaggerated sway of my hips, I cross the street and step into the house. Nobody tries to stop me or ask any questions. I have to restrain my eye roll at how fucking easy it is. I knew the Satan's maintaining their place of power for this long had gone to their heads, but this is fucking ridiculous. They're just asking for someone to strut in here and gun them all down. *Hmm, tempting.*

As I cross the threshold, I'm immediately bombarded by the deafening boom of horrendous rap music and suffocated by the stench of sweat, alcohol, and utter hopelessness. I'm in a narrow entryway, with stairs in front of me leading to the floor above. The room on my right is lit by flashing neon lights, and I can barely see through the dense crowd of drunk and high dancers. Ignoring them for now, I turn left into a brightly lit, old-fashioned kitchen, the countertops overflowing with bottles of beer and spirits.

There are plenty of people in here too, snorting cocaine off the small, linoleum-topped table, fucking in the corner, and getting wasted on cheap alcohol. I ignore them all as I do a sweep of the room, grabbing a beer and twisting off the cap on my way past. There are a couple of Satan's in here, unfortunately not the one I'm looking for. Taking in their glazed-over eyes and the red tinge around their noses as they watch me walk by, I'm guessing they won't remember even seeing me in the morning. *Good.*

Moving back into the hall, I glance up the stairs, taking a long tug of my beer before climbing them to a small landing with four doors leading off it. I put my ear to the first door, hearing the distinct sounds of people fucking before I move on to the next room. There aren't any sounds coming from behind it, but it's locked when I turn the doorknob.

Out of the final two doors, one is a grimy bathroom, with black grout in the sink, the toilet seat up, and what I'm pretty sure is piss covering the floor. Scowling in disgust, I toss my now empty beer bottle into the room, not giving a shit that it breaks, and tiny fragments of glass spread out all over the floor. I close the door and move on to the final room, hearing the sound of more sex coming from behind the door.

Now that I've got a general layout of the house, I head down the stairs and into the only room that's left, where the rest of the Satan's must be hanging out. It takes a second for my eyes to adjust to the darkness, but as I push my way through the packed crowd of dancers, I spot them spread out on chairs and couches along the back wall, ignoring the rest of the room while they put on their own show of fucking and snorting drugs. There in the middle, with a girl sucking him off, is Python, with his greasy hair slicked back and an overgrown beard that desperately needs a comb run through it. He's a large, burly man with a bit of a beer belly and a snake tattoo that winds around his neck. I think *he* thinks it makes him look intimidating. *I* think it just makes him look like a fucking idiot.

I have to force my face not to contort at the sight of him as I dance to the shitty music they have pumping through the stereo in an attempt to blend in with the crowd. He clearly doesn't give a shit about where Sheryl is or if she's okay. Not that I expected him to, but seeing him here, partying like it's any other night while he lets some random skank give him a blow job, just drives the reality home for me. Is this the life Sheryl and Grace have been living? Where the fuck do they even sleep? There's no way Grace could be in this house when there's a party raging like this.

All of it only serves to heat the blood in my veins, although I'm sure the shitty beer is helping with that too. I've had to rebuff several guys by the time I notice Python shove the girl away and tuck himself back in his pants. I watch as his eyes scan the room, and I give him a coy look when his gaze meets mine.

A cocky smirk lifts one side of his lips, and as I trail my fingers down the side of my neck and between the valley of my breasts, his eyes drop to follow. His smirk deepens, clearly pleased with what he sees. *Good.* I feel a warm presence at my back, and rather than moving away from whichever new asshole is trying his luck, I lean into him. Knowing Python will hate my dismissal of him, I look away instead of focusing on the guy behind me, not really seeing him as I mentally count down the seconds.

*Five. Four. Three. Two...*
"Get the fuck out of here."
*Right on time.*

62

Python's deep, possessive growl resonates from behind me, and without having to be told twice, the guy whose hands are on my hips flinches and scurries away through the crowd, and Python's hands replace his as he steps in front of me. I look up at him through my eyelashes, noticing his gaze glued to my chest. *Charming.*

"You must be new around here. I'd definitely remember an ass like that."

*Oh, how you make me swoon with your romantic words.*

Playing my part, I bite down on my lower lip and give him a lascivious look.

"Come join me and my guys."

*Fuck,* that is not what I want to happen.

I run my hand up the front of his leather jacket and press my body flat against his. This close, I can make out his pupils, dilated with a combination of lust and drugs as I grind my hips against his.

"Don't you want to dance first?" I purr.

With an arrogant smirk, he spins me and grabs hold of my hips, yanking them back against his pelvis as he attempts to grind his dick between my asscheeks.

His hands are everywhere—clasping my thighs, brushing my stomach, squeezing my tits. Thank god my back is to him, 'cause I don't think I could hide the hatred flaring in my eyes.

Once a new song starts up, he leans in, his beard scratching the side of my face as he grunts in my ear, "Alright, you've had your song. Maybe you should show me your thanks by getting on your knees."

It takes me a second to unclench my teeth and be sure I'm not going to chew him out for that sickening statement. As soon as I turn my head to look up at him, ready to take this somewhere more private so I can get on with what I came here to do, one of his fellow Satan's steps up to us.

His eyes dart from mine to Python's before he speaks up, "Python, gotta problem."

Anger sparks in Python's eyes, and he grits out, "fine" before spearing me with a look. "Don't move. I'll be back."

*Fuck.*

I'd been planning on luring him up to the bedroom without any of his men getting a good look at me. Sure, they're probably drunk and high, but I can't take the risk that one of them will remember me in the morning. The last thing I need is these assholes searching all over town for me. I can't risk making my move tonight... which means I'll just have to come back.

With tonight's plan officially ruined and with zero desire to hang around so I can suck that shitstain's dick, I push my way through the crowd and out of the house, quickly ducking across the street and into the abandoned lot where I left my duffel bag earlier. Frustration courses through me as I hastily remove the wig and change back into my pants and leather jacket. Once I'm ready, I swing the bag onto my back and get the fuck out of there.

By the time I make it back to my apartment building, the sun is starting to rise, the faint gray light of dawn only drawing unwanted attention to the grubby state of my street and the run-down, filthy building I call home.

I'm exhausted, frustration giving way to tiredness, as I step into the dark entranceway, barely even noticing the flicker of the lightbulb or the smell of damp and mildew in the stairwell as I climb to the top floor. There are the typical, varying sounds of people getting up and starting their day as I pass by apartments, but I'm so used to the constant hum of life in the building that it's nothing more than background noise.

64

Reaching my apartment, my eyes feel gritty as I unlock and open the door, dropping my bag and kicking off my boots before I pad into the kitchen.

"Morning." I yawn as I greet Luc, who is sitting at the small two-person table, looking annoyingly fresh as he munches on his cereal.

"You look like shit."

I toss a glower at my asshat of a brother as I grab my own bowl and sit down opposite him, but there's zero heat behind it. "Yeah, well, so would you if you had the night I had," I grumble, helping myself to the box of cereal and filling my bowl. I top it off with some milk before digging my spoon in and turning to lean against the counter. I watch him over the lip of my bowl. We both have our mother's red hair—although his is slightly darker—and blue eyes—some sort of deep Irish heritage thing I think—but that's where the similarities stop. His nose is broader, his skin darker and cheeks more defined, and even though he's only fifteen, he's already a good head taller than me. "How's school?" I ask around a mouthful of food.

"It's good."

I roll my eyes. Getting information out of him recently is like drawing blood from a stone. I guess that's just part of living with a teenager. I should probably just be grateful he doesn't leave the toilet seat up and his dirty clothes scattered all over the living room, although I do make a point of not going into his bedroom, so god only knows what state that's in.

"How's work?" he counters with a knowing look.

"It's good," I snark, throwing his own words back at him. It's not like I'm about to tell him anything more than that, and he damn well knows it. I don't talk about the club with him, and I sure as shit don't include him in my extracurriculars.

65

He chuckles under his breath, but I notice his gaze lingers on me for a moment before he finishes off his bowl and gets to his feet. He sets it in the sink and then reaches down to grab his school bag. Slinging it onto his back, he pauses before leaving the kitchen, and turns to look at me.

"You know, if you need me to help out, I can."

I'm shaking my head before he's even finished speaking. "No," I insist, lifting my head to meet his eyes. "I have it covered. Let me worry about money, and you just focus on school, okay?"

"I'm fifteen," he says with a frown, as if being fifteen somehow means he should be pulling his weight. He might be taller than me now, but he's still just a kid. Life has forced him to grow up faster than he should have; I'm not about to rob him of any more of his childhood.

"Yeah, and until you're eighteen, your job is to go to school." His school is a joke. I'm fairly certain even some of his teachers never graduated high school, never mind obtaining teaching qualifications, but it's the principle of the matter.

I pin him with a *don't argue with me* look, to which he rolls his eyes. It's not the first time we've had this argument, and I'm sure it won't be the last.

"Okay," he agrees on a sigh. "I'm off. I'll see ya later."

"Have fun," I call out just before the door slams shut behind him.

Luc is the reason I've fought so hard for what we have. He was only five when we ended up on the streets, and trying to look after him while keeping us both safe was the hardest thing I've ever had to do. His young age granted us nights in shelters I wouldn't have gotten otherwise, but I had to do things I'm not proud of so that we could get by. I couldn't bear seeing him go hungry any longer or continuing to run around in clothes several sizes too small with shoes that needed the toes cut out just so they fit him. These were all the reasons and justifications I needed to get through every back alley blow job, pick-pocketing people, and stealing food.

So, when Enzo first approached me with the offer of money for information, of course , I jumped at the chance. I was still too young to get a job anywhere, forcing me to take any cash-in-hand jobs I could find—which are few and far between and usually of the unsavory kind. Money in exchange for information was a lot easier and less degrading than some of the other things I'd had to resort to doing. It made a big difference until I was able to get a job in a strip club—one of the few places where you can actually earn enough to get off the streets and create a semi-stable home for yourself.

I get up on that stage every night and shake my ass so Luc can have a roof over his head, food in his belly, clothes on his back. So he can have the things he needs for school and the comic books he loves. So his life can be a little bit more normal than mine ever was.

It's to ensure he has a better life than I have—a brighter future than I can ever hope for. That's why I get up every morning and do what I do. It's why I don't piss off the Satan's or try to find a lesser-paying job that would let me keep my clothes on. Wanting him to live in a better world than the one we currently exist in is why I don't think twice when I'm draining the life out of some scumbag and pawning off their things. Luc is the reason for my existence, for every decision I make on a daily basis. He's the only thing in this world that matters to me. I'd die for him. I'd kill for him.

Finishing off the last of my cereal, I dump my bowl in the sink with Luc's before going for a shower. It's Friday, and I have just enough time to squeeze in a few hours of sleep before needing to be at work. I'm on the day shift today, which means I have tonight off. The Satan's go to Toxic on Friday nights, and while I'm not sure if I can approach Python there, I'm going to stalk him everywhere until the perfect window of opportunity presents itself again. I can't let him slip through my fingers next time, and if tonight isn't the night, then it's only a matter of another day or two until I get my opening. From what I can tell, the Satan's throw parties most nights. No matter what, Python will be nothing more than a decaying corpse by the end of the weekend.

***

I spend the afternoon trying out a few new dance routines in between serving customers. The day shifts are entirely different from the evening ones. Strip Tease is much quieter and the patrons more subdued, allowing us to practice new dance moves and show any new girls the ropes.

Once my shift is over, I change in the dressing room into a short red skirt, my thigh-high leather, heeled boots, and a black crop top, ready to hit Toxic and hopefully kill an abusive shithead. There's no better way to spend a Friday night, am I right?

Toxic is a large club housed in one of the warehouses down by the old, deserted docks. It's a popular spot on the weekends. Regardless of how broke the citizens of Black Creek are, they can usually still scrounge enough pennies together to get drunk on the weekend and pretend their problems don't exist for a little while.

The heavy bass of the music vibrates through the street as I step up to the door, paying the entrance fee before I pass by the bouncers and into the club. Multi-colored strobe lights illuminate the dimly lit, ample, open space, and I notice that there is already quite a crowd on the dance floor, and the bar is packed. I do a loop of the room, spotting the Satan's in the cordoned-off VIP section before moving to the bar and ordering a shot of tequila.

Downing it, I blend seamlessly into the crowd as I move onto the dance floor, swaying my hips and shaking my shoulders in time to the music until I find the perfect spot where I can hide among the other dancers while also keeping an eye on the Satan's, and more importantly, Python. The man himself is lounging in the middle of his crew of idiots, looking like the king of his kingdom as he surveys the room.

I watch for a while as he and his buddies do lines of cocaine, harass waitresses, and drink their weight in hard liquor. In the crowded venue, I notice Python is never left alone. At least one of his little followers is always with him, and he never comes out from behind the separated VIP area, meaning it's going to be next to impossible for me to get to him tonight.

I'm not one to easily give up, though, and I continue my pretense of dancing as the night wears on. As the hours pass by, the club only gets busier, and eventually, I have to accept that I won't get to relish in spilling Python's blood tonight. My thumbs stroke longingly over the hilt of the short blades hidden in the lip of my thigh-high boots. *Soon,* I promise them.

With a final glance in Python's direction, I sigh and turn away. There's no point continuing to stand here and watch him berate women and snort cocaine all night. Frustrated, I move over to the bar, figuring I may as well let my hair down and have a couple of drinks while I'm here. It is a Friday night, after all. If I'm not working, I may as well enjoy my night off. And nothing says *let's have fun* like another shot of tequila.

# OLIVER

*Chapter 5*

After being gone for over three years, it's weird being back here. Everything's the same, yet entirely different. How can a place change so much? Or maybe it's me that's changed? The last time I was here, I was a member of The Feral Beasts, the most feared and ruthless gang that ran the streets. After I left and everything went sideways, I started seeing myself in a new light. Being away from Black Creek gave me some much-needed perspective. It enabled me to re-evaluate the man I want to be and gain some further clarity for what I want out of life.

I was barely sixteen when I joined The Feral Beasts. Nothing but an angry, confused, lost kid who thought joining a group of violent thugs would provide me with the structure and aggressive outlet that I needed. And it did... initially, but over time, I came to see it for what it was—a bunch of lowlifes who cared about nothing but themselves. There was no line they wouldn't cross, and as they became more and more barbaric, I knew I had to get out. So when I saw my chance, I took it... even if it did result in me ending up locked up for two years. I haven't once regretted it.

I'd never planned on coming back to Black Creek. After the shit that went down in Crescentwood, I was done with gang life. Prison also gave me plenty of time to figure out what I wanted, and you know what I came up with? Nothing. Not a single damn thing. The truth is, I have no fucking clue what I want in this world. I just know I want to be a part of something bigger than myself. The anger and vengeance that was coursing through my veins the day I patched into the Beasts are still there, sitting like a lead weight on my chest, dragging me down. So when I got Cain's letter informing me of his plan for revenge, I knew I had to be involved. It's what I'd been trying—and failing miserably—to do when I joined the Beasts. However, this time, I'm not a sad, lost, lonely sixteen-year-old boy. This war is as much mine as it is Cain's, and I can feel it in my gut that this is what I'm supposed to do—even if it kills me. For Cain and Evie, but also for myself. I need closure. I need to come to terms with what happened that day and finally put it behind me so I can move on with my life.

I've been back in Black Creek for a month now, and it's amazing how quickly I've fallen into the swing of things. Most of Cain's crew is relatively new. He gave me the whole rundown when I first arrived, and I was shocked to hear how he'd ended

72

up recruiting some of them. Rescuing them from a facility that trains children to be killers? It sounded like insanity to me, yet you only have to watch some of the kids he's taken in—some of whom are barely eighteen—in the ring. They're lethal machines, able to obliterate their opponent within seconds.

Cain dubbed me his second in command when I returned, and I've been kept busy ensuring we have a firm control over the parts of downtown Black Creek that are ours, sorting out the new premises we recently moved into and starting up a fighting pit in the shell of an empty swimming pool in a long-abandoned gym across the road from us. It's been a huge success, with plenty of men—and even some women— coming to compete. Not to mention the outlet it has provided for the kids Cain rescued. They've quickly gained a name for themselves as being unbeatable in the ring, and people come from all over the city, and further afield, to fight against them, thinking they can win the title of victor—and the nice sum of cash we offer the winner. In fact, it has become such a popular attraction that we're now looking to expand and set up another one, ideally in larger premises where we could fit in a bigger crowd—which is why I'm here tonight.

Glancing around the large warehouse, I can't help but think how perfect this place would be. The vast open space lends itself nicely to what we have in mind, and there is more than enough space for a fighting ring, plus a large audience and even a bar. The fact that it's outside territory we already own is just an added bonus. We're not necessarily looking to take control of all of the downtown area. Still, it will undoubtedly make us appear as more formidable of an opponent if we occupy a majority of the city. Besides, we're playing the long game with the Antonellis, so we may as well keep ourselves busy by taking control of what we can of Black Creek until we're in a position to go after our real targets.

I'd been scouting out possible venues when I first came across this club. Looking at it from the outside, I had a gut feeling it would be perfect for our needs, but I needed to suss out the current gang in charge of this part of town before we could even make any moves to claim the land and the club for ourselves. So I've spent the last two days stalking them and finding out what I could. Once I'd confirmed they could easily be removed, I headed here, wanting to get the lay of the land inside the building before taking my proposition to Cain.

I lift my gaze to the large mirror hanging on the wall along the back of the bar. It gives me a perfect view of the VIP section on the far side of the room, where the current controllers of this part of the city reside, lording it up as they get trashed and put on a pornographic show for the rest of the club. The Satan's Advocates are a relatively minor, disorganized street gang who own a sliver of land by the old docks—where this warehouse is located. The ports have been out of service for years now, ever since the Antonellis took charge of the Tideside Docks on the opposite side of the river and declared that all goods coming into the city had to go through them.

I don't know much about the Satan's, but watching them the last couple of days has me confident that they pose no threat to the Rejects. Our guys will easily destroy them. A thrill of excitement rushes through me at the thought of confronting a rival gang and taking another step toward achieving our ultimate goal.

The bartender sets a glass of whiskey in front of me, the clunk of the glass against the wood drawing me out of my thoughts as he moves on down the bar. Lifting the drink to my lips, I take a sip, grimacing at the taste. Damn, you'd think more than two years of no alcohol would mean I'm not picky about what I drink, but this cheap swill tastes like shit in comparison to the fancy stuff floating around Crescentwood.

I down half the glass because, regardless of how crappy it tastes, it's still alcohol, and it's exactly what I need tonight. Observing the Satan's yesterday and today, and seeing the dilapidated state of their territory has not been fun. Just from what little I've noticed, I can tell that they are the typical, power-deluded, small-dicked assholes who try to claim every other street corner in Black Creek. They use their guns and a *because I can* attitude to terrorize the people here, forcing them to do whatever they want.

From what I can tell, they have every business in this part of town paying them a protection tithe—a pretty common thing in any part of the city—nevertheless what these people really need is protection from the Satan's. Only yesterday, I watched as one of them shot up a butcher's shop before dragging the owner's daughter out of there. I followed him back to their clubhouse—which had been just several run-down houses on a derelict street—where he proceeded to shove alcohol and drugs down her throat before fucking her and moving on to the next thing that caught his eye. I made sure I got the girl home in one piece, but I nearly blew my cover just to go in and rescue her. That shit is not fucking okay. I wanted to slaughter every single one of those assholes there and then. But we need to do this the right way, with the full force of the club, so we can make a statement to anyone who might think to rise up against us and properly claim Satan's Advocates territory as our own.

With my drink in hand, I turn in my stool to peruse the room. For the most part, the club is full of regular everyday men and women who are just trying to have a bit of fun on the

75

weekend. A loud roar of laughter draws my attention to the VIP area, where several booths are overflowing with raucous Satan's members. I've been casually keeping an eye on them since they walked in. From what I can tell, their lewd behavior is just more of the same as it was last night. Drugs and girls, just in a different location.

I noticed the change in the atmosphere, though, as soon as they walked in. Tension bled into the air, and most people have been keeping a safe distance from them ever since; never getting too close and frequently casting fearful glimpses out of the corner of their eyes. Not that I can blame them. The second they arrived, they picked out several scantily clad women and all but dragged them to their table, demanding they dance and put on a show for them.

I don't let my gaze linger on the group for too long, not looking to draw any unwanted attention. Nor do I have any desire to watch the show they are forcing the girls to put on. Downing my drink, I turn back to the bar, lifting the glass when I catch the bartender's eye in a silent gesture for a second one. A few moments later, another glass of cheap whiskey is set in front of me. With a nod of thanks, I slap a few dollar bills onto the counter and take a sip, letting the whiskey warm me up from the inside as I turn to face the room again. I'm not expecting to find anything different, however I do need to remain vigilant in case the Satan's start something. Besides, if growing up in Black Creek didn't teach me not to turn my back on a room full of strangers, then prison definitely did.

I'm doing a casual once-over of the club when I catch my first glimpse of her through the crowd. The strobe lights reflect off her auburn hair as she moves to the beat of the music. The way her hair catches in the glow has me mesmerized, the shiny strands a beautiful deep copper color as they sway with her movements.

From where I'm sitting, she has her back to me, so I can't get a look at her face, and with the dense crowd separating us, I can't see anything south of her shoulders. The unique shade of her hair is the only thing I can make out.

A shoulder bumps against mine as someone jostles into me at the crowded bar, and I glance away from the captivating redhead to scowl at them, giving them my long-perfected death glare. With a terrified expression, they mutter a quick apology before scurrying away, but it's too late. By the time I look back to the dance floor, she's gone.

Frowning, I knock back the last of my whiskey. I'm about to get up and leave—figuring I'm not going to learn anything I don't already know about the Satan's tonight—when the redhead herself slides up to the bar beside me. She is leaning her arms on the wooden countertop, thus her ass juts out in that way girls do that draws every eye immediately to her tight, round globes.

She's attempting to wave down the bartender on the far side of the bar, so I take advantage of her distraction to properly take her in. She's got on a tight black crop top that shows off her toned torso, and I catch a peek of a vine tattoo patterned with budding flowers peeking out from beneath her sleeve as it wraps around her upper arm. She's skinny, just like everyone in Black Creek, yet she's been blessed—or cursed, maybe—with voluptuous curves and a huge rack.

A short, red, leather skirt just about covers her ass, giving every red-blooded male in the house a hard-on. She's paired the ensemble with thigh-high black boots; the whole outfit making her look like my wildest fucking dreams. Believe me, two years in prison has given me plenty of time to fantasize about the perfect fucking woman and here she is, standing in front of me like God's hand-delivered her himself.

"A shot of tequila," she shouts at the bartender, having finally gained his attention. Not that it was much of a hardship with her tits sticking out like that. The guy behind the bar barely glances at her face, his eyes glued to her chest before he tears them away to fill her order.

"Make it two," I call out, throwing a few bills down on the countertop.

The woman turns to stare at me with a wary look as the bartender grabs a bottle of tequila and two shot glasses. She continues to scrutinize me as he sets the two glasses on the bar and fills them to the brim with the colorless liquid before lifting the dollar bills and moving off to serve someone else.

I'm barely paying him any attention, though, unable to tear my gaze away from the alluring woman standing beside me. Her eyes drop to my boots and slowly rise as she takes in my dark, worn jeans and black shirt. She takes her time investigating the tattoo sleeve on my right arm, although I doubt she can make out any of the finer details in the dark light of the club. I had most of it done while on the inside. Initially, it was just to cover up the Beast insignia that I couldn't stand to look at any longer, but it turned into a full arm and chest piece. There's not exactly a lot to do in prison, and getting various tattoos was a better use of my time than a lot else I could have been up to.

When she reaches my muscular biceps, she lingers there for a second before letting her gaze drift over my lean, toned chest that's easily visible through my form-fitting top. Finally, her eyes lift to my face, taking in the shadow of stubble dusting my jaw, the high rise of my cheekbones, and my messy, brown hair before her eyes connect with my pale-blue ones once again. Lust burns in her eyes and a flirtatious smile lifts her lips. Done checking me out—and clearly happy with what she sees—she grabs the two shot glasses off the bar, handing one to me.

"Cheers," she says, clinking her glass against mine before bringing it to her full, pouty lips, tilting her head back as she downs it in one.

Mimicking her, I throw back my own shot, hissing as the bitter substance burns its way down my throat. When I make eye contact with the redhead again, she's watching me closely as she licks a stray droplet of tequila from her lower lip. That simple movement draws my attention to her lips and sends a zing of need to my balls, the likes of which I haven't felt in far too fucking long.

When the bartender passes, making his way along the bar, I lift two fingers in the air, indicating another round.

"Are you trying to get me drunk?" she laughs, a warm, infectious sound that, even over the noise of the music, resonates with me. "Because you should know, I have a very high tolerance."

I don't know anyone in Black Creek who doesn't, but my lips quirk up at her joke, the muscles feeling stiff after the last few years of disuse. The bartender moves over to fill our shot glasses, and I hand him a few more bills as I watch the captivating goddess beside me. She tilts her head back when the glass touches her lips, extending the long column of her throat, which bobs as the liquid slides down it.

She turns back to look at me once more as she sets the empty glass on the bar. In the dark light of the club, it's impossible to make out the color of her eyes, but there's a slight glaze to them from the alcohol coursing through her system. Her tongue flicks out to run along her plump lower lip before her teeth sink into the flesh. *God, if that isn't the hottest fucking thing I've seen in forever.*

"I'm O—" I begin, but she presses her finger against my parted lips, cutting off my introduction.

"No names." She smirks coyly, and mischief brims in her eyes.

When she lifts her finger off my lips, I lean in, matching her lustful expression with a lascivious one of my own.

"If you don't know my name, what are you going to call out when I'm making you come?"

Her breath hitches at my dirty words, her teeth sinking into her bottom lip again, making me wish I was the one biting into the soft flesh.

"If that's where this night ends up, I'm sure I'll think of something," she purrs, her eyes half-lidded with desire.

I push to my feet, a move that has me looking down on her, and presses my body flush against her lithe frame. Grabbing hold of her hand, I pull her along behind me into the sea of bodies writhing against each other on the dance floor. Placing a large palm around her hip, I tug her in against me as she drapes her arms over my shoulders, swaying her hips in time to the music. We lose ourselves in the rhythm, every passing song and tease of her pelvis against my painfully hard erection only endeavors to skyrocket the tension crackling in the air between us. I don't know what it is about her, but I'm entranced by the sheen of her hair in the light, the teasing sparkle in her eye, and the flirtatious curl of her lip. It's possible I've just gone too long jerking myself off and maybe Cain's right by saying I need to get laid. In spite of that, there hasn't been a woman who has held my attention since I was released. At least, no woman until her.

She spins in my hold, pressing the curve of her ass against my cock. There's no way she doesn't feel how badly I want her. My arms wrap around her slim waist, my palms flat against her toned stomach as she grinds into me. I catch the dirty smirk on her face. She knows damn well what she's doing to me, the fucking tease. Dipping my head, I plant a kiss in the crook of her neck, and she tilts her head, granting me better access as I suck and nibble my way up to her ear.

"Two can play that game," I whisper into her ear before I trail my fingers up the inside of her thigh, slip under her short skirt and teasingly skim them over the front of her panties.

A soft gasp escapes between her parted lips, inaudible to anyone other than me over the sound of the music, not that she seems to care. Fuck, if the dirty noise doesn't have me grinding harder against her ass.

Slipping my fingers under the scrap of fabric covering her cunt, I find her already dripping wet as I circle her clit. Her head falls back against my shoulder, eyes drifting shut under my ministrations. I watch mesmerized as her lips part, her mouth dropping open as she gets closer to orgasm. A blush slowly works its way up her heaving chest as I slide my fingers lower and slowly push two inside her, eliciting a groan. She feels so fucking good spasming around my fingers. I can only imagine how fucking incredible she would feel wrapped around my dick, her wet heat sucking me deeper.

Her hand comes around behind her, slipping between us until she's rubbing it over the more than obvious imprint of my dick in my jeans. Applying just the right amount of pressure, she squeezes me through the thick fabric before dipping lower and cupping my balls.

I growl in her ear, pressing my thumb over her sensitive nub, rubbing tight circles until I feel her inner walls clenching.

"Fuck," she cries as she comes all over my fingers.

I don't give her time to recover before I pull out and spin her around. Placing my hand on her hip to steady her, I slide the other one into her hair, wrapping around the silky soft strands and tugging her face toward me. My lips slam down on hers, desperate to fucking taste her.

She opens up beneath me, her soft lips gliding over mine with our tongues dueling in a heated battle for dominance. She tastes like cherries and tequila. Total and utter temptation.

Her hands come up, fisting the front of my shirt and pulling me flush against her as I slide my hand round to her back, slowly moving it down until I'm cupping her ass, grinding my dick against her pelvis.

She breaks the kiss, taking a step back. As my hand falls from her body, she grabs it, searing me with a heated gaze before she spins around and tugs me behind her as she moves toward the back of the club. I have no idea where she's taking me, and I really don't care. All the blood has left my brain. It's been over three fucking years since I've gotten laid. Who can blame a guy for being led by his dick after that long? Since the second she sidled up beside me at the bar, my cock has one hundred percent been in control. It's driving every action, every word, and hell, it's about to get so fucking lucky.

She pulls me down a corridor, past the bathrooms, until she's pushing open a fire exit door, and we tumble out into a dark alley behind the club. The fresh air is a welcome relief from the stuffiness inside, but it does nothing to ease the heat thrumming through my veins especially when she spins around and pushes me against the wall beside the door.

With deft fingers she unbuttons my jeans, and pulls out my throbbing dick, wrapping her hand around it and gently squeezing before she grazes the pad of her thumb over the bead of pre-cum, smearing it as she pumps her hand up and down my shaft.

Without a second thought or any hesitation, she drops to her knees and licks her lips before wrapping them around me. *Hooooly fuckkkk*. I have to fight the urge to come too soon as she sucks me in deeper, the wet heat of her mouth feels like fucking heaven.

She looks up at me through hooded eyes as I entangle my fingers in her hair. The desire I see in her eyes has me thrusting into her, forcing her to take me further. She's not just doing this because she thinks she should; she's doing it because she fucking wants to. She's getting off on having me in her mouth as much as I am.

Her tongue is pressed flat against the underside of my shaft, and her cheeks are hollowed as she bottoms out, taking all of me. I can feel the tip of my dick hitting the back of her throat before she pulls back.

I try not to thrust and let her take control, but it doesn't last very long. Suddenly I'm fucking her mouth, her fingers digging into my thigh as she holds on for dear life. Her eyes never waver from mine, and I alternate between being captivated as I watch my dick disappear between her supple red lips and falling into the carnal need I can see burning in her glistening eyes.

Feeling the familiar tingling in my balls, I pull out and haul her off the ground. She's light in my arms as I spin around and pin her against the wall, my hand reaching between her thighs and tearing off her panties.

"As fucking amazing as that was, I believe I have a promise to keep," I growl.

She wraps her legs around me as I dig a condom out of my back pocket and sheath myself in record time before I line up at her entrance. I slam all the way into her as she cries out, crashing her lips onto mine.

*Jesus fuck*, she's the hottest thing I've ever felt. Did pussies always feel this good, and it's just been so long I've forgotten or is it all her? Maybe she's got a magical pussy. That or she's a venus flytrap, luring me in with her hot mouth only to kill me. Hell, I don't even think I'd care. What an awesome way to go out—with the most explosive orgasm of my life.

"Fuck," I groan, beginning to move.

I thrust into her, her hips lifting to meet mine as she continues to pillage my mouth. As she gets closer to the edge, she breaks off our kiss, her head dropping back to lean against the brick wall behind her. Licking down her throat, I bury my nose in the crook of her neck. I can already feel the familiar prickle at the base of my spine as she clenches tightly around me, her own orgasm nearing.

"Oh, fuck, yes," she cries out as her pussy spasms around me, practically sucking the cum out of me as I grunt into her neck, my hot seed hitting the latex condom.

There's no way sex has always been this good. No one could fucking forget this feeling of euphoria. *This* moment right here is the one that will flash before my eyes when I die, reminding me of how fucking incredible my life was.

"Okay, I believe you now," she pants, making me chuckle.

She unwraps her legs from my hips, dropping them to the ground, and I pull back, ignoring the silent cry from my dick as I withdraw from her comforting warmth.

Removing the condom, I chuck it in a dumpster and tuck myself away. "Wanna go back in and grab a drink?" I ask.

She glances up at me as she shimmies her skirt back down over her hips, shaking her head. "I'm done for tonight. I have an early start tomorrow."

"Well, can I at least get your number?"

She smirks but shakes her head again—an action I'm beginning to think she does quite often. "Sorry. I can't afford distractions right now, and you"—she rakes her eyes over me one final time—"would definitely be a distraction."

I open my mouth to respond just as the fire exit door bangs open, snapping my attention toward it as a rowdy crowd of clearly inebriated customers pile out. I swear I only take my eyes off her for a second, yet when I look back down the alley, the red-haired vixen is gone.

For a moment, I simply stand there, debating whether or not to go after her, but her words about being a distraction ultimately stop me. She was right about that. With all the plans Cain has, he's going to end up razing the city, and I can't let anyone alter my focus if we're about to rain down hell.

# SAWYER

## Chapter 6

Memories of last night still occupy my mind as I pull open the door to the women's shelter the next day. I hid in the alley and watched when the mysterious hottie from the bar discovered I'd disappeared. I saw the flicker of indecision in his light blue eyes, but it only lasted a second before a determined resolve replaced it, and he went back into the club. The wave of disappointment that washed over me was even more justification that I needed to stay away from him.

I'll admit, he definitely was not what I was expecting when I went out last night. He might not have been the blood and the sense of righteous justice I'd been hoping for, but he was certainly intriguing. The way his close proximity heated me up, it was like nothing I've ever felt before. Just looking at him, with his toned torso and muscular biceps had my panties damp, and I was practically coming as soon as he touched me. And holy hell in a handbasket, the sex was off the charts.

My job makes me cynical when it comes to men and sex, but I feel it's pretty accurate to say that most men are only concerned with getting themselves off. You rarely find someone who gives jack shit about a woman's pleasure. So, the fact that he not only thought about it but delivered in an exceptional way... well, that's a rare find.

He had the same hard edges as resident Black Creekians do, yet something was different about him. Not in a suspicious way like Enzo. Just... different. But like I told him, I can't afford distractions right now. Besides, he's probably tied up with one gang or another, and there's no way I'm getting involved in that shit. I know enough to know going out with a gang member is just asking for trouble. The gang will always come first to people like that. I've made many concessions in my life, but I refuse to settle for being an afterthought. I'd rather live the rest of my life single, even if it does mean I'll most likely die alone with twenty cats.

With a smile and a nod to the woman at the check-in desk, I head toward Sheryl's room, wanting to give her an update. I'm sure she's been a nervous wreck. She should have gone back to Python days ago, and I know the longer she's gone, the worse it will be for her if she does go back. Not that she is, but I can understand that the severity of her consequences for staying away for so long will be weighing heavy on her mind. She won't be able to settle herself until she knows he's dead and buried.

She pounces on me the second I step into the room. "Is it done?" Her eyes are wide with panic, and she somehow looks even paler than she did the last time I saw her.

"Not yet."

Running her hands through her hair in frustration, she chews on her bottom lip. "Maybe this isn't such a good idea. I was upset the other night. I-it wasn't that bad. I probably over-exaggerated it."

I plant my hands on her shoulders, waiting until her panicked stare meets my steady gaze. "He hurt Grace," I say the words slowly, reinforcing them in her mind. "He'll keep hurting her unless *you* do something about it." I pierce her with an intent look. "I promised I'd get rid of him, and I will. Just stay here, out of sight, for a few more days."

Tears well in her eyes, but she nods her head. I stay for a bit longer, checking on how she and Grace are both doing before I leave. It's clear she's not really in the mood to talk, and I've got things to be getting on with anyway. I have to work tonight, but tomorrow, Python is all mine, and this time I'm not going to let him slither through my fingers.

By the time I leave Sheryl, it's late afternoon, and as I walk into the apartment, I find Luc sprawled across the sofa, looking bored out of his mind as he stares abjectly at the TV.

"What's wrong?" I ask, frowning.

He sighs, barely sparing me a glance as he mutters, "Nothing."

*Oh, well, okay then.*

Just about managing to hold back the roll of my eyes, I state, "It's clearly something. Just tell me."

His lips thin as he finally shifts his attention to me. "I'm so fucking bored."

"So do something else," I reason, quickly losing patience now that I know there's nothing really wrong with him beyond usual teenage grumpiness.

"Like what?" he argues. "There's nothing else I can do."

"I don't know," I grumble. "Read one of your comic books." His face scrunches up, not liking that suggestion. "Or play a game on your phone." That idea earns me another unimpressed glare. "I don't know, Luc." I sigh. "Is there anyone from school you can hang out with?"

He just glowers at me in response. "You know there isn't."

I let out a heavy exhale as guilt swarms through me. He's slowly lost all of his childhood friends over the last couple of years, as they've become embroiled in gang business. They always tried to rope Luc in too, but when he wouldn't budge, they just dropped him. I know it can't be easy for him to resist that level of peer pressure and slowly lose the people you thought were your friends. I'm beyond proud of him for standing up for himself and refusing to be so easily led astray, but the guilt weighs heavy on my soul. It's because of me that he's got no one to hang out with and that he's stuck mainly inside this tiny apartment when he's not at school. Honestly, it would be enough to drive anyone crazy.

I remind myself that I'm just trying to keep him alive, and that assuages some of the guilt I'm carrying, but it doesn't loosen the knot in my stomach when I look into his incensed, stormy-blue eyes.

"Well, why don't we play a board game?" I offer. I have several hours to kill before I need to leave anyway.

The anger in his eyes softens a little, but he still looks pretty pissed off as he reluctantly agrees, and I go to fetch something from our measly collection. We found them in the

90

storage cupboard when we first moved in, and over the years, we must have played them hundreds of times. There isn't much else to do around here. Besides, it's always just been Luc and me—the two of us against the world—and until his teenage hormones kicked in, we liked it that way.

After humming over our choices, I grab the Scrabble box and move to sit on the floor. Luc joins me a moment later, and for half an hour, all is right in the world again as we laugh and tease and make fun of one another, arguing over possible made-up words just like old times.

"Thrubble is not a real word," I argue while laughing.

"It so is."

"Use it in a sentence then," I challenge.

His lips purse as he thinks it over for a second, and I just shake my head.

"Oh, I'm going to go thrub—"

The squeal of tires against asphalt on the street below cuts him off, and I stiffen as I look toward the window, suddenly on alert. Car doors bang as I quickly climb to my feet and move to peer out the window.

My mouth goes dry as I find two cars parked across the middle of the road outside my building. I count ten burly men with weapons surrounding them as their eyes roam over the building, but what terrifies me is the man standing at the front of the group. With his snake tattoo prominently on display, he'd be recognizable anywhere.

"Go to your room," I bark to Luc as I spin around.

"What? Why? What's going on?" He asks, a slight tremor to his voice.

"Just go," I snap as I hurriedly stuff the board game under the sofa. "Hide somewhere and stay quiet." He hesitates a second longer before getting to his feet and moving toward his room.

91

Just before he crosses the doorway, though, I grab his upper arm and pierce him with an intent look. "No matter what happens, or what you hear, do *not* come out. Got it?"

His lips part on a gasp as he stares into my eyes. I can see the protest on his lips, but thankfully, he must see how fucking serious I am right now, and he just nods his head in agreement before I gently nudge him into his room.

I stand and watch as the door closes behind him, my heart hammering in tune to the sound of footsteps as the men hurry up the stairwell. Forcing myself to focus, I scan the room for any other signs that someone other than me lives here, letting out a small sigh of relief when I don't spot any of Luc's stuff sitting out.

If it's possible, my body coils even tighter when I hear the sounds of the first men reaching my floor. *Fuck, they really are here for me.* I'd been hoping it was just a coincidence, but as I hear the thundering footfalls in the hall, the chances of this being a coincidence get slimmer and slimmer.

The boom, boom, boom of a heavy fist knocking against a door makes me jump, and it takes far longer than it should for me to realize it's not actually my door but my neighbor's. The noise is followed by the sound of the door being kicked in and people yelling before several gunshots go off. The whole time, I just stare at my kitchen wall—the one that's adjoined to my neighbors—envisioning in my mind's eye what is likely playing out next door and feeling so goddamn thankful that it's not me they're here for. With Sheryl having been gone for so long, it was a distinct possibility. Although, I'm not even sure if Python knows who her friends are or that she even has any.

I'm not sure how long I stand there, listening to the indistinguishable sounds coming through the thin wall. Time loses all sense of meaning. It could be mere seconds or half an hour later before I hear the sounds of retreating footsteps thumping their way down the stairs, followed by the rumble of an engine starting and car doors slamming.

It's only when a deathly quiet falls, so heavy that for all I know, I've gone deaf that I finally react to the close call. My legs tremble, my whole body shaking as I sag to the floor in relief. I'm very aware that my neighbors are most likely lying dead next door, however all I can think of is *thank fuck it wasn't me.*

...

Eventually, the shaking stopped, and the fear and relief gave way to anger. Waves and waves of red-hot, molten fury. Outrage that we should have to live in such fear; at the knowledge, we aren't even safe inside our own homes. I don't know what my neighbors did to piss off the Satan's, and I don't care. It might not have been me they came for this time, but it could be next time, which scares me. The entire ordeal only incentivizes me to kill Python. Honestly, I want to destroy his whole fucking crew, but I'm just one person. There's no way I could take on an entire gang of criminals. For now, I just need to worry about the head of the snake.

My anger warms me for the whole night, getting me through my shift in the club and all of the next day as I plot and plan, and the next night, I watch from the shadows as a party rages—I swear it's all they fucking do—within the thin timber-frame walls of the Python's house. I can hear the music pounding and feel it vibrating through the asphalt all the way across the street, where I'm once again hidden while I watch tattoo-covered men dressed in leather and half-naked women filter in and out of the party.

93

I've got Raven hidden in the shrubs at the far end of the street for a quick getaway. With my thigh-high leather boots, black booty shorts, and matching crop top, not to mention the same honey-blonde wig as last time, covering my distinctive copper locks, I look more than ready to get down and dirty with the Satan's—which is exactly what I want them to think I'm here to do.

Running my thumb along the lip of my boots, I let vengeance heat the blood in my veins as I finger the hilts of the two small daggers I have securely tucked inside. I can practically taste the sweet aroma that comes from purging the world of yet another scumbag. It's a distinctive flavor—a mixture of sweet and spicy. It's heady and intoxicating, and it gives me a head rush like nothing else.

With adrenaline giving me a natural high, I stride confidently across the street and into the house. I head straight for the kitchen and search through the various bottles of spirits on the counter until I find a sealed bottle of whiskey. Unscrewing the cap, I bring it to my lips and down a decent portion of it before making my way into the living room. Anticipating that Python will be lounging in the same spot as last time, I push my way through the dense crowd of wasted dancers until I spy him amongst his crew, at the back of the room, exactly where I knew he would be. They appear casual, at ease, but I see the way Python warily eyes up the various people in the room, determining if they are a threat—or could be of use to him— before moving on.

I stop when I'm just off-center of his line of sight, far enough away that I don't look suspicious, but close enough to gain Python's attention when I start swaying my hips and openly drinking from the bottle. I lose myself in the music, the lyrics of *Gasoline* by Seether washing over me as I hold the whiskey bottle loosely between my fingers and alluringly trail my fingers across the bare skin of my abdomen, skimming the top of my booty shorts. I teasingly dip my fingers beneath the waistband and let my head fall back, my eyelids dropping to half-mast. Through my eyelashes, I peek at Python. His eyes observe my every movement with a carnal desire, and the corner of his lips quirk up in a sleazy grin that says everything about the dirty thoughts running through his head.

I don't have to put on a show for long before he says something to the men surrounding him and gets to his feet, stalking toward me. Everything about him screams predator. He thinks he's the most threatening person in the room. Little does he know he's caught in my trap, and he won't escape alive.

The song switches to *Figured You Out* by Nickelback as his hand comes to rest low on my hip, giving it a possessive squeeze as he pulls me in.

"You disappeared on me." There's a threatening weight to his tone, and I know if I don't play this right, he'll lose the thin thread of control he has over his temper.

I don the personality I use to work at the club and smile coyly at him, ensuring none of the hatred I feel for him is visible on my face. "I came back, though." I peer up at him with innocent, sultry eyes and allow my fingers to brush over his chest, making it clear that I came back *for him*. This is true, just not in the way he thinks.

He assesses me for a long moment before choosing to let go of his anger, a sordid grin curling around the edges of his lips. "Hmm, well, I'm sure you can find a way to make it up to me." There's a dangerous edge to his voice, one that says I have no choice in the matter. It makes my spine straighten, even though I know tonight will never get that far.

Forcing a submissive, innocent look to my face, I look up at him through my eyelashes as I bring the bottle of whiskey to my lips again, taking another deep swallow before I run my tongue along my lower lip, catching a stray droplet. He tracks the movement with dilated pupils before he smirks. His expression is a slimy thing that I'm sure he thinks has women buckling at the knees but only makes me suppress a shiver of disgust as he wraps his meaty hand around the bottle and tugs it out of my grip, not even bothering to ask if he can have some first. But then men like him don't ask for things. They just take them.

Tilting his head back, his eyes stay focused on me as he chugs a quarter of the bottle, finishing it off before he shoves it into the arms of some random person as they pass by. His free hand claims my other hip, and I bring my hands up to rest on his shoulders, scraping my fingers teasingly over the bare skin of his upper arms. He grinds against me as song blurs into song, and I fantasize about chopping his fucking hands off with every squeeze of my ass and lick of my neck. I picture my skin washed red with his blood, the feel of his heart against my palm as it stutters to a stop, and by the time he tries to push me to my knees, expecting me to happily suck him off in the middle of his goddamn living room, I'm so fucking ready to get this over with.

"On your knees," he growls in my ear, his words a clear demand.

When I resist, his fingers dig painfully into my shoulders, but I grit my teeth, pushing past the urge to dick punch him. Instead, I laugh, a noise that's the perfect balance of drunk and seductive. "Baby, what I have planned for you is more than a quick face fuck." I slip my fingers underneath his shirt, digging my nails into his skin before dragging them down over his slight potbelly. I bite into my plump lower lip as I look up at him through my eyelashes. "It's going to take all fucking night."

His eyes are glazed over with alcohol and laced with desire as he snatches my hand and starts dragging me across the room and up the stairs. I can hear the sound of people fucking coming from behind some of the doorways while others are fucking right out in the open. Still, I pay them no attention as he pulls a key out of his pocket and unlocks the last door at the end of the corridor, flicking on the light as he ushers me in.

He purposefully locks it behind him and tucks the key back into his jeans pocket, and I watch every move with narrowed eyes. When he turns to face me, I let him lead me to the bed, pushing me down onto the mattress. His hands grope me everywhere, leaving fingerprint bruises on my tits and ass, while I let out obscene-sounding moans that any idiot could tell are obviously fake. He's too concerned about his own pleasure to give a shit, though.

He rolls onto his back and cocks a brow at me as his hand moves to undo his leather belt, letting it hang loosely as he pops the button of his jeans and pulls himself out. He strokes his less than impressive length while I resist rolling my eyes as I gasp. "Oh my."

He laughs maliciously. "Come on. Show me what a whore you are."

I move to straddle his thighs, wrapping my fingers around him and working him up until his head falls back against the pillow and his eyes drift shut. I'm already touching him more than I ever wanted to, but as I slide the thin blade out of my boot and aim it at his dick, I can feel my own excitement coating my panties.

I nick the loose skin of his ballsack, and he jolts, hissing through his teeth. "What the hell?"

"Oops," I giggle drunkenly. "Sharp nails."

"Well, watch it."

I wait until he relaxes back against the pillow again before debating what I want to do next. Part of me wants to drive the blade right through the bead of precum forming at his tip and into his urethra and see how much he fucking likes that. Another part of me wants to just slam it through the center of his shaft, right into the mattress below, and sit back while he screams in agony.

Unfortunately, castration will make it too obvious that it was a woman out for revenge who murdered this sorry sack of shit, and I can't have anyone pointing fingers in Sheryl's direction. So instead, I climb up his body, grinding my still fully clothed pussy against his dick. His eyes pop open as I pull off my crop top, and he drinks in my tits as they bounce in front of his face.

With him distracted, I link his fingers with mine and push them above his head, pinning them against the wooden headboard.

"Oh yeah, just like that. Take off your panties."

I smile down at him, and he probably thinks the wildness in my eyes is because I'm as caught up in this as he is. He doesn't suspect a thing... until I drive the dagger through his palms, into the softwood of his headboard, trapping him.

His eyes widen to the size of saucers, and there's almost a second's delay before he starts screaming bloody murder. I jump off him, quickly moving to turn on the stereo, letting some god-awful rap shit blast through the room as I turn it up to a blaring volume, effectively blocking out his screaming curses.

Spinning to face him, I watch as he stares up at where his hands are pinned to the wood above his head, blood dripping down into his hair, looking like some fucked up version of Jesus on the cross. He tries to push against the handle, wincing and quickly stopping. My blades aren't even that long. It probably wouldn't take much effort to wiggle it free from the wood, but despite the *tough-guy* persona he puts on in public, he's clearly a fucking wimp.

I move to climb back on top of him, slipping my other blade out of its sheath. My grin is positively vicious as I loom over him, ignoring the murderous look in his eyes. I flash my dagger at him, pushing his top up so I can trail the tip lightly down the center of his abdomen, moving closer to his now flaccid cock. I fucking revel in the gratification that floods my body when a spark of fear enters his eye and sweat beads along his hairline.

Why is it men will do practically anything when you point a knife at their dicks? You could literally point it at any other body part, and they'll challenge you, goad you, call your bluff... but so much as wave it at their cocks, and they turn into statues, muttering fake apologies and placating assurances not to do it again. Not that I have any idea what this asshole is saying to me over the sound of the shitty music. Everyone saw him come up here with a girl. No one will even think to check on him until morning... After all, what could a mere woman possibly do to a big, strong gang leader? Hmm, let's find out, shall we?

Getting bored of teasing him, I move my blade to the upper right quadrant of his abdomen and push the blade into his flesh. A drop of blood forms, and as I dig deeper, forcing the blade downward, that droplet becomes a slow, steady stream that flows faster with each inch I carve into his stomach until his midsection and my hand are coated in blood.

I stop just above his pelvis and use my hand to wipe the blood away, frowning when I find the line isn't straight.

"Asshole," I snarl. "You moved!"

His eyes have rolled back in his head when I lift my head to glower at him, and his breaths are coming in sharp, pained inhales, making his stomach rise and fall in rapid movements.

Shaking my head at the genuinely pathetic display of manliness, I get back to the task at hand, and I don't stop again until I'm done. I admire my handiwork for a long moment before focusing on Python, noticing his skin is coated in a layer of sweat, and his face is deathly pale.

"Oh dear, you're not looking so hot."

I'm fully aware he can't hear me over the blasting of the music, but I don't really care. Doesn't mean I can't have a little fun. After all, this is one of the few moments in my life when I actually get to let go a little and enjoy myself, when *I'm* in control; when *I* hold all the power. When I'm holding some asshole's life in my hand, I get to gain back some semblance of dominion over my own goddamn life. So yeah, I'm going to enjoy every fucking second of it.

Leaning forward, this time, he doesn't even look at my now blood-spattered tits as I wrap my hand around the dagger sticking out of the headboard and give it a hard yank.

His hands collapse onto the pillow, unmoving as his eyes begin to droop. He's close to passing out, and well, we can't have that.

I give his cheek a hard smack, and his eyes fly open, blinking rapidly as he tries to orientate himself.

"Pay attention, motherfucker."

He looks at my lips, but I'm pretty sure he can't understand what I'm saying. No worries, the manic look in my eye and savage grin is all I need him to see.

With a flick of my wrist, I slash the sharp blade across his neck, and his eyes flare for a moment as the life starts to drain out of them. I watch, fascinated as blood pools around the horizontal slice across his throat before it spills over, dripping down the column of his throat before soaking into his shirt and onto the sheet beneath him.

I'm not sure how long I sit there for, listening to him gurgle and gasp as he slowly drowns in his own blood. I watch as his breathing becomes shallow until his chest stops moving altogether. Only when he lies still beneath me, do I move, wiping the blade against his jeans to clean it off his blood before tucking it away inside my boot.

I've just grabbed my crop top from the bed when I hear noises in the hall. The thudding of boots. A scream. Gunshots. The sound of something heavy crashes against the bedroom door, jolting me into action as I hastily climb off the dead gang leader. If it's one of Python's men, I'm dead. There's no two ways about it.

Confused about what could possibly be going on, I decide in a split second that there's no way I could make it out the window in time, and clutching my top to my chest, I scurry into the corner of the room. Making myself as small as possible, I press my back flat against the wall and bring my knees up, ensuring my daggers are within reach. I force tears to my eyes as what sounds like a boot smacks against the wooden door, breaking the shitty lock. The door swings inward, and with tears streaking down my blood-stained face, I lift my head. I make myself look as innocent as possible as two muscular men—one who looks like he can't be any older than eighteen and a middle-aged man with gray, thinning hair—that I don't recognize as Satans' members storm into the room with their weapons raised.

They see Python first, and I note the surprise on their faces as they share a glance with one another before the older one notices me, jutting his chin in my direction. Their guns are still raised as they round on me, but instead of the tense lines around their eyes, there's a confusing wariness.

The younger guy moves to turn off the shitty music, and even though the heavy bass of the music from downstairs still vibrates through the floorboards, it's not loud enough to cover up the broken sob that escapes my lips as I let my chin wobble. *Damn, maybe I do have transferable skills after all.*

"What the fuck happened in 'er'?" the older guy asks, his gaze bouncing back and forth between me and the dead Satan's leader.

"I... he... " My voice cracks and I bury my head in my hands, sobbing. Well, pretending to.

"Razor," one of them says. "Look."

Lifting my head slightly, I peer through the slits between my fingers as the two of them lean closer to the dead body, inspecting it.

"Jesus, fuck," the older guy—Razor—exclaims. "How the hell did this even happen?"

They both stare at the body for a second longer before I feel their gazes on me, and I let out another shoulder-trembling sob.

As the older one makes a move toward me, I snap my head up, setting my features into one of fear as I try to back away from him, pressing my back flush against the wall. I don't even have to try that hard to be afraid. I am. I might be able to seduce men and lower their defenses, but I know the extent of my skills, and there's no way I could take on two large men like this and expect to get away unscathed. Don't get me wrong, I'll put up one hell of a fight if they touch me. I'm just not confident it's a fight that I'll win—my defensive skills are mediocre at best.

Seeing my terrified expression, Razor stalls, slowly putting his gun away and lifting his hands, palms forward in a gesture that he means me no harm. I watch him closely as he crouches down in front of me. His arm flexes, drawing my attention to the tattoo there, and I can just make out the Reaper Rejects insignia. *What the fuck? Why are the Rejects here?*

"We're not going to hurt you," he says, and I know he's trying to put me at ease, but I don't buy his bullshit. My blades are in my boots, but I can have them buried in his throat in a split second if he so much as looks at me wrong. It's his little buddy behind him that I'll have a more challenging time taking down without the element of surprise on my side. "We just want to know what happened."

I begin to blubber, mumbling nonsense because, well, I have no idea how to explain my way out of this one. "B-bathroom... dead... b-blood everywhere." I heave out another sob, glancing up between wet eyelashes to see the deep lines of confusion carved into his forehead as he studies me.

"Ehh, okay, let's get ya out of here, yeah? Get some whiskey in ye."

He doesn't move, continuing to look at me until I give a shaky jerk of my head.

"Alright, love, put your top on, and I'll get ya out of here."

I'm honestly a little confused by his behavior, but it's about to get me out of this room, so I don't overthink it and instead pull my top on, ignoring the icky feel of the dried blood crusting on my skin. I get to my feet, making them appear weak and shaky, and without sparing him a glance, I let the two Rejects escort me past Python and out of the room.

# Chapter 7

The bouncer on the door nods his head when I pass, and as I step into the large, open room, the noise of the crowd ricochets off the tiled walls. Men and women scream encouragement at whichever fighter they have their bets on tonight, drowning out the sound of *Monsters* by Shinedown blaring across the room from the overhead speakers.

As I glance around, I notice the place is packed tonight, and I have to push through the crowd as I cross the room. They hardly notice, though, since everyone is too focused on shoving each other as they jostle for a better view of the fight taking place in the middle of the room.

I started the underground fights when the Reaper Rejects only consisted of myself and a handful of others who had suffered at the hands of the Antonellis. Back then, it was nothing more than guys from the neighborhood meeting up once a week in an empty lot to try and prove themselves. But they've grown exponentially since then. When I took over old Beast territory a year ago, I made the fights a regular thing that drew a small but reliable crowd. Things really amped up when I helped my old friend, Beck, rescue his girlfriend from a compound where they were teaching kids how to become killers for hire. We ended up rescuing a bunch of those kids. I managed to find homes for many of the younger ones, but most of those who were older didn't have anywhere to go. When they asked if they could stay here, I had to tell them about my plans. I had to explain to them that if they did choose to stay, they would be putting themselves in danger once again. I honestly expected most of them to leave—and I wouldn't have thought any less of them if they had. Even though every one of them was a trained soldier, they'd already lived a life that wasn't theirs, and I assumed they would just want to enjoy their newfound freedom. I was wrong. Every single one of them agreed to help me, and by the end of that day, they all wore the Reaper Rejects tattoo with pride.

I suddenly had more members than I knew what to do with and finding somewhere large enough to house us all became my number one focus. When I came across the dilapidated apartment complex, I knew it would be perfect for our needs. Over the last few months, I've watched as my men have accepted the new kids into the crew, and we've slowly learned to get along—like one giant, dysfunctional family. The kids I rescued have grown the most. When they first arrived here, they were constantly on edge, jumping at every sound and

106

resorting to violence to solve every problem. I can't even begin to imagine the hell they were put through in that compound.

As I watched them struggling to cope with this new life they'd found themselves in, I knew they needed an outlet for all the confusion and anger they were feeling. I might not know what they had to endure, but I do know what it feels like to be an angry, confused, lost teenager, to feel that simmering rage pulsing beneath your skin with no constructive outlet. It can lead to dangerous things. So as soon as we moved into the apartment complex, I instructed the guys to gut the sports center opposite it and turn it into a suitable fighting ring.

We operate pit fights out of the swimming pool, and we knocked down the wall into the gym area, opening the floor space so we could put a bar along the far wall and squeeze in as many customers as possible.

I encouraged the kids to satiate their need for violence in the ring, giving them an outlet for everything they were feeling but didn't know how to process. I don't think I'd fully appreciated just how deadly these kids were until the first time I watched one of them in the pit. He was like an oncoming storm. His opponent never stood a chance against his precise strikes and forceful blows, and the fight was over in mere seconds. Although, it drew one hell of a crowd. After that, the whispers began about the unbeatable Rejects, and since then, our numbers have grown by the week, everyone coming to watch— or try their hand—against the deadly force of the Reaper Rejects.

A roar goes up from the crowd as the fight comes to an end, and people move to collect their winnings as the fighters are helped out of the pool. Bypassing the jostling audience as they move to refill their drinks before the next fight, I climb up the steps to the low platform I had built along one side of the room, intended for me and my officers and providing an

107

uninterrupted view into the fighting pit, and around the rest of the room.

A woman dressed in booty shorts, with her tits hanging out and a tray of drinks in her hand, meets me at the top of the stairs.

"Evening, Cain," she purrs, smiling seductively.

I let my gaze run over her subtle curves and perky breasts, winking as I take a glass of whiskey from her and move to join Oliver on one of the lounge seats. He's been checking out the Satan's territory all week and I haven't had a chance to catch up with him.

He raises his chin in greeting as I approach before his gaze roams over the adrenaline-pumped crowd on the floor below. "Hey, man."

"How's things?"

I settle on the seat beside him, looking down into the swimming pool as two new fighters drop into it and another round begins to the chorus of hoots and hollers.

We both watch the fight for a bit before he speaks. "Satan's territory looks promising. Small-scale gang; not very organized and cocky."

I nod my head. "And the docks?"

"They would definitely work. There's a nightclub in one of the buildings that attracts a good crowd on the weekends." One side of his lip quirks up in a mysterious smirk before he continues, "We already know it's drawing people in so it shouldn't be too hard to add regular fight evenings to the schedule."

We lapse into silence as the fight gets underway, a young blond man who's all attitude and mediocre muscle, is up against a middle-aged brute of a fighter. The two of them circle one another for several moments, the young guy losing patience first as he goes in for an uppercut that snaps his opponent's head back.

Blood gushes from the older fighter's nose and drips onto the already stained swimming pool tiles at their feet. Unperturbed, he spits blood into his opponent's face, going straight in for a round of powerful jabs to his chest and abdomen. The two fighters get more and more aggressive, the young one becoming increasingly desperate as he resorts to trying to gouge his opponents eyes out and rip his ear off with his teeth every time the guy gets too close to him.

"How have things been here?" Oliver asks as the young blond fighter is taken to the ground, his body slamming against the bottom of the pool with a painful sort of thud.

"Our shipments were light again," I inform him, my jaw ticking in irritation. It's been an issue for the last few weeks, and I've a fair idea who's behind it. The Grim Bastards have been a pain in my backside since I took control of the firearm distribution chains in and around Black Creek, and I'm pretty sure they've been stealing from me for the last few months. Somehow they've been gaining access to my shipments before I've been notified of their arrival and can send men to pick them up.

The Grim Bastards are my only other real competition for control of Black Creek—other than the Antonellis, but they're a whole different ball game. Between the three of us, we essentially rule the city. The Antonellis have a monopoly on all things gambling and sex. They run a prosperous casino down at the Tideside Docks, as well as multiple high-end sex clubs. When the Beasts left Black Creek, the Grim Bastards took control of their drug distribution channels, while I already had the necessary connections that made it easy to negotiate deals with those who operate the arms trade on the West coast.

109

Since I started running the arms trade in Black Creek, I've been working to reduce the number of firearms on the streets. Honestly, I don't trust anyone other than us to sell them. I've made it crystal fucking clear to my men who they can and cannot sell to. Namely kids, but I get my men to use some common sense when they're trading, and not just look at the green that's being handed over. I can't say the same happens in the other gangs that buy the guns off us, so I've been restricting how much they can purchase, and slowly reducing that figure.

Of course, I'm not stupid enough to think I can rid Black Creek of all guns. Not only would that put me out of business, but it would be fucking impossible. Nor do I think for one second it would make a difference. If I didn't provide them, someone else would, or they'd just be replaced by equally destructive weapons. I'm just trying to police their distribution.

However, the Grim Bastards are a problem I'm going to have to deal with. Soon. I can't let that sort of disrespect stand. The difficulty is, part of me doesn't give a shit. I didn't get into this business to contend with rival gangs, argue over borders or dispute the consignment of firearms. No, I'm in this game for exactly one thing—revenge. Vengeance. Retribution. Whatever you want to call it. It's a hatred I've been harboring for eleven years now, and with every passing day, it burns brighter, scorching my soul and turning it to ash.

"I'll get some men on it."

Oliver has fallen into his role as my second in command with surprising ease. Sure, having been a member of the Feral Beasts for years, he more than understands the hierarchy and what the role requires, but I know he has been confused and feeling a little lost since his release. Like me, he's only in this for revenge. To correct past mistakes and make up for what we couldn't prevent when we were barely more than children ourselves.

When this is all behind us, I imagine he'll move on and find a life for himself far from Black Creek. Like Beck did. He was one of the lucky ones who actually made it out of this cesspit alive. Got himself a good job and a nice girl to love. He even got himself three other guys with whom he's supposed to share her. Don't ask me how that shit works. I couldn't imagine sharing a girl with anyone for anything more than one night. Even then, I can be a possessive bastard. I like a girl's attention to be solely focused on me when we're fucking. Nothing wrong with that.

I give a sharp nod of my head, knowing he'll get the job done. It's not my main priority right now, though. Neither is taking over Satan's territory—although that is important. No, my main focus has been on finding a way into the Antonelli empire. Their part of the city is separated from the rest of us by a winding river that opens up into the docks and is the namesake of our city of criminals—Black Creek. They've set up their own little kingdom over there, controlling everything that comes in and out of the docks and running high-end, high-stakes gambling nights, where the buy-in costs more than most Black Creek residents earn in a year.

The Antonellis wronged my family a long time ago. They forever changed the course of my life when they attacked our house and took my sister. On that fateful day, they stole the other half of my soul. Where I am cloaked in darkness, my sister was all radiant glow. She was the bright spark in my life, the one thing that kept me grounded, that prevented me from stumbling across that moral line and falling into devilry. In the absence of her light, I've succumbed to the darkness, bathed in immorality, and painted myself in blood.

Back then, Reaper Rejects only had four members. Four kids who thought they wanted nothing more than to grow up but were blind to the harsh realities of life. We thought we knew it all, thought we were invincible when we were actually ignorant to the horrors of this world.

Now, we are a hundred men strong, and every single one of us is ready for war. We're willing to fight for our cause, to die for what's right. I will sacrifice whatever is necessary to avenge my sister, to destroy the men who stole her, and obliterate the dynasty that has been the source of all my pain.

As if he can sense the hostile anger pouring off me, Oliver glances my way, watching me closely for a moment as if he thinks I'm about to storm out of here and head straight for the Antonellis before a cry from the pit has him focusing on the fight once again.

My hand is squeezing the whiskey glass in a death grip as a deafening roar goes up from the crowd, signaling the end of the fight, and the muscles in the back of my jaw are so tense that I have to work to relax them before taking a sip of my drink. I've been on this path of revenge for a long time now, but the closer we get, the more impatient I become. Now that we have sufficient manpower, I'm ready for us to take our next steps, but unfortunately, we can't go storming into the Antonellis' district just yet. We need to be smart about how we attack them. I might have plenty of men at my back, ready and willing to fight this fight with me, but the Antonellis will have many more people than us.

The Don—Giovanni Antonelli—is my main target, but between his right-hand man/bodyguard and son, not to mention the numerous underlings he has working for him, he won't be an easy man to get my hands on. Besides, killing him isn't enough. His son, or someone else, will simply take his place, and the cycle will continue all over again. Every single one of them are vermin infecting this city. They *all* need to be eradicated.

With the fight over, and a lull while people top up their drinks before the next one begins, Oliver turns his attention my way. His own features are tight as he asks, "Any update?"

I know he's as impatient as I am to move forward. Nothing is worse than all this sitting and waiting.

"Nothing new."

His shoulders drop at my news, but it's nothing either of us didn't expect. The men I planted within the Antonelli organization several months ago are still too new to have made any significant progress yet, and unfortunately, any information they have been able to relay back to me hasn't been all that useful.

I wish there were another way in, an alternative plan we could be working on in the meantime, but I don't know what. The Antonelli empire is like an impenetrable fortress. We can easily get into their part of the city, and with the right clothes and enough money, into their casino and clubs, but then what? It's not like Giovanni himself hangs out on the casino floor all day, and even if he did, the second I would make a move toward him, I'd be gunned down before I could do him any harm.

But they have to have a weak spot, some way that I can get close to them. Everyone does. No stronghold is entirely impregnable. If I look long and hard enough, I'm sure I can find a crack somewhere, a chink in their armor, their Achilles heel. All it takes is patience and perseverance, and while mine may be running thin, I'm nowhere close to giving up.

A roar goes up from the raucous crowd below, pulling me out of my thoughts as another fight comes to an end. Damn, I was so deep in my thoughts I hadn't even realized another one had begun.

The heavy bass of the music has been turned up, and I can feel the tiled wall behind me vibrating. A server wearing only a bra and booty shorts climbs up the stairs, swaying her hips with each step in the sky-high heels she has on that make her toned legs look like they're a mile long as she carries a tray with two new drinks on it. Without saying a word, she places them on the glass table between our seats, giving me a coy smile before she moves away. Her ass shakes from side to side, my eyes glued to the round globes as she disappears down the stairs again.

She barely gave Oliver a passing glance, nor did he look away from the fight that was getting underway. As I sit and watch him, I notice the tense set of his shoulders and the straight line of his spine. Despite the fact we're perfectly safe here, he's on edge. It's a stance I've noticed in him often since he returned. I'm not sure if it's just being back in Black Creek, our ever-present responsibilities, or the weight of whatever he's been through in the last few years, but I've yet to see him actually just sit down and relax and enjoy himself for a night.

When he first returned, girls were all over him—a fresh face, instantly given the title of my second, and the perfect balance of dangerous yet elusive, who wouldn't want a piece of him? After two years in prison and several months in a male-only halfway house, I thought for sure he'd be all over that. Fuck knows I'd do nothing but drink and fuck for a month if I'd been locked up that long. But Oliver barely spared them a passing glance, more interested in getting down to work and making himself useful. I dunno if he felt he had something to prove and didn't want to get distracted, or what, but he's barely stopped working for a second since he got back. I am all for a strong work ethic, but the dude needs to learn to enjoy himself a little. Fuck knows, in this life, you could well end up dead tomorrow.

114

Reaching toward him, I clap a hand on his shoulder, shaking off my own dark thoughts as I smirk at him. "You need to loosen up a bit, O." I jerk my head toward the staircase where the waitress disappeared. "She looks like she'd be a bit of fun for a night."

He chuckles, shaking his head. "Yeah, and she only had eyes for you. Besides, I'm not interested."

Another small smile curls the corner of his lips slightly, and this time understanding dawns.

"No way," I laugh, shoving his shoulder. "You finally got yourself laid. About fucking time, man. Jesus, I was beginning to think all that time locked up in your cell with only your hand for company had affected the goods somehow."

"Shut the fuck up, asshole," he snorts, shoving me right back. "The *goods* work just fine, thank you very much."

I shake my head at our banter, huffing out a breath of laughter. "Yeah, well, now that you know for sure, you should have a drink and enjoy yourself." I spear him with a serious look. "Tonight we get drunk, and tomorrow we'll go after the Satan's."

\*\*\*

From the darkness, I stand alongside my men as we watch the raging party unfold before us. From what Oliver has told me, this sort of thing is expected at the Satans' clubhouse. Having seen enough, I lift my hand and signal for my men to advance. We're all dressed in black, camouflaged in the darkness. We have two teams surrounding the house. I'm with my men out the front, watching as party-goers go in and out of the front door, and the flashing of multi-colored strobe lights light up the window into the front room, which is jam-packed with people dancing drunkenly and grinding all over one another. Oliver is

115

with the other team around back, ready to take out any of the Satan's members who try to escape that way.

No one notices us as we close in on the house, but as we enter the pool of light from the house, the first of the party-goers spot us. Their eyes widen, and jaws drop when they do. It's a typical reaction, given the neck warmers, pulled up to the bridge of our noses, decorated with a skeletal design that makes the bottom half of our faces appear skull-like. That, and the AR-15 semi-automatic rifles slung over our shoulders aimed, ready to fire.

Of course, we're only after the Satans' members. Many of these people are just here to party, score drugs, or are gang hangarounds with nowhere else better to be. Unless one of them comes for us, we'll leave them alone.

People start to push past us, rushing out of the house as we enter, wanting to get away before bullets start flying. The music is so loud in here that the terrified screams in our presence don't alert Python or his men to the present threat, and the guy who I'm guessing was meant to be manning the door is too busy banging some chick against the wall.

As more and more people start to push and hurry past him, causing a scene, he finally stops thrusting into the girl he's fucking. His look of confusion contorts into shock when he sees us, and before he can so much as pull his dick out of the chick, I lift my gun and shoot him point-blank in the head. Blood splatters over the wall and the girl he was fucking. With the silencer in place, the circular hole in the front of his head is the only indicator that a gun went off at all.

As he collapses to the ground and my team spreads out, shooting at anyone resembling a Satan, more screaming starts, and anyone who wasn't running for the door before is now.

The ground floor of the house descends into mass panic as everyone flees and the Satans' members left standing start to return fire. Most of them are high and drunk, making their actions slow and uncoordinated, easily giving my men the advantage as they pick off the Satans' members one by one. Within no time at all, the ground floor is empty, bar the dead bodies scattered over the floor. It's kind of jarring, seeing the place deserted, with the music still blasting. The blood spatter and corpses dotted around the area only add to the macabre atmosphere our presence has caused.

"No sign of Python," one of my men shouts into my ear. I don't turn the music down or off, not wanting to alert anyone upstairs to the chaos that's ensuing below them. With a jerk of my head, two of my men—Razor and Fin—head up the stairs, weapons at the ready.

While they clear out the upstairs, I direct my men to search the rest of the house as Oliver steps through the back door, doing a quick once over of the kitchen before his eyes meet mine. Unable to talk over the music, I nod my head in a silent gesture that all is good, and he returns it with a sharp one of his own before moving back out the door, directing his team to search the other properties on the street.

I take my time, moving from room to room, counting the number of bodies, and taking in the state of the house. It's apparent no care has been given to it. Mold grows in the corner of the living room, kitchen cabinets are missing their doors, the banister is missing several balusters, and some idiot has punched a hole in the wall. The whole house stinks of weed, cigarettes, and alcohol.

Having done a loop of the ground floor, I make my way up the stairs, noticing more dead bodies slouched on the stairs and against the hall in the landing. Peering into the first bedroom, two more men with Satan tattoos lie face down on the mattress. One has his jeans and boxers shoved halfway down his ass, and the other is naked from the waist down. I barely spare them more than a passing glance as I walk past the doorway, moving on to inspect the next room. Before I can reach it, though, a noise from the bedroom at the end of the hall gains my attention—most likely Razor and Fin finishing up. I make to move toward it as Razor escorts a young woman with long ash-blonde hair out of the room. Her eyes are rounded in fear, and she's soaked in blood, making what I can see of her pale skin appear ghost-like. It's not an altogether surprising find, given we just massacred the entire house. If she was fucking some guy in the room when my men stormed in, she could have gotten caught in the crosshairs, although it is a surprising amount of blood. It almost looks like she slipped and fell face-first into a pool of it.

I'm faintly aware of someone finally turning off the goddamn music downstairs, and a heavy silence falls over us as I take in the girl. Before I can say anything, Razor's words have my eyes snapping up to meet his. "Boss, you might wanna check this out." He tilts his head toward the room behind him, and as I close the distance between us in several long strides, he moves to the side, giving me a clear view of the room.

*Holy shit.* This was definitely not the work of my men. Blood saturates the bed, dripping onto the floor. There's splatter on the wall behind the bed frame, and lying supine in the middle of it all, is a Satan's Advocate member—with his shirt pushed up to his nipples, and his pants and boxers shoved down, his limp dick lying out in the open.

"What the—" I begin, moving into the room.

"The Reaper was here," Fin states. Not that he needs to. His calling card is etched plainly into the man's skin for all to

118

see. I run my gaze over the confident slashes across his stomach. It's obvious there was no hesitation here. Whoever sliced him open was experienced and sure of themselves.

I've heard of the Reaper. Everyone has. He's been taking out gang members for the last few years, although I've just never seen his handiwork up close before. It's impressive. Completely in contrast to gang kills which are usually quick and efficient. For me, personally, there's next to no emotion involved when I kill someone. It's a means to an end—like tonight—but I don't need to be a psychologist to know that just by looking at the brutality inflicted on Python's body whoever the Reaper is, their kills are driven by emotion.

But what's his motive? It's not a question anyone seems to know the answer to. His kills can be anyone from a gang leader, to a random mid-level member, to a simple hangaround who barely has anything to do with the gang. There's no obvious pattern other than the fact they all have affiliations—even if somewhat tenuous—with one of the various gangs in Black Creek. Surely, if he just wanted to eliminate us, he'd go for the leader every time. I get the impression whoever the Reaper is, he's trying to make a statement. I just don't know what it is he's trying to say.

Once I've taken in every inch of the R carved deeply into his abdomen, I lift my gaze to look at the man's face. Python. The leader of the Satan's. I guess that explains why he wasn't downstairs. His neck has been cleanly sliced, again showing no signs of hesitation, and the man himself stares sightlessly at the ceiling above him.

"Boss," Razor speaks up after a long moment. I was so caught up in analyzing the handiwork of the Reaper that I almost forgot he and Fin and the girl were still here. "We found the girl in here when we kicked in the door."

119

I raise an eyebrow in surprise as I turn to look at the blood-soaked girl trembling beside Razor. Razor's a large man, much like myself, except where my body is honed out of muscle, he's carrying his fair share of the weight. But it works for him. It gives him this formidable appearance and makes everyone think twice before messing with him.

Beside him, the girl looks tiny, even though, in her heels, she's probably around six-feet tall. She's dressed in a short black skirt and a matching top that exposes her toned abdomen, highlighting the flare of her hips. Her milky skin is splashed with red, giving her a grisly appearance, and beneath the blood which is quickly drying on her skin, I can just about make out the faint markings of a tattoo along her shoulder and across one side of her chest. It should probably make her seem like a victim—the lone survivor of a massacre, but it doesn't. For some reason, it suits her. Like she was born to bathe in the blood of gang members.

She's shaking all over, and her pupils are blown, leaving a thin line of the strangest color of blue ringing them. She's most likely in shock. What I don't understand, though, is why the Reaper would leave behind a witness. That makes no sense at all.

I watch her closely, noticing the way her gaze bounces over me, taking in my six-foot-five frame, broad shoulders, narrow waist, the minuscule bits of ink on display along the back of my hands. Slowly, her eyes travel up to my face, skipping over the neck warmer covering the bottom half. It doesn't seem to bother her, the half-skeleton look. Rather she takes in my dark wavy hair, straight, thick eyebrows, and what she can see of my broad nose before she finally meets my gaze.

Behind the fear and panic in her eyes, there's something else, but I can't put my finger on it, and she averts her gaze before I can figure it out.

"You saw the Reaper?" I bark. She might be a scared girl, but I need to be the leader of the Rejects right now.

She jumps at my harsh tone, but when her eyes flick up to meet mine, there's a defiance in them that surprises me.

"N-no."

My eyes narrow, not believing her. I take a giant step toward her, the heavy sole of my boot echoing around the otherwise silent hall as my close proximity forces her to tilt her head back to look up at me. "It's in your best interest not to lie to me."

It's a small, barely perceptible movement, but her lips flatten in annoyance. As I open my mouth to ask her again, my phone goes off in my pocket. I fish it out, intending to cancel it, but when I see Oliver's name, I know it's him checking in, and I need to answer.

Huffing out a sigh, I look up at Razor. "Take her downstairs. She's not to leave until I talk to her."

Razor gives a sharp nod of his head in understanding before he wraps his meaty hand around the girl's thin upper arm, escorting her along the hall and down the stairs.

I never expected to nearly cross paths with the Reaper tonight. Hell, for all I know, he could have slipped right past me earlier, blending in with the other party-goers as they fled the house. He's barely more than a myth whispered in quiet tones on street corners. If it weren't for his signature kills, I'd think he didn't exist. But now that someone might have seen him, I need to find out more. I honestly don't give a shit who he is. If he has a vendetta against gangs, then perhaps he'll be willing to help me take out the most corrupt one of them all. I've been wracking

121

my brain, trying to figure out an alternative way of taking down the Antonellis, and it almost seems like fate that the Reaper— the very man who hates us all—may have left behind an unknown witness for me to stumble across. *This* could be what I've been waiting for.

As the blonde-haired girl drops out of view, I can't help but wonder if she could be the key to everything.

## Chapter 8

I let the brute of a man—Razor—lead me down the stairs and into the kitchen, where a bunch of other men wearing the same creepy skeleton face coverings are dragging dead bodies out the back door. They are leaving behind a red trail of blood which, unsurprisingly, looks like it belongs on the once white, but now gray with grime, linoleum floor.

He grabs a wooden chair from the scuffed up table in the corner of the room, pulling it out and gesturing for me to sit down. I do. I need to get out of here, but I can't just make a run for it—I'll never stand a chance if I do. I have to bide my time, and hope the opportunity presents itself before the sinfully gorgeous man comes back to question me. I could hardly get a word out past my dry throat when I looked at him. It's ridiculous because I couldn't even make out half of his face, but I didn't need to, to picture his curved lips.

There was an air to him that is common in men from Black Creek. That cocky attitude that many unrightfully walk around with, but on him, it seemed fitting. Like he'd earned the right to be that arrogant. Not that that makes any sense. I know absolutely nothing about him. Reaper Rejects is a name that's only started to make waves in the last year, but with each passing week—as they seize more and more territory for themselves—those whispers have gotten louder. Beyond being aware of their existence, I don't care to take the time to learn about each individual member. Although Razor—who is currently filling a chipped mug with tap water for me—called him boss. Which can only mean one thing—he's the king of the Rejects. That would definitely explain his authoritative attitude and the cocky swagger. It also means he's trouble.

As I glance down at the bloodstains trailing out the back door, it's painfully obvious that the Rejects have murdered all of Python's men, which means they officially own our little strip of Black Creek. Even more reason for me to stay away from them and their unjustly rugged leader. God knows it's only a matter of time before I end up killing one of his men for abusing his wife or beating up his kid. I'm actually surprised I haven't already. I've crossed paths with most of the gangs in Black Creek... when one of their members met their deaths at my hands.

"Drink this, girl." Razor sets the mug down on the table in front of me, but I make no move to lift it. He eyes me up before chuckling under his breath. "I ain't poisoned it or nothin'."

Still.

126

Another moment passes where he continues to watch me closely before asking, "What's your name?"

I know I have to give him something, but I make a show of chewing on my lower lip, acting as though I'm weighing up the pros and cons of divulging that piece of information before I hush out, "Jessica."

He leans across the table. "Jessica, you ain't done nothing wrong. Cain just needs to know what you saw tonight, okay?"

*Cain.* That must be his name. I have a sudden urge to say it aloud, wondering how it sounds on my tongue, but I bite down against that instinct and instead I slowly nod my head as I mentally piece together a plausible story. Razor watches me carefully, taking in every twitch of my lips and wrinkle of my forehead. *Fuck. Dammit. I'm not going to get out of this without telling them something.*

Fate must be on my side tonight, as the screen door behind him squeaks open and a young guy—what the hell is with all the kids?—pops his head in. "Razor, I need your help for a sec."

Frowning, Razor nods his head, and the guy ducks out of the kitchen again. Razor returns his focus to me, tapping his finger against the wooden table top. "I'll be back in a sec. Sit tight." He goes to stand, but before he pushes open the screen door, he turns his head to spear me with a harsh look. "I'm serious. Don't fucking move from that chair."

His boots stomp against the flimsy wooden decking as he heads outside, and I sit quietly, listening until his footsteps fade away. The kitchen is empty now, all the men probably hard at work burying bodies in the backyard.

Seeing my opportunity, I listen out for the noise of approaching footsteps as I carefully pick my way across the

127

kitchen, walking on my toes so no one can hear the tap of my heels against the floor.

As I approach the hall, I hear the sound of a voice coming from upstairs. Cain's distinctive, deep rumble as he talks to someone, followed by the sound of heavy boots against the floorboards. I don't waste any time, slipping out the front door and into the night, sticking to the shadows as I rush down the sidewalk toward my bike at the far end of the street.

I can hear men shouting to one another from within passing houses, voices that can only belong to Rejects. If there are any Satans still alive, they'll be hiding in the cover of darkness, just like me.

Once I reach my bike, I quietly unzip my duffel bag and switch the short skirt and heels out for leather pants, boots, and a matching jacket. As I'm yanking the trousers over my hips, I hear a commotion behind me. Raised voices followed by the banging of a screen door against the wood as someone steps out of a house.

I'm too far away to make out everything that's being said, and I don't waste time squinting in the dark to try and see who is talking or to whom, instead shoving my feet into my boots. No doubt whoever it is is looking for me, and they're getting the other Rejects on the job. The wind changes directions, blowing my way, and I distinctly hear the words "blonde girl" and "missing," and know I need to get out of here ASAP.

*Fuck.*

I hurriedly tug on my leather jacket, ignoring the gross feel of Python's blood crusted on my skin as I zip it up before pulling the blonde wig off my head. I stuff it in my duffle, jam my helmet on my head, and as the bike roars to life, easily heard all the way on the far end of the street, I twist the throttle and take off, flying down the road. The sound of the engine drowns out any shouts thrown my way, and I don't dare look back to see if anyone is following me. Instead, I race through the city, making last-minute turns and weaving in and out of the sparse traffic as I constantly check my mirrors until I'm confident no one is following. Only then do I slow down to a leisurely speed and turn my bike homeward.

\*\*\*

Despite my late night, I'm up early the next morning, munching down a bowl of cereal when Luc stumbles bleary-eyed and still half-asleep into the kitchen.

"Morning." I grin brightly at him, and he just scowls, mumbling something incoherent as he grabs himself a bowl and empties the last of the cereal into it. Damn, I need to make a list and go shopping today. And I need to stop by and let Sheryl know Python will no longer be a problem. None of the Satan's will bother any of us again. But will the Rejects be just as bad as them? Worse? Only time will tell.

I wait patiently until he's nearly finished with his breakfast and looking more alert. "Don't go to school today," I say as he shovels the last spoonful into his mouth.

His brows tug together as he looks at me, his eyes clouded with suspicion.

"Why?"

"Just don't, please? Stay home for a day or two."

A crease forms between his brows as he stares me down. "Does this have anything to do with what happened the other day?"

I purse my lips, mulling over my answer before I respond. Of course, when he stepped out of his room after the Satan's left our building the other day, he had a bunch of

129

questions for me, none of which I answered, much to his chagrin. After a tense moment, I huff out a sigh. Things were so much easier when he was younger, and he just did as he was told or could easily be distracted by the prospect of spending the day watching cartoons instead of going to school.

I try to keep Luc out of as much of my life as possible. He doesn't need to know the seedy things I get up to. He already knows about the club—he needs to know where he can reach me in case of an emergency, but he doesn't need to know the rest of it. The problem is, he's getting older and more inquisitive, and he's starting to put some of the pieces together, and that terrifies me.

"Reaper Rejects have taken control of Satan territory," I finally tell him, giving him part of the story, but nowhere near the whole thing.

His eyes widen in surprise. "How do you know that?"

"It's none of your business how I know that," I snap. "I just do. So until we know what they're planning on doing, just stay home."

He studies me for a long moment, with a slight frown, before finally nodding. "Okay."

The tension drops out of my shoulders, relief that he should be safe here—or as safe as one can be in Black Creek—overcoming me.

"But only if you stay home too."

*Fucking asshole.* I scowl at him. "I have to work tonight."

He shrugs his shoulders like it's no big deal. "Call in sick."

"You know I can't do that. We need the money."

He quirks a brow. "Seriously? I'm sure we can survive if you miss one shift."

130

I open my mouth to protest, but he talks over the top of me. "Don't think I don't know about the shoebox full of cash hidden under the floorboard beneath the sofa."

I gape open-mouthed at him for a second. "How do you know about that?"

The infuriating shithead just shrugs a shoulder. "There's more than enough to cover what you'll miss out on tonight."

I have to force my lip not to curl back in an angry snarl, and instead, I try to suck in a deep, calming breath. "That's supposed to be for a rainy day. If there's an emergency or something."

He glances out the grimy window at the gloomy sky above us. Droplets of rain splash against the pane, leaving water marks as they trail down it. "Looks like a rainy day to me."

I roll my eyes, even as I huff out a chuckle. "Fine, I'll stay home today, but I have to go in tomorrow."

His face lights up with a grin, and it brings a rare smile to my own lips. "Pajama and movie day, like old times." His eyes flash with excitement as he dumps his bowl in the sink and drops onto the sofa, channel surfing until he finds something he likes.

Shaking my head, I clean our dishes before joining him, and that's how we spend the day, watching old movies and chatting about absolutely nothing. It's reminiscent of when we first moved in here. It was the first apartment we'd ever lived in. The first time we'd had a place that was just ours, and we would frequently spend the whole day on the sofa, watching TV or playing games, and pretending the world outside our tiny apartment didn't exist. We'd never had the luxury before of being able to block out the rest of the world. Usually, it was just there, staring us in the face, whether we wanted to deal with it or not.

So to be able to carve out time for just ourselves... it was fucking perfect.

Unfortunately, the real world comes calling the next day, and Sheryl has obviously already heard the news when I step into the women's shelter that evening on my way to work.

"You did it," she exclaims in a hushed whisper. Her bony hand squeezes mine with a surprising amount of strength. It's been nearly a week since she showed up here, and her bruises are healing well, but they're still visible without any makeup.

I glance furtively around us as I drag her into a quiet corner of the communal hall. Grace is sitting a few seats down, scribbling on a piece of paper with some broken crayons. She gives me a toothy smile and a wave, which I reciprocate before focusing back on Sheryl.

I notice a sparkle in her eyes that wasn't there the other day, and she can barely contain herself as she wraps me in a tight hug. "I can't believe you actually did it," she whispers. "Thank you."

When she leans back, I give her a soft smile. "Do you know what you're going to do now?"

Shaking her head, she says, "Not yet, but Beatrice has offered us a room for now, in exchange for helping her out. I can look for jobs in the meantime."

"That's good. I can ask at the club, if you want. Some of the girls help each other out with daycare when they're working, so it wouldn't be a problem with Grace."

She thinks it over for a second, but I can already tell she's not fond of the idea.

"It's not that I don't want to, I just... " She swallows roughly. "I don't know if I'm ready for that sort of attention yet." Her hands are shaking and I quickly wrap mine around them, giving her a reassuring squeeze.

"Hey," I say sharply, waiting until her eyes raise to meet mine. "I understand. You don't have to explain anything to me."

She gives me a watery smile, sniffling as she leans in to give me another hug. "I don't know how I'll ever repay you."

"You don't have to," I assure her. "I was only doing what needed to be done... besides, if I hadn't, it looks like the Rejects would have."

Her eyes are rounded in surprise when she breaks off the hug. "I'd heard rumors, but I wasn't sure if they were true or not."

"Well, they're true. They raided the Satan's clubhouse. Killed them all."

She gasps, her hand coming up to cover her mouth. "While you were there?"

"Yup." I pop the p, ducking my gaze so I don't have to see the concern in her eyes.

"Shit, did they see you? What are you going to do?"

"It should be fine," I assure her, even if I'm not entirely convinced of that. "I was wearing a disguise, and I got out of there before they could ask me anything. Chances are, they'll be too busy gaining control of their new territory to go chasing after some chick."

She pinches her lips, and I can tell she doesn't quite believe me, but thankfully she doesn't argue and we move over to join Grace while she draws a picture of a knight coming to save the princess from her tower. As I listen to her tell the story that accompanies the picture, I sigh, wishing life was that easy. Part of me wants to warn her that men are not heroes. That they don't come encased in armor and ready to dive into battle for you, but I also don't want to tarnish her optimistic outlook on the world. God knows, life will quickly suck the hope out of her as

133

she grows older, so why not let her hold on to a fantasy for a little bit longer.

***

The same whispers about the demise of the Satan's are running rampant when I walk into the club later that night. It seems everyone has heard about the Rejects, and the question on everyone's mind is... what does this mean for us?

"My sister lives in Reject territory, and she says as long as you don't go asking for trouble, they leave you in peace," Jezebel informs everyone while we're sitting at our individual dressing tables, getting ready.

"I've heard they run these really successful fighting challenge nights, and they hire girls for the winners," Lori adds. Lowering her voice, she whispers, "Apparently, they pay very well, too."

I do my best to ignore them as they speculate back and forth. The way they talk reminds me of Grace and her knight. They make the Rejects sound like they're the good guys, here to save us or some such shit. Even if only a fraction of what they're saying is true, it doesn't make them good people. They still run a gang. They still murdered a bunch of people the other night, all for the sake of gaining more territory.

Dolled up to the nines and dressed in my best hooker heels, I leave the gossiping hens behind in the dressing room. As I'm passing the office, I can hear Drew talking to someone. That's not unusual, but the deep cadence of the other person's voice strikes me as familiar. I pause, lingering by the door, needing to hear his voice again. I can't make out their words, but I can decipher Drew's voice through the wooden door before there's the scraping of chair legs. Realizing they're about to exit

134

the office, I duck into the bathroom next door just as I hear the door handle turn.

More muffled voices as the two men step into the hall, and I crack the door open a fraction to peer out as I hear the click of Drew's office door shutting, followed by two sets of footsteps moving away from me. I can only see their backs, and ignoring Drew on the left, I focus on the guy on the right. I only catch a quick glimpse—tall, muscular, dark-haired, gorgeous ass—before they both disappear, and I'm left perplexed, trying to work out who he was and why he sounded so familiar.

The rest of my shift goes by as usual. No Rejects stop by, and I have to assume they're all too busy to have any downtime yet, but I'd imagine in the coming days and weeks, we will start to see more of them coming in. It's only a matter of time, and the thought makes my palms sweat. Mainly in case Razor, the young kid who was with him, or Cain, stops by. Sure I had on a wig and heavy makeup, but up close, they would probably be able to figure out the girl they're looking for is me.

At the end of the night, after Drew locks the front door behind the last customer, he calls out, "Listen up, everyone. I know you're all tired and want to get home, but I wanted to let you all know, a liaison for Reaper Rejects stopped by today."

That immediately gets my attention as my thoughts drift back to the guy I saw leaving his office earlier. He must have been a Reject. Maybe one of the ones I saw the other night. It would explain why his voice seemed familiar.

"They've offered us protection in case there is any backlash from their takeover, and they've asked me to tell you that they are looking for waitresses to help out with regular cage fighting matches they'll be hosting at Toxic starting next week. If anyone is interested in helping out, please put your name on the sign-up sheet in my office."

I notice Viv and Jezebel exchanging a look, and I remember her words from earlier. More money would be nice, but I'm not about to walk myself into a room that's guaranteed to be full of Rejects when they're most likely still looking for me. In a few weeks, they'll have forgotten all about the girl covered in blood from the Satans' clubhouse and move on. Sure, like most people in Black Creek, they're curious about who the Reaper is—such a fucking stupid name, by the way—and probably thought I'd seen him. Ultimately, I'm sure they have more important things to be focusing on than chasing after a ghost.

I've heard whispers that the gangs think the Reaper is some sort of vigilante, out to annihilate all of them. How self-centered is it to think it's all about them? But it's not like they pay any attention to the deaths of non-gang members. I also make a point of not carving my mark into jobs I get paid to do—jobs like the one I had last week, where the shithead was a lawyer, where someone will notice and report him missing. I need the world beyond Black Creek to assume he was in the wrong place at the wrong time, that he got caught up in something he shouldn't have, or messed with the wrong person. If the authorities got wind that someone was going around murdering well-to-do people, they'd descend on the city. The sparse police force here doesn't give a shit. They're as corrupt as the rest of us. Every one of them is in someone's pocket, but it wouldn't take much to have the FBI sniffing around, asking unwanted questions.

The same discretion does not apply to jobs like Sheryl's. Jobs that I take on because I refuse to let the abusive men of this town beat us down. Jobs where if I don't intervene, there will inevitably be dire consequences. Like Sheryl, most of these women have no money, no security, no one they can rely on or turn to for help. Of course, killing their abusive partner doesn't mean they won't end up with someone similar, but the asshole gets what he deserves for putting his hands where they don't belong. A lot of these men are, in some way, affiliated with one street gang or another—as are most of the men in Black Creek—so naturally, that led people to assume the Reaper was anti-gang. And don't get me wrong, I am. I think it's a toxic environment that breeds misogyny and violent behavior... it's just not the reason why I'm killing these fuckers.

## Chapter 9

It quickly becomes apparent that the Rejects are looking for me. Well, for a skinny blonde girl who was known to hang out with the Satan's and may have been seen covered in blood the night they were slaughtered. It's seriously annoying as it means I have to keep a low profile for the next few days, only leaving the house when I have to. I'm confident my red hair will throw off most of them, but if I accidentally end up face-to-face with Cain or Razor, I can't be sure that they won't recognize me.

I don't even understand why they're so hellbent on hunting me down. I'm just some witness. For all they know, I was too shocked to even remember anything—assuming, of course, that I saw anything at all.

It's seriously messing with my routine. I had a new voicemail on the spare burner I keep stashed away, hidden from Luc, with a new job for *the Reaper*, but I haven't been able to risk doing any investigative work to see if it's a job I can take on. And it's a paid one too, so I really don't like the possibility of losing out on money over this whole bullshit.

All of the women's shelters in and around Black Creek have the contact details for my burner phone, and the women that run the shelters know what I do—hell, I've personally helped some of them out. Of course, only Beatrice knows the person behind the phone is me. Everyone else just offers the number out if they feel the woman could benefit from my services, or they place the call themselves if they are particularly concerned about someone.

If a potential client does contact me, I get them to leave their details, and do a little research into who they are before deciding whether or not I'll take the job. Unfortunately, I don't have the time or resources to help out every woman that contacts me, so it often depends on how many other jobs I'm working at the time and the severity of the case. Of course, if a woman or child appears to be in imminent danger, I'll do everything I can to prevent something tragic from happening, and most of the time, I can get the job done before it's too late.

There was only once when I didn't act quick enough. Luc had been really sick with bronchitis one winter, and I was scared to leave him for too long. By the time I had hunted down the shitstain who was abusing his pregnant girlfriend, it was too late. She'd been missing for two days when I caught up to him, and while the girl's friends were out looking for her, I immediately knew what had happened. In the voicemail I'd received from the shelter, the woman had sounded really concerned for this woman's safety and hadn't been able to persuade her not to go back to the asshole.

When I found him, hanging around outside the Grim Bastard's compound, he acted like nothing had happened. Like his pregnant girlfriend wasn't missing. It sickened me. It made me so mad, I can only describe his death as a rage kill, funneled by pure emotion. It's safe to say there was nothing left of him to be found by the time I was done, and his screams of agony still soothe my battered soul. But that woman died because I didn't act quickly enough, and that knowledge will haunt me for the rest of my days.

So, yeah, the fact that I'm having to take precautions and sit back when some woman could be getting the shit beat out of her, pisses me the fuck off.

"Did you hear about that girl the Rejects are looking for?" Luc asks me. It's been a week since the Rejects took over Satan territory, and other than them spreading word about the blonde woman they're looking for, it's been surprisingly quiet. A few skirmishes broke out initially, but they were quickly squashed. "What do you think that's all about?"

"No idea," I shrug, not wanting to engage in this conversation with my brother. I get he's curious; it's unusual that they're searching this hard for a girl. Everyone is wondering who she is and what she means to the Rejects.

"It's just weird that they're looking for a girl, isn't it?"

"She probably just stole from them or saw something they didn't want her seeing."

His gaze is fixed on the TV, and I can tell, even though he brought the conversation up, he's not that interested in it.

141

"Yeah, you're probably right. At least it keeps them busy, right? Means they can't stir up shit for any of us."

"Exactly." If only they weren't busy pursuing me, then all would be great.

"Bet you've never been so glad to have hair that looks like it belongs on a Pokemon character."

I'm sitting beside him on the couch, and I jab my foot into his thigh, glowering playfully at him while he chuckles.

"Don't you have homework or something," I gripe.

He quirks a brow, throwing me an *are you serious* look. "I know it's been a while since you were in school, but you do remember what a farce the education system in Black Creek is, right?"

He's right. I dropped out of school when our mother died. Murdered. When our mother was murdered. But I remember what a sham it was. School was nothing more than a daycare for parents to send their children off to so they could work or get stoned in peace for several hours each day. I learned a hell of a lot more living on the streets than I ever did inside a classroom. Still, I've insisted Luc attend until he's eighteen. It might not exactly be educational, but it's what kids do. Besides, it's got to be better than working some shitty, dead-end job that you know you'll be stuck doing for the next forty years of your life. I don't want Luc to feel trapped like that at such a young age. Admittedly, I don't ever want him to feel like that, but I'm not sure how I can prevent it, so for now, I'm settling for delaying the inevitable for a few more years.

Rolling my eyes, I snark, "Then sit there and watch your TV show in silence like a good little boy."

His face scrunches before he barks out a laugh and returns his attention to the TV, enabling me to get back to mentally figuring out what I'm going to do about my Reaper

Rejects dilemma. Except, there's nothing I can do but lay low for a few more days and hope they get bored with chasing after someone they'll never find.

***

After another couple of days of only leaving the house to go to the club and get groceries, I've had enough. I couldn't continue to sit there twiddling my thumbs. The voicemail on my phone with some new asshole's name was calling to me. Chad Greenway's death at my hands is exactly what I need to help me let go of all this frustration.

Which is why I'm currently tailing him on my bike as he drives through Antonelli territory. From what I've gathered, Chad is a partner at a hedge fund firm, and when he's not working, he likes to gamble away his obscene bonuses and frequent upscale sex clubs, like the ones the Antonellis run. Then, when he's thrown away all his money, he likes to go home to his wife and take his shitty decisions out on her. Classy guy.

I slow down as his car comes to a stop outside Bella Antonella, the Antonellis' casino. I continue past the entrance and pull the bike over to the side of the road several blocks down, watching as Chad—a balding man in his forties—gets out of the backseat and strides into the building. Unfortunately, I can't just strut into the casino and cozy up to Chad until I can convince him to leave with me. Not only do the Antonellis have bouncers on the door and security cameras that would easily pick me up, but they would probably be able to smell the poverty on me from the sidewalk. Their establishments have a particular class about them. Their patrons wear expensive suits and fancy dresses. There is no chance I'll get inside that casino dressed in what I'm wearing. Even as I watch, some asshole with his hair slicked back escorts a lady through the front doors with what looks like diamonds clasped around her neck and wearing a gorgeous evening gown. No, I won't be able to get to Chad inside the casino.

I sit and wait—an incredibly dull but essential part of my job—and several hours later, looking worse for wear with the top button of his shirt undone, his tie hanging loosely from his neck, and his hair disheveled, he storms out of the building and gets into his awaiting car. Perking up, I start the engine of the bike and follow after him as he goes a couple of streets over to Belle Donne—one of the Antonellis' sex clubs. I'm wondering if I could sneak in there. It would be dimly lit, and I'd easily blend in with the working girls—the perfect place to kill him, especially if I made it look like an accident.

Once he's stumbled inside, clearly drunk off his ass, I scope out the exits, noting the bouncers and security cameras on the front door, as well as the bouncer and camera covering the staff entrance around back, before I head home. I need to do more research before I do anything else. At least I've got his routine down. I've been following Chad for the last few nights now, and it's always the same—casino, sex club, home. I told his wife to make up an excuse to leave town for the next two weeks, so hopefully, she's done that and won't have to suffer at his hands tonight when he gets home. That gives me another week and a half to get the job done. Now I just need to figure out how to get inside that club.

*** 

The next night, I walk onto the stage at Strip Tease to *S&M* by Rihanna and lose myself in the music as I twirl in my sky-high heels, grinding my hips, tensing my abs, and pushing out my tits.

The place is packed tonight, and I noticed several tables of Rejects members when I walked in. They've been stopping by the club the last few nights, all with easy-going, jovial smiles. They don't cause too much of a ruckus, and I haven't heard of any of them getting aggressive or physical with the girls. If anything, they seem to almost have some level of respect for us. It makes me suspicious, to say the least, and I definitely don't trust them.

I'm halfway through my routine when I feel eyes on me, which sounds ridiculous because I probably have the eyes of at least half the men in the room right now, but this is different. Whatever this is, it burns my skin and makes my heart race. As I lift my feet, swiveling around the pole, I squint through the light, trying to pinpoint who is looking at me, but I can't make out anyone obvious.

I can't shake the feeling of eyes on me for the rest of my dance, and by the time my set ends, I'm trembling. My legs feel shaky and unstable as I carefully descend the steps from the stage, but before I can so much as take a breath, a heavy weight crashes into me, throwing me back against the wall with a thud that knocks the air out of my lungs.

Slowly, my eyes crawl over the broad-chested, tatted-up asshole pinning me to the wall, along the dark scruff of beard dusting his jaw, until I meet his searing green eyes, fuming with rage. I suck in a gasp, my eyes widening. *Oh, fuck.* Anger radiates off Cain like thermal energy, heating the air between us. His eyes hold me immobilized, and suddenly I realize it was his gaze I could feel burning into me on stage.

"You," he snarls, his voice sounding more beast-like than human. Before I can gather my thoughts to figure a way out of this, he's wrapped his large, inked hand around my upper arm in a firm grip, and I nearly stumble in my high-heels, struggling to keep up with his enormous strides as he storms into the back hallway, heading for Drew's office.

He pushes open the office door and shoves me into the room, practically throwing me onto the sofa as he looms over me. I hurry to push myself upright and glower at him, biting my tongue so hard I'm surprised I don't taste blood. See, this is why I stay as far away from gang members as I can. The malevolence pouring off him is stifling, and the tense way he's holding himself tells me he's trying really hard to hold himself back. Back from what? From hitting me? From hurting me? He might look like temptation with his black jeans that mold to his thighs and his t-shirt that looks like a second skin, but he's everything that's wrong with this world. He's so used to people cowering beneath him, obeying his every whim, that he can't stand the fact I'm not whimpering and begging for forgiveness at his feet.

"Why did you run away?" His words are a harsh bite, spat out through gritted teeth.

"You just murdered a whole bunch of men," I snap. "Do you really think I was going to hang around so you could kill me too?"

The words are out of my mouth before I can rein in my temper, and there's a dangerous flash in his eyes before they narrow on me.

"I wasn't going to kill you." He says it like it should be obvious—like how could I possibly think such a thing. Of course, silly me. How could death by machine gun possibly have crossed my mind when fifty-odd men, half-hidden behind gruesome, skeleton-designed neck warmers and carrying automatic rifles, are stomping around the house, killing every gang member they cross? "Tell me what you saw."

146

I press my lips together, scrutinizing him, and when I don't immediately obey his command, his anger sparks again.

"Fine," he snaps, digging into his pocket and producing a wad of cash. He flicks through it, and he's standing close enough that I can tell he's holding more money in his hand than I make in a month. He peels off three one hundred dollar bills and holds them out to me expectantly.

I sneer at his outstretched hand. "I don't want your fucking money."

His brows lift in surprise for a split second before he masks it with a scowl, more of that perpetual anger of his simmering in his emerald irises. Without saying a word, he stuffs the money back in his pocket, and in one large stride he closes the distance between us. I press my back flat against the sofa and tilt my head back so I can maintain eye contact with him, refusing to let him intimidate me, even as my heart hammers against my chest and a little voice in the back of my head tells me to behave.

This close, his whiskey and leather scent envelopes me. It makes no sense because he's not even wearing leather, but it's a distinct, homely smell. Despite the glower I'm throwing his way, I can feel the smell seeping into my skin, my body reacting instinctively to it. My muscles uncoil and relax, and I find myself wondering if I could bottle that smell and spray it on my pillow at night. It would be the perfect way to fall asleep.

I shake myself out of that ludicrous thought and focus back on the brute towering over me. I'm not going to get out of here without giving him something. I don't know why he's so hellbent on finding the Reaper, but I highly doubt it's even crossed his mind that he might be staring him—well, her—in the face right now.

My tongue flicks out to lick my bottom lip, and his eyes dart down to my mouth, tracking the movement. It's the first sign of interest he's given—if that's even what this is. Even though I'm wearing next to nothing, he hasn't given me more than a cursory glance. In fact, his gaze has hardly left my face at all.

Sighing, like he's won, I say, "I didn't see anything."

At the sound of my voice, his eyes snap to meet mine, but he doesn't back away, only stares at me intently until I continue talking.

"Python and I went upstairs, and I went to the bathroom before..." I lick my lips again, putting my fantastic acting skills to use as I pretend to be shocked and horrified as I think back to that night. "When I came back to the bedroom, h-he... I found him like that."

I drop my gaze, sniffling as I pretend to wipe my eyes. I'm just a meek girl who's traumatized by what she witnessed in that room.

He's silent for so long that I peer up at him through my eyelashes, needing to get a read on him. His eyes are narrowed in suspicion, and I can practically see the thoughts running around in his head as he tries to suss me out.

"Why was the door locked?"

Uhhh. "I panicked when I heard people screaming and running out of the house." It's a total guess. Over the cacophony of rap music, the sweet melody of Python dying, and the heady sort of concentration that comes with killing a man, I didn't hear a damn thing that was going on outside that room. But there's no way a whole group of Cain's men stormed in there, looking the way they did, without causing a panic.

My words are met with another long moment of contemplative silence before his next question. "How do you explain the fact you were covered in Python's blood?" The

148

skepticism is clear to hear in his voice, but he's got no reason not to believe me. More importantly, he's got no proof that I'm lying.

"I-I thought I could save him." I let my chin wobble. "I t-tried to stop the bleeding, b-but it was too much." My voice raises in pitch, making me sound half-hysterical. "I-I didn't even see what was"—I scrunch my nose in disgust—"*carved* into his abdomen until I heard someone kicking down the door."

"So you never saw who killed him?"

I shake my head. "No."

"What about someone at the party? Did anyone stand out or seem to be paying particular attention to Python?"

Other than me? "No. Not that I saw, but I wasn't really paying attention to anyone else."

He purses his lips as he thinks for a moment, before finally giving a sharp jerk of his head. "Fine." He doesn't sound happy, but at least he seems to believe what I'm saying—for now. "You can go back to work."

With my heart lodged in my throat, I scurry toward the door without a backward glance. On my way out, I grab ahold of the handle, turning it roughly in my hand as I pull the door closed behind me, but the handle is old, and I know that if you twist it hard enough, the latch sticks. I wait a moment until I hear his voice, then I push the door open ever so slightly. It's not enough for me to see into the room, but there's a slither of a gap between the wooden door frame and the door, allowing me to hear what he's saying to someone on the phone.

"She's lying, O... I'm not sure. I can't place it. I just... there's something off with her."

*Fuck.*

Not wanting to be caught eavesdropping, I pull the door closed again and jiggle the handle, engaging the latch before silently moving away and getting back to work. Cain's words play on repeat in my head, and I constantly run my gaze over the various Reject members, wondering who it was he was talking to. And why. Why is he so set on finding the Reaper? What does he want with him—with me? Knowing he's devoting so much time and energy to finding me makes me antsy, and I can't settle for the rest of the night, moving on autopilot as I deliver drinks, perform on the stage, and give lap dances.

## Chapter 10

I feel like a paranoid schizophrenic, looking all around me as I stealthily make my way to the garage where I keep my bike. Cain's words about not believing me echo in my head for like the fiftieth time since last night, and I'm worried he will have someone watching me, digging into my life. I can't have him—or anyone—finding out who I am. And more importantly, I can't afford to bring trouble to Luc's door.

Thankfully, I don't see or hear anyone behind me as I approach the garage door and bend to yank it open. I need to complete this job ASAP. The longer I work it, the greater the chance Cain will discover who I am—or at least realize I'm up to something. It's all good, though, because I have a plan for Chad Greenway, and I'm going to execute it tonight.

Pulling on my helmet, I walk the bike out of the garage and close the door behind me before taking off down the street, heading for the Antonellis' part of town. I'm not sure if it's psychological or real, but I swear, you can tell when you've hit Antonelli territory. In fairness, you do have to cross over a bridge to get to it, but it's more than that. There's a shine to the buildings that you don't see where I live, and the same grime doesn't seem to coat the streets.

When I'm a couple of blocks away from the Belle Donne, I park up at the side of the road and duck into an alleyway to change. I've brought fishnet tights and the shortest booty shorts I own, along with my laciest bra. I have absolutely no idea what high-end hookers wear, but it's the best I could do, and I'm hoping any discrepancies won't be noticed in the dim light of the club.

Once I'm dressed, I pull out a wig—this time one with long, dark brown, wavy hair. The color matches the brown contacts I put in before I left the apartment, the ensemble hopefully enough to disguise me from any security the Antonellis might have and prevent anyone inside the club from identifying me. Ready, I throw on a cheap trench coat that I can afford to discard once I'm inside, and amble across the street toward the Belle Donne.

My next hurdle is getting inside. I'd already written off the front door as my entry point. With the cameras and bouncers, there's no way I'd easily get in, a fact I quickly confirm as I come out on the opposite side of the street to the club. Besides, I doubt that's how the working girls get in and out of the club. No, my guess is, much like at Strip Tease, they use the back door.

Hurrying across the road, I stick close to the shadows provided by the adjacent building as I sneak down the alleyway running along the side of the club. As I go, I scan my eyes over the rest of the brick building, debating if there's an alternative way in—an open window, a hidden roof entrance—but I don't have time to scout the place out any further. Ideally, I would have taken my time to scope out the best way in, but Cain has forced my hand, and is making me act sooner than I'd like with this job. Just one more reason to be angry with that asshole. He's completely messing with my life, and for what? So he can chase after some ghost? Who does he think he is? Surely, it must have crossed his mind that hunting down someone who kills gang members might result in his own death. It's just idiotic.

Unable to spot a suitable alternative way into the club, I continue down the alley to the back of the building, where the staff entrance is. Crouching behind a dumpster, I take in the burly guard on duty, blocking the door and the security camera attached to the wall behind him.

I chew on my bottom lip as I debate what to do, but the way I see it, I only have one option, and I'm just going to have to hope on a wing and a prayer that it works.

With nothing else for it, I step out from behind the dumpster and stride toward the bouncer, my heels clicking against the cobblestones with every step. His head snaps in my direction, his eyes raking over me as I step into the pool of light surrounding the door.

I lick my lips in a nervous gesture as I look up at him with doe-like eyes. "Ahh, this is the staff entrance for Belle Donne, right? It's my first night, and I've managed to get myself all worked up and disorientated."

155

The guy just stares down at me with an impassive expression. "I wasn't informed we had anyone new starting tonight."

I let my eyes widen in shock, a flare of panic flashing across my face. "W-what? No, I definitely have the right start date. Oh my goodness, I can't believe I'm screwing this all up already. I can't afford to lose another job." I force tears to well in my eyes as I duck my head and sniffle. Why are so many men suckers for a crying woman? Not that I'm complaining, ninety percent of the time, it works in my favor. And as the guy huffs out a restrained breath, I know it's working on him too.

"It's alright, little lady. There's no need to cry about it, they probably just forgot to inform me. Why don't you go on in and talk to Franny in the office. She'll get you sorted out before you start."

I swipe under my eyes and look up at the frowning man like he just hung the moon for me. "Oh, thank you! Thank you!"

He gives me a tight smile in return as he ushers me through the door, and as it clangs shut behind me, I let the whole helpless woman look drop from my expression as I glance around, taking in the back hallway of the club.

Thankfully the hallway is empty, and I hurry along it, not needing to be caught now that I'm through the door. The whole *I'm new* thing will only work for so long.

Finding the door into the main club, I push it open and slip inside, relief lifting my shoulders as I find the interior of the club lit only by dim lamps, providing a seductive atmosphere that matches the soft, sensual music and breathy moans I can hear in the quiet seconds between songs.

The room I'm in is made up of booths, with translucent curtains draped around each one, providing a modicum of privacy for its occupants. Unable to determine if Chad is behind

156

any of them, I hurry across the thickly carpeted space toward the only other door in sight.

The next room's atmosphere is entirely different from the one I just left behind. The music is faster and louder, intended to get the blood pumping and adrenaline flowing. The room is lit only by overhead neon lights, which flash, giving it an eerie quality. In the split-second flashes of light, I can make out people grinding on one another in the middle of a crowded dance floor and others making out against the booths lining the far walls.

I take my time, pushing through the crowd and squinting into the dark corners of the room, looking for anyone that resembles Chad. I come across several possibilities, but when I get close enough, I realize they aren't him and continue on my hunt. I'm not sure if it's the music or knowing I'm getting closer to my prey, but I can feel the need for bloodshed humming beneath my skin, like a visceral reaction to the shitstain's close proximity. It heightens my senses and seems to draw me across the room as if some baser part of myself instinctively knows where he's hiding.

As I move into another room which is set up like an upscale theater, with its red, velvet, circular booths, all facing a stage, and golden table lamps that give out a low light, I spot my next victim, lounging in the middle of the room as he watches two naked women putting on a show on the stage. As I focus on them, I realize it's basically a live porn performance. *Whatever helps him get his rocks off, I guess.*

I grab a drink from the tray of a passing waitress, sniffing the glass. *Damn, they have the good stuff here.* There's none of the harsh scent of alcohol. Instead, all I can smell is vanilla and oak. I almost feel bad as I empty the mini tube of benzodiazepines I crushed up earlier into the glass and dip my finger into the liquid, mixing it in with the alcohol.

With the drink in hand, I approach Chad, sitting alone at his table. "Enjoying the show?" I ask in a husky voice, holding the glass out for him. My words snag his attention as he gives me a once-over before reaching out to take the drink, bringing it to his lips.

He swivels the whiskey around his mouth before swallowing, giving a casual shrug in response to my question.

"Perhaps I can help you find something more suitable?" I offer in a seductive purr.

His eyes rake over me once again, making goosebumps rise along my skin. "I'm after something... specific."

I raise a brow and quirk my lips, leaning into him in such a way that makes my tits squish together, threatening to burst out of my bra. "I can be *anything* you want." The words taste like vomit in my mouth, but whatever gets the job done.

He gives me another long, assessing look before knocking back the rest of his drink. A thrill of excitement pulses through me as he empties the glass, handing it off to someone before gesturing for me to lead the way.

I notice a hallway lined with doors on my perusal through the club, so I lead him in that direction, knowing they could only be there for one purpose. I find the hallway with ease, and as I stride confidently along it, I note the red light that's activated beside some of the doors, obviously indicating that they are occupied. Finding an empty one, I open the door and step in, feeling his presence behind me as he follows me in. The loud click of the latch signifies that I finally have him alone as I do a quick scan around the room, taking in the plush king-sized bed occupying most of the space, as well as the wall of various sex toys, whips, paddles, and handcuffs—*kinky*—before I spin in my heels to face him.

Before I can plant my feet again, I'm knocked sideways, stumbling from the shock of the blow. My cheek smarts from the crack of his hand across it, and I can feel the sting of a split lip. He descends upon me while I'm still trying to comprehend what the hell just happened, knocking me back with another punch to my cheek. *What the fuck? Is this what he gets off on?* Apparently, it is. As I glance up at him, I can see the hungry look in his eye. He enjoys the power he gets from beating on a woman; he feeds off the high. It's fucking disgusting.

He lifts his hand to strike me again, but before he can do so, a strange look crosses his features, and he stumbles to the side.

"W-what the... whuts happenin' to mee?" His words begin to slur, the drugs finally taking effect, and he collapses to his knees at the end of the bed. Both benzodiazepines and alcohol are central nervous system depressants. They make you drowsy and uncoordinated, and in high enough doses, can repress your respiratory system—at least, that's what a quick internet search told me before I bought a little baggie of Xanax off some kid who hustles on the street corner down from Strip Tease.

I watch impassively as Chad slumps against the bed. His eyes repeatedly drift shut before fluttering open, like he's struggling to stay awake, and the rapid rise and fall of his chest gives away the difficulty he's having breathing. I wasn't entirely sure how many pills it would take to finish him off, so I ground up as many as I thought would dissolve in a drink. Looks like I've gotten the concoction just right, though.

He groans weakly before vomiting all over himself. He tips onto his side, crashing against the ground, not giving a shit that he's lying in his own vomit, and I patiently wait until his

159

chest stops moving before I jump into action. When he's finally lying unmoving, in a heap on the floor, I give it another minute while I wipe the trickle of blood from my chin, wincing as my tongue glides over the already swollen cut on my lip before I pull open the door to the room, stepping into the hall and screaming, "Help! HELP! He's not breathing. Please, someone help!"

It takes a second, but eventually, doors start to swing open, and people spill into the hallway, drawn by curiosity to know what's happened. As the hall fills with people, some just standing there peering into the room, while others move toward a very dead Chad, I melt into the crowd and slip away, rushing toward the back entrance of the club. A slight smile of achievement curls up the corner of my lips as I reach the door leading into the back hallway, but it's wiped clean when I crash into a hard chest.

A small *oomph* escapes my lips as the air is pushed out of my lungs, and my hands clasp onto a set of muscular forearms to steady myself. Blinking, my eyes take in a crisp white shirt and black tie before they crest over a smooth, angular jawline, high cheekbones and pitch black hair before meeting steely chocolate-brown eyes.

"Uhh, sorry," I stutter, swallowing around a sudden lump in my throat. I gesture with my thumb over my shoulder. "I think there was, ehh, an accident or something. Someone needs help."

His eyes dart over my head, looking toward where I just came from.

"I'll handle it." His gaze drops back to meet mine, narrowing as they take me in. "Do I know you?"

My eyes roam over his face, and it takes me a second, but recognition hits me like a semi-truck, knocking any

160

remaining oxygen from my lungs. How the fuck did I not realize it at first?

"Emm, I don't think so," I croak. "I'm new."

I move to take a step back, away from him, wanting to put some much-needed space between us, but his large, coarse palm comes up to grasp my face, his fingers pressing firmly into my cheeks as he leans down to study my face. My heart rate skips a beat, thinking he's figured out who I am, but after a second, I realize he's examining the cut on my lip. His face pinches, a predatory look flashing in his eyes as they move up my face, stopping on what I imagine is the beginnings of a bruise on my cheek. At the realization, his fingers loosen on my skin, but I swear I can still feel the zing of them, even after he's let me go.

He opens his mouth to say something, but he doesn't get the chance to say whatever is on his mind before more calls for help, the voices becoming more alarmed with each passing second, drawing his attention to the chaos behind me. He straightens up, giving me a final frown and quizzical look before he takes off down the hall.

I'm frozen in place as I watch him go, seriously shocked at who he is. I mean, I've got no idea who he is. But I know who he is *to me*. He's older looking than the last time we met, but then that was eight years ago, and we were in a dark alley. Not to mention that he was pointing a gun at my head, so no wonder I didn't immediately recognize him.

As he disappears, I blink out of my shock, and remembering where I am, I slip out an emergency exit door at the side of the club and disappear into the night. The cool air whips across my face, blowing the fake brunette strands in all directions as I sprint the few blocks to my bike. I shove a pair of pants over my outfit and toss my wig in the duffel bag, pulling

161

on a leather jacket before securing the bag across my back. Not wanting to waste any more time, I swing my leg over my baby and tug on my helmet before giving the engine a rev and taking off down the street.

The cold air bites my skin, mixing with the adrenaline still flooding my body and making me feel alive, as I let out a loud whoop that is quickly swallowed by the wind. Damn, there's nothing quite like the thrill that comes from killing a scumbag like that. Anger licks along my skin, heating me from the inside out as I run my tongue over the cut on my lip, remembering the sting of pain when he hit me.

Once Raven is parked in my garage, I take out my burner phone and fire off a text to Chad's wife, letting her know the job is done before I rifle through the compact side unit where I keep some tools for the bike, and a bottle of cheap whiskey, strictly for occasions like tonight.

I pull off the lid with a pop and knock back a mouthful. Images of the man from tonight clash in my head with long-buried ones from eight years ago. The way he'd looked at me tonight was so similar to then. That ice-cold gaze that froze me in place, his chiseled jaw that looks like it's been carved from stone.

He said he'd handle it when I mentioned there was a problem, so he must work for the Antonellis in some capacity. Hitman plus club manager? That's an eclectic mixture of skills. But then who am I to talk—stripper and avenger of battered women—those two things hardly go hand in hand.

I wonder if he recognized me. *God, I hope not.* I bury my face in my palms and let out a long, weary groan. That's the last thing I need. As if it's not bad enough that Cain's got a stick up his ass when it comes to me. *Ha, fuck.* Even the thought of having not one but *two* gang members looking for me makes

162

my palms sweat, and I quickly try to drown out the anxious feeling by taking another swig of whiskey.

The bottle is empty, and I'm just this side of tipsy by the time I stagger into the night and make my way home.

···

I'm working the late shift at the club the rest of the week, which would be fine... if some overbearing, tatted-up asshole didn't keep stopping by whenever I'm working to sit silently in the corner and follow my every move. It's driving me fucking insane. What the hell is he even doing? Trying to intimidate me? Ha, there's no chance of that.

I can feel his eyes tracking my movements every night, feel them burning into me when I'm on stage, delivering drinks, giving lap dances. Hell, I even feel the lingering tingle of his gaze along my skin when I take my break.

After three nights of this nonsense, I'm like a raging bull when I step into Strip Tease on Friday and find him already sitting at his usual table. Despite knowing I need to be careful, I throw him a hateful glare, which he returns with a knowing smirk before I stomp over to the bar.

"What's up your ass tonight?" Mike asks when he sees me.

"He's here every night," I grumble, not having to explain any further who *he* is. "Doesn't he have better things to do?"

Mike just shrugs as he dries a tumbler before storing it away under the counter. "No idea. None of them seem too bad, though—the Rejects."

Of course, he thinks that. When they come in, many of them spend time at the bar talking to him. I've seen the way he

163

interacts with them, laughing and chatting. He already acts as though they're all buddies.

I snatch up a tray of drinks and move to distribute them to waiting customers around the room, as usual ignoring the searing heat of my skin as Cain trails me with his eyes.

The night goes on like that—me ignoring him, him watching—until the last customer leaves, and Drew locks the front door while the rest of us wipe down the tables and straighten everything up for tomorrow.

Once I've wiped the last table clean, I head toward the dressing room to change and gather my belongings, which is, of course, when Cain decides to finally make his move—just when I was starting to think I was done with him for the night. He calls out, "Drew, give Red the keys. She and I have a few things to discuss before she leaves. She can lock up when we're done."

Gritting my teeth, I turn to glare at the insufferable asshole.

"Oh, uhh, sure," Drew agrees hesitantly. He's not about to argue with a Reject, though. Not that I would expect him to. He gives me a long look as he hands the keys over, silently asking if I'm okay—he's a good person like that—and I give a nod and small lift of my lips to let him know I'm fine. I can handle myself against this asshole. While I prefer to lure my men with false pretenses, I have just enough self-defense skills to get me out of a tight corner. Although I have to admit, I've never had to fight off someone like Cain, who's all bulging muscle, and toned features. He's built more like a Viking warrior than a Black Creek thug, so I don't for one second think I could win against someone like him. But I could hopefully catch him by surprise. Not that I think he's asking me to stay so he can try to attack me. Nope, if I've learned anything from his incessant stalking the last few nights, it's that this asshole prefers to use silent intimidation to try and break me.

Neither of us moves or says anything until the last of the staff leave, most of them giving me curious or questioning looks as they pass by. When we're finally alone, I quirk a brow at him. "What is this about?"

"Dance for me." It's an order, given to me by the current overlord of our little part of town, and more importantly, a decider of fates for the people who work at Strip Tease.

It only makes rage simmer within me, though, and no doubt he can see the pits of anger burning in my eyes as he smirks at me. Pursing my lips, I have to swallow down my snort of refusal. I can't afford to piss him off and cause problems for Drew or anyone else who works here. The Rejects may seem like decent guys, but as I said, I don't trust them, and I definitely don't trust their leader. It wouldn't be fair to Drew or the others if I caused problems for them just because I've gotten myself into a tight spot with Cain. Besides, it's only one measly dance... how bad can it be?

I hesitate for another second, calculating my options, but ultimately, I'm just delaying the inevitable. I *know* what I need to do; what I *have* to do. There's no other choice—not if I don't want to end up fired or get my colleagues in trouble.

Biting my tongue, I make the only move I can—I head toward the stage.

"Ah-ah."

I freeze, gritting my teeth. *Fuck.* It takes me a second to compose myself before I look over my shoulder at him. He's leaning back in his seat with his legs spread wide, the intent clear to read in his cocky expression.

165

"Here." He points to the spot between his thighs. *Fucking asshole*. He knows I can't refuse; knows I won't risk the other's livelihoods.

*Fuck.* I seriously don't want to get that close to him. If the feel of his eyes on me is enough to scorch my skin, then being within touching distance of him is going to send me up in flames.

I glare daggers at him, making it clear how much I want to tear out his trachea and jam it up his ass as I spin on my heels and stride toward him, planting myself between his spread thighs. I ignore the way my muscles tense, and the fine hairs on my arms stand on end as if his close proximity has sent a bolt of static electricity through my system. It doesn't help that, while he's fully dressed, I'm wearing nothing more than a thong and a scrap of fabric claiming to be a bra. Even though he's barely paid any attention to my body, I feel the need to put more layers between us. Not because of him, but because of me. I can't trust the way his presence affects me; how it makes my heart race. My heated skin begs for his touch, and while I'm reluctant to get any closer to him, my body is practically singing for joy at our closeness.

He raises his eyebrows in an expectant look when I make no effort to move. There's no music, and honestly, this is awkward as fuck. Huffing out a breath, I start to sway my hips, shifting my weight from one leg to another as I fixate on a point on the wall just to the right of his head. One dance. Three minutes. That's all, and then I'm getting the fuck out of here.

I slowly countdown the seconds in my head—the only way for me to time myself, and it provides a sufficient distraction from the gorgeous asshole watching me intently and, more importantly, the disturbing response my body has to his nearness. I lose myself in the movement of my body, in the heat of his gaze, in the passing seconds as I tick them off one by one until he breaks the trance I was in.

"I know you're lying."

It's a statement. One delivered with absolute confidence.

"Is that so?" I challenge, finally allowing myself to meet his gaze. His bright green eyes bore into me, stalling the breath in my lungs.

He leans forward just as I bend my knees slightly, bringing our faces within inches of one another. "The question is, why?"

I don't answer him, meeting his watchful gaze with a steely one of my own as I stand back to my full height, peering down at him. I have to be careful here. I can't push him too far, but I also can't just spill all my secrets. He might know I'm lying, but he's got no proof, and that thought bolsters me.

As he sits back in his seat, I make an effort to soften my expression, stepping in to him. My thigh brushes against the coarse material of his jeans, and I have to ignore the way my skin reacts to that simple touch. Reaching out, I trail my finger down the front of his shirt before placing my palms on his chest and leaning in close to him.

"Maybe I just wanted to get the attention of a big, bad gangster," I volley, whispering the words seductively in his ear before pulling back to gauge his reaction. "Or maybe you're making up excuses to seek me out."

His expression darkens, and in a lightning-fast move, his hands snap out and reach around the back of my thighs, dragging me into his lap. My hands clasp his shoulders to stabilize myself while I work to hide my surprise at the feel of his semi-hard erection in his pants.

"Now, what would I want with a slut like you?" he snarls venomously. "Not good for anything except putting on a show and spreading your legs."

Despite the angry flare his words spark within me, I smirk down at him, appearing completely unaffected as I shift in his lap, deliberately rubbing my core over his dick.

"Are you sure about that because the hard-on in your pants says otherwise."

Using sex to disarm men is the most effective weapon I have. It's shocking how easily a man can be distracted when a hot girl flirts and rubs herself against him. I have to admit, though, this is the first time I've been turned on by someone I'm trying to charm. Heat pools in my core as I rub myself against him, and I have to work hard to push aside the cloud of lust threatening to consume me. *He's a Reject*, I remind myself. *He's an asshole. He's been trying to intimidate you all week. He wants to find the Reaper.*

It's enough to snap me out of the lusty haze and focus back on the task at hand. Intent on distracting him, so he forgets all about why he's here, I flick my tongue to lick along my bottom lip, and I lean in to run my nose up the column of his neck, ensuring my nipples graze against his chest.

"It's okay if you are," I whisper in his ear, sucking on his ear lobe as I subtly shift my crotch over his dick, feeling him grow beneath me. My pussy clenches yet again, and I have to mentally chastise myself. He might be downright fuckable, but he's abso-fucking-lutely off-limits.

His hands grab hold of my hips, squeezing tightly as he takes over control of my movements, using me to get himself off. I see the flare of heat in his eyes, and I have to bite back my own groan of pleasure every time the rough fabric of his jeans presses against my clit. I'm honestly no longer sure where this

168

is going. As heat surges through my body, I almost forget why I'm trying to distract him.

He's rock hard beneath me now, only making my pussy clench hungrily. Just when I'm convinced I have him in the palm of my hand and he's about to come in his boxers, he jumps to his feet, making me stumble as I try to get my legs beneath me before I fall to the ground.

My head is still spinning from the sudden change when he snatches my arms behind my back and bends me over the table, so my cheek and tits are pressed against the hardwood, my ass in the air.

I'm so caught off guard that I don't even react as he leans over me, the heat of his body warming my back as he whispers in my ear. "I told you, I don't have a need for worn-out hooker pussy." His words are a low, warning snarl that penetrate through my sex-addled brain.

I start fighting against his hold on my wrists, but it's futile. His grip only tightens as he kicks my legs apart with his feet, shifting, so he's easily holding my wrists in one hand. His other one slides down over my ass before he trails his fingers across my hip until he reaches my inner thigh, teasing the sensitive skin there.

My breaths come in rapid pants, both wanting him to touch me where I need him most and wanting him to fuck off. It's a confusing battle that annoys me to no end.

His fingers dance along the lining of the cheap thong I'm wearing before he brushes them over the fabric along the seam of my pussy. I buck against his touch, inadvertently pushing my ass against his still hard cock, and hating the evil-sounding chuckle he emits.

He rubs over my clit more deliberately, and I know he can feel how damp my panties are as I fight not to writhe or moan under his touch.

"Maybe you did just want my attention," he purrs in a husky voice that sounds as smooth as expensive whiskey. He slips his fingers beneath the scrap of fabric, finding me soaking wet as he pushes three fingers inside me.

I'm gritting my teeth so hard, I'll be lucky I don't crack one. He somehow seems to know that I'm fighting my body's natural reaction and that only encourages him to work me over harder, thrusting his fingers into me in fast, deep strokes until I can feel my pussy fluttering around him.

"You're so close to coming," he murmurs, and I can hear the lust in his voice. Despite whatever the fuck this is, he's not as unaffected as he would like me to believe. "All over my fingers. Is that what does it for you? Getting finger fucked by gang leaders? You need someone violent and in control to make you come?"

I can't even grit out a "no," too afraid that if I open my mouth, I'll say something different or simply moan in such a way that will be enough of an answer to how much he's affecting me.

Just as my orgasm feels like it's about to unfurl from my lower belly, he stills his fingers inside me. "Is that why you were with Python that night? Thought he would give you a good fucking?" His voice has lost that husky quality, the anger in it now abundantly clear. "Or was your pussy merely a distraction? You should know," he growls in warning, "I'm not like Python or any of those other meatheads. Your saggy cunt won't keep me from finding out what you know or from hunting down the Reaper. You're only making things worse for yourself by lying, so this is your last warning. Next time I won't be so nice."

170

He pulls out of me, finally releasing his hold on my wrists, and I spin to glower at him.

"Go fuck yourself," I snarl furiously, feeling the heat of anger and embarrassment coating my cheeks.

He smirks smugly. "No need, I've got plenty of women who will happily get me off, and they'll do a hell of a better job than you could."

With that, he strides toward the staff entrance at the back of the room. I can't do anything but stand on shaky legs and watch him go. Before he slips through the door, he calls out, "Don't forget to lock up."

When I'm alone, I sink into his now vacant chair, dazed. *What the fuck just happened?* How did that take such a turn for the worse? I still can't wrap my head around how I went from being the one in control to being bent over the table while he finger fucked me, and I'm not the slightest bit happy that I can still feel the delicious stretch of his fingers or the fact I'm fucking furious he stopped before I could come.

*Chapter 11*

The outer door bounces off the frame as I slam it behind me and stomp down the alley to the main road. I run my hand through my hair, tugging at the short, black strands in frustration as I force out a long, slow exhale through my nose. My bicep flexes as I tense the muscles in it. I want to scream my rage to the heavens, let out all this pent-up anger in the ring. But more problematic is the voice in my head, urging me to go back and finish what I started. The tightness around my crotch isn't helping the situation either.

Refusing to give in to whatever hold the red-headed witch has on me, I force my feet forward toward the Escalade I have parked at the side of the road just outside the club. The street is dark and vacant at this late hour, but I'm hardly paying any attention to my surroundings as I climb in behind the wheel and slam the door closed behind me.

My hands clench the steering wheel tightly as I take a second to try and clear my thoughts. I couldn't believe my luck when I walked into Strip Tease and saw her on stage. It took a minute for me to recognize her without the wig and blood coating her body, but when she swung her hips and tilted her head back, exposing her face to the lights above her, I knew immediately that she was the girl from that night. Razor told me her name was Jessica... clearly a fake. Her paperwork at the club says Red, although that's obviously not her real name either. What does she have to hide, that she can't even give her real name to her employer?

Releasing a heavy sigh, I let my head fall back against the headrest as my mind involuntarily drifts back to the feel of her grinding against me, the brush of her tits against my chest. "Ugh," I groan. That was *not* how I envisioned tonight going. I got her schedule from the manager, and I've made a point of turning up at the club every night she's been working this week, letting it sink through her pretty little head that I own her. There's absolutely nothing she can do or say to prevent me from showing up night after night. When I took over the Satan's territory, all of the businesses within this five-block radius effectively became mine. They're under my rein, my control. If I decide they should shut their doors and close up shop, then they will do so, under threat of death should the owner disobey. Those same rules apply to Strip Tease. Of course, I have no intention of actually doing any of that. These are hard-working people just trying to make a living. Who am I to barge in and screw with their livelihoods?

Now, if they stand in my way against the Antonellis, like the red-headed vixen is, then that's a different matter. And yet, my intimidation tactics don't seem to be phasing her in the slightest. Every night, she's thrown me hateful glares and scornful looks, the likes of which no one has dared aim in my direction since before Evie disappeared. I admit, even as a prepubescent, the other kids on our street were fearful of me. I've always been tall for my age, and I perfected a *not to be messed with* expression at a young age. When I started lifting weights in my teens and added a hefty bulk of muscle to my lanky frame, it only added to the intimidating image. Throw in the tattoos covering nearly every inch of visible skin and the fact I'm the leader of a group of ruthless gangsters quickly taking control of the city, and well, it's safe to say most people buckle beneath my demands. But not *her*.

Since the silent intimidation tactic didn't seem to be working, I decided an up-close and personal approach was required, but *holy fuck*, did that backfire. Instead of forcing her to tell me what she knows about the Reaper, I only succeeded in exposing how much the girl gets under my skin. Although, it's apparent that I affect her too. She put up a strong front, but there was no denying the way her body melted beneath my touch.

Loosening my right hand from around the steering wheel, I bring it to my lips, smelling her sweet scent as I suck a finger into my mouth. I can taste the residual essence of her as it dances across my tongue, only heightening my need.

*No!* She's a liar, and she's getting in the way of my agenda. She can taste like the world's best cream pie, but I won't allow her to interfere any longer.

I grit my teeth as I put the car into gear and head away from the club. My thoughts are a conflicting mix of anger and lust as I race across town at breakneck speed, needing to put as much distance as possible between the tempting seductress and myself.

Despite the twenty-minute drive to the new premises I acquired for the Rejects, I'm still reeling with anger, frustration, confusion, and worst of all, desire, as I stomp into the front lobby, where I find Marcus and a couple of other newer recruits putting on tactical gear, clearly on their way out.

"What's going on?" I ask.

"There's a new shipment coming in. We're going to catch the Grim Bastards in the act of stealing it." He tosses me a malicious grin as he checks his handgun, loading bullets in the chamber before securing it in his holster.

I perk up at that news. Killing some thieving fuckers is exactly what would brighten my mood. Meeting his grin with a wicked one of my own, I ask, "Where's Oliver?"

"In the office. We're all heading out in a few."

With a jerk of my head in acknowledgement, I head past him toward the office, relieved to feel the last remnants of lust leaving my system as it's replaced with a need for blood and violence.

"You're going after the Grim Bastards?" I ask Oliver as I step into the office, finding him slipping his own gun into the holster at his waist before securing a knife to the strap on his other thigh. He's dressed in full, stealth, tactical gear, just like the men out in the lobby.

"Yeah, I've had a couple of guys keep a lookout for the delivery, and they called an hour ago to say it was on its way to the drop-off point." He turns to face me, giving me a quick once over. "I called you."

I pull my phone out of my pocket, frowning when I notice the three missed calls. *Damn,* I was too caught up in playing games with the stripper. I didn't even realize my phone had gone off. I would have been pissed if I'd missed the chance to go out on this job.

"I'm coming with," I tell him, moving behind my desk to grab my own gun belt out of my drawer. I'm already dressed in dark clothing, which will suffice. As I affix it around my waist, I catch Oliver giving me a knowing smirk. He knew I'd be pissed if I'd missed out on this. We both live for the adrenaline rush that comes from staring death in the face, from destroying our enemies and living to fight another day. He might not take part in the fighting pit or the cage, but that doesn't mean he doesn't revel in the bloodshed the same way I do. After all, we grew up on violence and chaos. It's been a daily part of our lives for as long as we can remember. Brutality is in our blood; it's at the very core of our essence, the very center of who we are. Without that deep-seated viciousness, pining for vindication, we're nothing but lost souls without a purpose.

I throw on a leather jacket over my ensemble, and when I'm ready, I meet Oliver's gaze, the two of us sharing an intense look filled with malice and excitement for the battle ahead.

*Oh yeah, this is exactly what I needed tonight.*

We meet the other three members of our team in the lobby and head out to the parking lot, where we all get into one of the Cadillacs. Since Oliver is the one with the game plan, he climbs in behind the wheel, and I take the seat beside him while Marcus, Rampage, and Tank climb into the back. The three of them joined my crew nearly a year ago. Rampage and Tank are two of the eighteen-year-olds who agreed to join me after I rescued them, and Marcus had been at the compound that night, pretending to be a guard. I nearly shot the fucker when he ran

177

toward me across the asphalt, thinking he was trying to stop the kids from escaping. It was only when I spotted the young boy cradled in his arms, that I realized he was helping him. He worked tirelessly alongside me and my men, helping us rescue every single one of those kids that night, and he even trailed us back to Black Creek, ensuring we found safe homes for as many as we could.

After about a month of him hanging around, showing no signs of leaving, I pulled him in for a chat. I'd seen the dark shadows in his eyes, caught glimpses of the haunted look he wore sometimes. I know exactly what causes that. Only a loss like no other can hollow a man out, so he's merely skin and bones; a shell existing for the sheer purpose of existing. It didn't matter to me who it was he lost, I could sympathize with his pain regardless. Not wanting to pry, I never asked him about his past, but I did fill him in on my own. It's safe to say, he was on board with my plans for vengeance by the time we were done.

The drive is silent as Oliver directs us toward the north part of town. I stare out the window, not really taking in the rundown buildings and various vagrants as we make our way through Grim territory. There's a storage facility just beyond the city limits, effectively in no man's land, where I rent a container. Every month, I get the guys from up north to drop off a crate's worth, which I delegate among my men to sell.

There are supposed to be precisely one-hundred guns in each shipment, but for the last few months, there have only been eighty. Meaning someone's helping themselves to *my* guns before I set eyes on them. I've already looked into the guys up north and confirmed it's not them who are trying to swindle me, which means someone is getting to the shipment before my men can get up here to collect it. There's only one group of people that could be—the Grim Bastards.

For the most part, we leave each other be, but they've been making a lot of noise recently about their reduced gun supply, and I'm pretty sure this is their underhanded way of expressing their displeasure.

"Remember, we don't know if the Bastards have been informed the shipment is here yet, so everyone be on alert," Oliver states, slowing the car down so the security barrier can scan our license plate before lifting to grant us entry onto the property.

The place is dark and vacant as we drive past numbered units with roll-up shutters. Instead of going straight to my container, we park several rows over—out of sight of any lurkers—and quietly slip out of the Cadillac.

"Stay alert," I state in a low whisper, ensuring my voice doesn't travel as I repeat Oliver's words. I scan our surroundings, listening carefully for any sounds that could indicate anyone else is here.

"Here, take these." Oliver holds out his palm, containing five small Bluetooth earpieces, so we will be able to keep in contact if we have to split up. With a final look at my men, we head out, ready to kill some motherfucking thieves.

I lead the way, with Oliver watching my six, Rampage and Tank behind us, and Marcus bringing up the rear. When we reach the end of the row, I peer around the side of the building, my gaze darting around the dark expanse of space as I squint into the darkness, trying to discern any moving shadows. Nothing. No one in sight and no sounds alerting us to anyone nearby.

Giving the signal that it's all clear, we move around the side of the building, past the next row, again checking it's empty before moving on. I can't hear anything but the regular beating of my own heart and the steady exhale of my even breaths. Even the crunch beneath our boots as we move over the loose gravel is barely discernible.

As we come upon the edge of the row of units before the aisle containing mine, I crouch low, aiming my gun as I duck my head around the side. I quickly pull back as a round of bullets goes off, blindly firing off a few shots of my own, which undoubtedly go wide.

With my heart hammering in my chest at the near-miss, I turn back to face the others. "Take Rampage and Tank and go around the other side." My words are barely more than a whisper, not wanting them to be carried on the wind to our attackers, as I give Oliver the order. He nods before indicating for the guys to follow him, and the three of them slip around the other side of the wall we're hiding behind, quickly disappearing out of sight.

I take a second to formulate a plan in my head. "Cover for me," I bark out in a low voice before lifting my gun and keeping low, I run across the open space toward the wall marking the end of the other row of storage units. Guns go off all around me, including my own, as I shoot at the three men standing in the middle of the aisle. I manage to take one to the ground before I dive behind the wall.

Adrenaline pounds in my veins as I hurry to right myself, finding Marcus in the dark as he ducks behind his own wall again. I take a quick second to assess myself, ensuring I've got no injuries, before speaking quietly into the Bluetooth headset. "There's three men and an SUV in the middle of the aisle and at least one guy on the roof."

"We have eyes," Oliver responds a moment later. "We can take out the man on the roof, if you two can handle the others."

I share a look with Marcus across the open space, and he gives a confident nod—we've got this.

"We're on it."

I wait until I hear a round of gunshots going off, knowing that it will be Oliver taking out our threat on the roof before I step out from behind the wall with my gun raised. I notice Marcus doing the same out of the corner of my eye as I press down on the trigger, aiming at the two fuckers blocking the way to *my* guns.

They were already turning away from us, most likely to investigate the shots they heard from the other side of the aisle, making it easy for Marcus and me to eliminate them.

As the last one falls to the ground, I stride toward the three bodies, keeping my weapon aimed until I can kick their guns away. Satisfied that they're definitely dead, I lift my head to take in my surroundings. Marcus has already rounded the SUV, making his way toward the roll-down shutter of my storage unit.

"Boss," he says, glancing over his shoulder at me. "They must have had a key. The lock has been undone, but it's not broken."

*Fucking assholes.* How the hell did they get a key? It explains a lot, though. Initially, I'd dismissed the storage facility as to how they were getting a hold of my guns, but having ruled out every other possibility over the last few months, I was left with no other option.

He bends to grab the handle, ready to yank the door up, but he glances back at me before he does so. With my gun at the ready in case more of these fuckers is hiding in there, I give him a quick jerk of my head, and in one swift motion, he yanks open the door, pointing his own weapon into the dark room.

Before either of us can move, something rushes out of the darkness. Someone's making a run for it. *No fucking chance,*

181

*asshole.* I dive toward them, catching whoever it is by the collar and yanking them back.

Marcus moves to flick on the light inside the unit, the single bulb enough to show me the shithead's face as it crumples in panic. He's young enough, probably early twenties, and the look on his face is enough to tell me he's new to this life. Most likely massively regretting his decision to sign up right now.

"You with the Grim Bastards?" I demand in a low growl.

His eyes dart from side to side as he tries to work out his best way of getting out of here alive. He must have some functioning brain cells as he eventually stutters out, "Y-yes."

I'm aware of Oliver and the others closing in behind us, so there shouldn't be anyone else left alive.

"Well, you tell that motherfucking scumbag that if he steals one more gun from me, he can consider it an act of war." I lean in, so my face swallows up the asshole's entire field of vision. "And trust me, I'll be the one that finishes it, with his head on a spike."

I toss him toward the car, glowering at him as he falls to his knees before quickly righting himself and running the short distance to the car. We all stand and watch as he drives off, veering all over the place in his hurry to get away.

"You don't think he'll just bring more back up?" Oliver questions.

"Maybe. Let's hurry up and get the fuck out of here, just in case he does."

Glancing away from where the Grim's car disappeared, I turn and toss my car keys to Rampage and Tank. "Go bring the car around so we can load this shit into the back of it."

Tank snatches them out of the air before Rampage can get a hold of them. "I'd better do it. Fuck knows this angry bastard

182

will find something to rage about in the thirty-second drive over here."

He rushes back toward the car with his laugh lingering in the air as Rampage cusses him out. I ignore their antics as I investigate the crate, happy to discover it hasn't been tampered with. There's a crowbar on the ground beside it, and I scowl at it before kicking it away.

"I want all new security in this place," I tell Oliver. "Cameras, better locks. The works."

"You got it."

I'll have to make arrangements for my shipments to get delivered elsewhere, which will be a fucking headache, but I've got no doubt Grim, the President of the Bastards, will fail to heed my warning tonight. He'll be back, even if it's just to snoop, and I want to catch him in the act when he does.

When Tank has returned with the car, we don't waste any time loading the shipment into it and getting the fuck out of there. Less than an hour later, I'm sitting on an old, worn couch beside Oliver in the middle of what used to be a reception area, but we're in the middle of converting it into a place where we can all sit and chill when we're not working.

The lights are turned down, and there's a bunch of strippers dancing to some heavy tune. The guys had the party ready for us upon our return, and the alcohol has been flowing steadily since we got back. Now that I no longer have the Grim Bastards to distract me, my thoughts return to the redhead.

"The stripper isn't going to give us the Reaper's name," I tell Oliver, sighing as my mood plummets. He knows all about her, of course, but I want to be the one to deal with her. The one to break her. She's holding out on me, lying to my face, and I won't fucking stand for it any longer.

His beer bottle is lifted halfway to his mouth, but he pauses, turning to look at me. "Is that where you were tonight?"

I give a nod of my head. "I've spent all week trying to get under her skin, and nothing is fucking working."

Oliver snorts. "You mean the big, bad Cain couldn't get a mere woman to fall at his knees and tell him whatever he wanted to know?"

I frown, because he's right. I've always been able to scare or seduce information out of people, and neither has worked on this woman. Her stubbornness lights a spark of anger within me, and my hand clenches around my beer bottle. There's always a way to get what you want, and eventually, the stripper will spill her secrets to me. I just have to try a different tactic.

## Chapter 12

I sit there for a long time, trying to understand what just happened with Cain and, more importantly, what it means going forward. It's becoming pretty damn obvious that he isn't going to let this go. For whatever reason, he's intent on finding the Reaper, and he's decided I'm his best chance at getting the answers he seeks. I'd hoped if I continued to tell him I didn't know anything that he would drop it, but somehow he knows I'm fucking lying, and like a dog with a bone, he's going to keep hounding me until he gets answers.

A headache is forming behind my eyes as I struggle to think of a suitable solution. Unable to come up with anything, I groan in frustration as I get to my feet. By the time I'm changed and have locked up behind me, it's nearly three a.m. as I make the familiar walk back to my apartment, I swear I can feel eyes on me, and I constantly peer into the darkness around me, trying to identify where it's coming from. I know, whoever it is, isn't Cain. The way this person's eyes dig into my skin, it lacks Cain's intensity, the heat that scalded my skin, but it's no less distracting, making the hairs on the back of my neck stand to attention.

The eyes follow me until I slip into the doorway of my apartment building, and when I've reached my place, I make a point of not turning on any lights so I can peer out the window to the street below. I catch a flicker of movement at the corner of the street, but when I squint in that direction, I see nothing but shadows. After a few more moments, when there's no more movement from outside, I turn away from the window. I might not see anyone, but I know they're out there. Watching. But, who are they? And more importantly, what do they want?

***

Someone's following me. The eyes I felt on me last week when I left the club have tracked me every time I step foot out the door ever since. But every time I turn around and peer into the shadows and dark corners provided by buildings and alleyways, I don't see anything.

Whoever it is must be one of Cain's men, but considering what happened at Belle Donne and my run-in with the guy who nearly killed me eight years ago, I can't be completely confident it's not someone on the Antonellis' payroll.

Maybe someone followed me home that night, or they've tracked me down since. Just thinking about it has panic flaring to life, and a desperate need to flush them out takes over me.

I've spent all week trying to decide if it's wise to confront whoever it is and working out how to actually do that, but ultimately, I've decided I need to know. I can't do any of my extracurriculars if my every move is being watched, recorded, and reported back to some asshole. I haven't even been able to check in on Sheryl and Grace in case this shithead stalking me connects the dots between us, leading him back to Python. Not being able to do what makes me feel truly alive pisses me the fuck off. I feel like a caged animal pacing her pen. If this asshole is acting under Cain's orders, then I'm going to tear his balls off, and if it's the Antonellis, well, *fuck*, I hope it's not an Antonelli. Bad things happen to those who catch their attention.

"See ya later, Kenny." I wave at the bouncer as I exit the club, having just finished the day shift and more than ready to get home and curl up with a glass of wine and some shitty TV show for the night.

On my way down the street, I pop into the corner shop to pick up a few things, and that's when I feel the hairs rise along the back of my neck. It's the same instinctual response I've had all week when I know I'm being watched. My lips purse in annoyance. It's always the same. Whoever it is, leaves me alone when I'm at home or in the club, but the minute I dare step foot on the streets, they find me.

I catch a flicker of movement in the periphery of my vision and snap my head toward the end of the aisle. *I could have sworn I saw someone duck out of sight.* Anger licks along my spine as my hand clenches the bottle of wine tightly. Working on loosening my grip, I carefully set the bottle back on the shelf before leaving the aisle. I've had e-fucking-nough of

189

this shit. I refuse to be corralled and intimidated by a fucking ghost. If this is Cain's way of thinking he can get me to confess what I know, then he's going to be sorely disappointed. I don't scare that easily, and he's going to have to do a hell of a lot better if he thinks he can bully me into spilling my secrets.

I take my time, wandering up and down a few of the aisles, pretending to peruse the shelves as I make my way toward the staff-only door at the back of the shop. Once I reach it, I duck inside, taking in the storage room stocked with excess inventory until I find a fire exit door at the back of it. *Perfect.* I hastily cross the room and push it open, stepping out into a narrow alley that runs along the back of the buildings on the main street. There's nothing but wheelie bins, upturned crates, and trash bags back here, and I quickly flatten myself against the wall, behind the door, ignoring the pounding of my pulse at the base of my neck as the door bursts open and a young man with a short cut, white-blond hair steps out.

He curses under his breath as he stares toward the opposite end of the alley, running a hand through his buzz cut. Not wasting any time, I jump toward him, catching him off guard as I tackle him from behind. I get him into a chokehold the way Hadley taught me, but his reflexes are quick, and he jabs me in the gut with his elbow, momentarily winding me. Distracted, my hold loosens, and he easily slips free. In a blur of movement, he spins to face me, reaching out to grab me by the neck and slam me against the wall.

The force knocks the air from my lungs as I stare at him, shocked at the sudden turn of events. As I scramble to gather my thoughts, I notice the dark shadows that crawl across his irises for a moment before they start to lift, and his eyes widen in surprise as he blinks and returns to the present. *What the fuck was that?* Not having the time right now to dwell on it, I slam my fist into the crook of his arm and step swiftly to the side, breaking his hold on me.

His eyes follow the fast movement, an eyebrow lifting in surprise. I raise my hands, ready to fight him off if he steps even a toe in my direction, but he doesn't make any further attempts to try and corral me. Instead, his posture relaxes, his shoulders dropping. The subtle change only has me more on edge, and I clench my fists tighter, ignoring the sting as my nails dig into my palms as I prepare to defend myself.

He lowers his hands, letting his arms hang loosely by his side, and his gaze runs over me in an assessing manner as I stand there, confused, perching on the balls of my feet. Despite his seemingly relaxed manner, I'm half expecting him to pounce on me, but instead, he surprises me by saying, "Impressive. Not many people know how to get out of a chokehold like that."

Ignoring that weird remark, I spit out, "Why the fuck are you following me?" I still don't lower my fists, but I do take a second to look him over. He's young, younger than me. In fact, if I had to guess, I'd say he isn't much older than Luc. There's something about him, though, that I can't quite put my finger on. Maybe it's to do with whatever I saw in his eyes. It's almost like there's a dark aura around him, hinting at the terrible things he's capable of. It seems crazy, given just how youthful he looks, but whatever it is is enough of a warning that I don't let his young age fool me.

He ignores my question while tilting his head, and asking, "Where did you learn to fight like that?"

With my brows furrowed, I continue to assess him for a tense moment. "Listen, kid—"

"Bones."

When I just stare at him in confusion, he explains. "My name is Bones. You know, like Jon Jones, the MMA fighter."

I scrunch my nose up. "I'm not calling you that."

The kid's shoulders visibly deflate, making him look every bit of his adolescent age, and *fuck me*, it almost makes me feel bad.

"Who has you following me?" I ask instead, refusing to let him lure me into a false sense of safety. He's already proven he's got impressive fighting skills, and the energy exuding from him tells me he's no stranger to violence.

He refuses to answer, flattening his lips as his childish demeanor slips away, and he once again becomes the guy that chased me outside. I narrow my eyes on him. "Cain?"

He still doesn't respond, and I run my gaze over him, trying to find something identifiable, but he's wearing a long sleeve top and pants, so I can't spot a Reject tattoo, and honestly, I have no idea what someone who works for the Antonellis would look like. A mafia idiot dressed in a suit with that air of arrogance about them? If that's the case, the kid is definitely not with the Antonellis. Despite the slash of violence surrounding him, there's a strange, boyish charm about him, but it's deceiving and makes me question my actions.

I decide to take a gamble. "I know it's Cain," I state, hoping I'm right. "Tell him to fuck off and leave me alone."

The kid's lips lift up in a delighted grin like he's finding all of this hilarious. When he doesn't do anything but smile broadly at me, I spear him with a deadly look before turning on my heel and stomping down the alley, figuring he's not going to hurt me. He must belong to Cain, and if that's the case, his orders will be to follow me and report back. I don't believe Cain would send one of his minions to torture the information out of me. No, I, without a doubt, believe the insufferable asshole would rather do that job himself.

Before I exit onto the street, I call out over my shoulder, "And stop fucking following me!"

***

The kid had enough common sense not to follow me the rest of the way home the other night, and I don't get the same tingle of awareness when I'm out and about the next day. It feels fucking fantastic like I can finally breathe again, without the oppressive weight of eyes on me. I almost feel like a new woman as I step out of the apartment building on Saturday to run some errands and grab some groceries, and my mood is better than it has been in days as I think about the lovely, relaxing bubble bath I have planned for tonight.

Once I've done all I need to do, I pop into the shelter to check on Sheryl and Grace—who are both doing great—before I head home. I'm humming under my breath as I reach the top of the stairs, stepping onto the fourth-floor landing. The only way this day could get any better is if I had a voicemail with some shithead's name on it, waiting for me to pluck from the face of this earth. Reaching the door to my apartment, I set the grocery bags on the floor to fish out my keys. I pause with the key halfway inserted into the lock, frowning at the peeling green paint on the door as I hear voices coming from inside my apartment. Luc knows not to let in anyone he doesn't know, so I can't work out who he could be talking to.

My body is tense, coiled like a spring ready to unfurl as I jiggle the key in the lock until it swings open. Without the wooden barrier between us, the voices within the apartment become clearer. I hear Luc's distinctive laugh, followed by another male voice that I can't immediately place. Snatching the

193

bags off the floor, I barge into the room, coming to a stop when I find the kid from yesterday lounging on *my* sofa.

My eyes immediately narrow on him in suspicion, the two of them turning to face me as they stop talking mid-conversation. I should have fucking known he wouldn't just leave me alone. But involving Luc? Hell to the fucking no!

"What the fuck is he doing in here?" I bark at Luc, tearing my gaze away from the kid to look at my brother. The smile on his face drops off, and his eyebrows climb up his forehead as he gapes at me.

"Bones?"

"I needed to talk to you," the kid speaks up, garnering my attention.

I glower at him. "Well, you could have waited outside, on the street." Dismissing him before he can argue, I snap my attention back to my brother. "What did I tell you about not letting strangers into our home?! Do you have any idea who he is? God, Luc, he could have hurt you, or worse." Concern for my brother makes my voice crack.

"Whoa," Bones says. *Fuck me,* nope, I'm not calling him that... What did he say his name was again? Jon? Jon holds his hands up in a placating gesture. "I'm not here to hurt anyone. I just have a message for you."

"Well, get on with it so you can get the fuck out of my apartment," I snap. He's probably only a few years older than Luc, but knowing who he works for, the people he associates himself with... well, I can't have him corrupting my brother.

"Cain told me to tell you to be at Toxic tonight."

I pinch my lips, not appreciating the demand.

"Who's Cain?" Luc asks, his eyes bouncing between Jon and me. Of course, Luc knows nothing about my issues with the leader of the Rejects. Nor do I want him to know.

"No one," I blurt out before Jon can think to inform him who the fuck he really is—assuming he hasn't already. I continue to stare Jon down until he gets the message—spill a word of who you are or my beef with the Rejects, and you'll fucking regret it. A look I can't place flashes across his face, but he nods in concession before making a move toward the door.

I want to ask him what Cain wants, but I can't voice the question aloud with my brother standing right beside me, so instead, I let him slip past me toward the door. Just before he disappears down the hall, he turns back to look at my brother. "I'll let you know the next time we're playin' a game, yeah?"

Luc grins. "Sounds good."

"What the fuck does that mean?" I bark at Luc as the front door clicks shut.

He narrows his eyes on me. "What the fuck is your problem?" he demands. Luc rarely argues with me. For the most part, he's pretty good at doing what I say, knowing I'm only trying to do what I think is right to keep us both safe. But apparently, he's not feeling so agreeable today.

"Do you know who he is?" I volley back.

"A Reject? So? He was nice to me."

I throw my hands up. Of course, that idiot told my brother who he was. *God, I'm going to fucking murder him.* "Just because he was *nice* to you doesn't mean he wouldn't hesitate to put a bullet in your head if you pissed him off," I argue. "And there's absolutely no way you're hanging out with him."

He snorts out a pissed-off chuckle. "You can't control every aspect of my life, Sawyer. I'm nearly sixteen, so I can be friends with whoever I want; do whatever I want. Hell, maybe I'll sign up to join the Rejects. They seem like pretty cool people."

I stomp toward him, steam practically pouring out of my ears. "Over my dead body," I snarl. "I will not let you end up like every other kid in this town—pedaling drugs on a street corner until you get gunned down in a drive-by, all to make some useless point to a gang that doesn't give a shit about you. You deserve a better life than that."

I see the anger melt out of him as his shoulders deflate. "I know," he grumbles. "You're just trying to protect me. I'm not a kid anymore, though. I don't need you to mother me."

I give him a ruly grin and cuff him around the chin. "I'm never going to not worry about you."

Our argument may be sidelined for now, but I know it's not over. He's been pushing my boundaries more and more recently, and I know I'm going to have to start loosening the reins, but *man*, it's hard. Everything I do is for him, and the thought of something happening to him... well, it's not even worth thinking about.

He reluctantly lets me pull him in for a hug, giving me an awkward pat on the back. I don't let just anyone see me emotional, and I rarely hug people, but my brother is the exception. When I'm outside of this apartment, I need to don my hard-ass bitch face. It's the only way to deal with the daily shit Black Creek throws at me; to handle the shitty customers in Strip Tease; to ensure everyone I meet knows I'm not to be messed with. But when I'm in here, with Luc, I want to be as open with him as I can be. There are parts of my life he can't know about—it's just safer that way—but that doesn't mean I can't be emotionally available for him; be a sister—someone he can vent to and spend time with. I'm the only constant in his life, and I'm doing my best to wear two hats—one of a sibling and another of a mother figure.

All we have is each other, and I think it's helped us to become as close as we have, but it is tough at times. Especially as he has grown older and he feels the need to figure out who he is and find his place in this world.

As he pulls back, he raises an eyebrow. "So, who's Cain?"

I groan, turning away from him and grabbing the grocery bags I dropped on the floor earlier, dumping them on the kitchen counter before I start to unpack them. "He's the leader of the Reaper Rejects," I admit, deliberately not looking at him.

"What?!" he exclaims in shock. "What the hell does he want with you?"

"Nothing," I lie. "He's been stopping by the club, and Drew asked me to liaise with him, if he had any questions."

It's a bold-faced lie, but I'm sure as fuck not about to tell my fifteen-year-old brother that Cain's men caught me killing Python, and now he won't leave me the fuck alone.

"Bet you're loving that," he jokes. He knows how much I hate any and everyone associated with gangs. They're a fucking stain on this town. The ordinary, everyday people of Black Creek would be better off without any of them.

"You've got no idea. Mac 'n' cheese for dinner?" I ask, changing the subject.

"Yeah, sounds good."

As I start lifting out what I need for dinner and Luc buries his nose in a comic, I mull over Cain's demand for me to meet him tonight. After the way our last interaction went, I'd honestly rather avoid him. I've never had a man turn the tables on me like that before, nor has someone I so vehemently despise managed to make my body respond the way it does around him. All I could think about was the feel of him inside me; how easily he had me coming apart beneath his touch. And the whole time he was playing my body like a fiddle, all I wanted to do was rip his head off. It's a very conflicting set of emotions, and I've no idea how to deal with it, yet I can't just keep reacting to Cain's

197

moves. I need to make some of my own. My guess is, despite his order, Cain isn't expecting me to show up tonight. He's seen enough of my defiance by now to know I'm not one to simply bend to his commands... which is exactly why I'm going to be at Toxic tonight.

I fill the next few hours with making dinner and cleaning the apartment. When the sun has long since set, and while Luc is engrossed in some end-of-the-world-type movie on the TV, I head out into the night, dressed in a skin-tight tank top and black skinny jeans with rips in the knees. I've paired the outfit with my trusty chunky-heeled boots so the outfit toes the line between sexy and badass and finished it off with a gun secured in my shoulder holster, hidden under my jacket, and my trusty blades in my pocket—just in case.

"Wasn't sure you'd actually go," a voice says from the darkness, startling me as I step onto the pavement outside my apartment building.

"Jeez," I chastise. "Are you checking up on me?" Before he can answer, I shake my head and hold up a hand. "You know what, I don't wanna know."

Jon's grin gets even wider, and as I turn and stroll down the street, he moves to my side, easily keeping pace with me.

"I like you. You're a bit of a secret badass, aren't you?"

I quirk a brow, refusing to tell him anything more about me.

"Your brother is pretty cool too."

"Stay away from him," I snap, scowling in his direction. "I mean it. I don't want him caught up in any of this shit."

"What shit?" It sounds like a genuine question, which confuses me.

"In anything to do with the Rejects," I explain.

198

Jon shrugs his shoulders. "We're not that bad, you know. Cain's not the jackass you think he is."

Of course, he thinks that. He's a fucking teenager. His brain hasn't fully developed yet, so he's practically programmed to make stupid decisions and trust the wrong people.

"Have you been to one of our fight nights?" he asks after a moment of heavy silence. When I just give him a questioning look, silently saying, *seriously? What do you think?* he laughs. "You'll love it."

He talks my ear off the whole way there, and it makes me wonder how the hell he ever shut up long enough to follow me without giving himself away. He actually seems like a decent enough kid, although some of the things he says are a bit weird, making me wonder what sort of childhood he had growing up. Anyway, it's none of my business, and the questions quickly drift from my mind as we reach the old docks and turn onto the street Toxic is on. He flashes his Reject's tattoo to the bouncer at the door—which apparently grants us both free entry—and we walk into Toxic.

The intoxicating combination of sweat, testosterone, and adrenaline hit me as soon as we step inside. Looking around, the entire ground floor of the club has been completely revamped. Where the dance floor used to be—where I danced with my mystery man only a couple of weeks ago—there is now a sizable octagonal ring, surrounded by a metal cage. The cage runs all the way to the roof, four floors above us. A staircase at the edge of the warehouse leads up to the first floor, which runs like a landing around the outer edges of the room, enabling people on the floors above to lean over and watch the fight as well.

A smaller dance floor has been erected at the far side of the room, opposite a bar, which has been upgraded and looks like it stocks more than just the cheap stuff. It's impressive, and it must have cost a fortune to do.

The place is already packed, and a fight is currently underway by the sounds of the roaring crowd.

"Oh, we're just in time," Jon exclaims with an excited gleam in his eye. Without further explanation, he grabs my hand and yanks me through the crowd. He shed his jacket as soon as we stepped up to the bouncer, so his Reject's tattoo is prominently on display on his forearm, and the crowd parts easily for us until we're standing ringside.

My eyes widen in surprise, and I watch, captivated as two men fight each other like wild animals in the ring. They're both shirtless, sweat and blood coating their bodies. It's only when I stare mesmerized at the dark-haired fighter, casting my eyes over the various tattoos inked across every available surface of his torso, that I realize it's Cain.

"It's no-holds-barred fighting," the kid explains, and when I tear my eyes away from the fight to look at him, he's staring in awe at the fighters. Feeling my eyes on him, he turns to look at me. "They can literally do anything, and it's allowed. Biting, kicking, twisting." He grins, and in the dark room, with the stench of testosterone in the air, it looks creepy as fuck. "They can even gouge each other's eyes out."

*That's not at all disturbing.* I return my attention to the cage fight in front of me just in time to see Cain sock the guy in the face, following it up with a blow to his instep that sends his opponent crashing to his knees. Cain smashes his knee into his competitor's face, simultaneously slamming his fists down on his back, and the guy collapses to the floor as a roar goes up from the crowd.

"Holy fuck," I murmur in awe.

"Yup. I can't wait until I can get my chance."

At his words, I spin to gape at him. Sure, he was able to handle his own against me the other day, and he's got some muscles on his arms, but he's nowhere near as broad as either Cain or the other fighter. Besides that, he seems way too fucking young to be in that ring. He could die, for Christ's sake. What asshole would let one of his men voluntarily go into the ring all so he can, what, claim bragging rights? Fuck no.

I plan on telling him exactly that. Entirely unaware of the anger sparking within me, Jon simply sighs, saying, "But Cain won't let us until we're eighteen."

*Huh*. Well, just right. "More like twenty-one," I grumble. It's not that I'm a stickler for the law or anything, but I can't look at him without picturing Luc, and there is absolutely no fucking way I would be letting Luc anywhere near this place before he's twenty-five. Even then, if I could chain him up at home, where I know he's safe, I'd do exactly that.

"Come on." Jon gestures toward the bar. "May as well get a drink."

I open my mouth to protest as I look around me to see where Cain went. Another fight is starting up in the ring, and I scan the throng of people surrounding it, trying to pick him out of the crowd. It takes me a second, but I catch sight of him just before a door on the far side of the room swings shut behind him, a *staff-only* sign making me sigh as I turn back to Jon and reluctantly agree to a drink while we wait.

When we finally make it through the crowd surrounding the bar, I order a beer. The kid does the same before turning to look at me. "So you're the girl that saw the Reaper?"

I raise an eyebrow in surprise. I didn't expect him to know anything about me. Isn't that the usual hierarchy in gangs? It strikes me that he might know something of use, so I deflect with a question of my own.

"Why is Cain so interested in the Reaper?"

Jon grins at my deflection. He seems to like that I hold my own against him. "Who wouldn't be? A badass like that who can literally kill men in their own beds without getting caught?" He shakes his head, the awe apparent in his voice. I wonder if he'd be just as impressed if he knew the Reaper was a woman.

"Doesn't he kill gang members, though? Shouldn't you want to stay as far away from him as possible?"

"He ain't ever killed a Reject." He smirks, bringing the bottle up to his lips.

I snort, shaking my head, thinking, *only because none of you have given me a reason to... yet.*

We sip on our beers for a bit, and I gaze around the room. Another fight is underway in the ring, and the dance floor is quickly filling up. Looking to the floor above me, people are pressed up against the railings running alongside the metal wire of the cage, their fingers wrapped around the thin metal as they shake the wire fence, screaming for whichever fighter they're rooting for.

Along with the heavy techno music, it's a heady atmosphere, doused in pheromones and tinged with violence. It's a form of escape that's offered here. A chance for people to leave the dreariness and misery of their everyday lives at the door, and revel in their sins. All around me, men and women are giving into their basic needs—fighting, fucking, forgetting. I can taste the bad intentions in the air. If the gateway to hell were anywhere on earth, it would be here in this very club. I can practically feel the evil spirits as they coax and taunt us, daring us to give in to our desires—for just one night.

My heart rate picks up to match that of the music's, most likely in tune with every other warm body in this place, and I feel the itching desire to get up and move. I rarely let myself indulge in such frivolity. The only time I come to a club is when I'm pursuing a target, and even though I'm here with a purpose in mind, it doesn't change the fact that tonight is the first time I've been in a club in years when I don't have to constantly be on alert, watching my six and keeping an eye on whoever I'm stalking.

Don't get me wrong. I'm no idiot. I'm still very much aware of everyone around me. One always has to be vigilant in Black Creek, but as I polish off my beer and signal the bartender for another one, I figure, while I'm here, I may as well let my hair down a little. Fuck knows, I deserve to have some fun.

The bartender sets two new beers down in front of us, and I down mine before jumping to my feet. "Let's dance."

With a cocky grin, the kid hastily gulps down his own before following me out onto the dance floor. I lose myself in the pounding bass of the music, letting it flow through me until it's controlling my movements, my breathing, my heartbeat. I don't even realize I've closed my eyes until a set of hands land possessively on my waist.

Scowling, I turn around to bite the asshole's head off, but the words stick in the back of my throat as I come face-to-face with my mystery man. A coy smile plays at the corner of my lips, matching his lascivious smirk.

"I was hoping I'd see you again."

I cast a quick look around me, not spotting Jon anywhere, but as the sex-dripping mystery man strokes his thumb back and forth across the strip of bare skin between my top and jeans, I immediately forget all about Jon and Cain and why I'm here. Just that small bit of contact has my blood warming, an excited thrum humming through my veins. What is it about him that makes me feel so alive? So carefree?

"Is that so?" I barely recognize the seductive purr of my own voice.

He steps in closer, his hips pressing against mine, our chests grazing. I have to tilt my head back to look into his face. There's a mischievous twinkle in his pale blue eyes that's a contrast to the hard lines around his eyes and lips, reminiscent of an arduous life. There's a seriousness about him that resonates with me. As if, like myself, he was never able to let loose and just be a kid or an irresponsible teenager. He looks like he's carrying the weight of the world on his shoulders.

There's a dusting of dark stubble along his jawline, similar to the last time we met, and I wonder if he always keeps it like that or if he shaves in between. He pushes his thigh in between mine, using his strong hold on my hips to move them in time to the music, matching my movements with smooth ones of his own. The crowd around us falls away. The entire world does. What *is* it about him that makes me lose all common sense? That makes me forget about everything around me? I could get lost in him, drown in the pools of his eyes, suffocate in his fresh, alluring scent.

He ducks his head, his lips brushing over mine enticingly. His hand moves to cup the side of my head, and his fingers slide into my hair as his lips sweep across mine again, adding a flick of his tongue to the mix this time. His taste is intoxicating, like cinnamon and dark chocolate—sweet and sinful.

I fall into him, my arms winding around his neck as I pull him closer and deepen our kiss. I still don't even know his name or anything about him. But that's the thing about reveling in your sins—the who, or what, or why don't matter. It's all about the moment. About the way his fingers dig into my hip, the sweep

204

of his tongue across mine, his hungry groan, my breathy moan. The other details don't matter—at least, not right now.

I'm not sure how long we stand there, tasting one another, ignorant to the world around us, but eventually, his phone buzzes in his pocket, and he breaks off our kiss with a wry look. He fishes it out, glancing at the screen before saying, "Give me a sec." He moves to walk away, but at the last second, he snatches my wrist, searing me with a pensive look. "Don't go anywhere."

Before I can respond, he walks off, quickly swallowed up by the crowd. I'm not left alone on the dance floor for long before Jon reappears, tapping me on the shoulder and pulling my attention away from my mystery man's retreating back.

"Sorry, wanted to watch my buddy in the ring." He gestures with his thumb toward the cage, where a guy who looks to be of similar age to Jon is easily demolishing a guy twice his age and double his size. *What the hell?* "Cain's this way." He jerks his head for me to follow him, and I glance briefly over my shoulder, looking at the spot my mystery guy disappeared. As nice as it was to lose myself in him, a distraction like that is the last thing I really need right now. So, with a heavy sigh, I follow Jon, leaving all thoughts of cinnamon and chocolate behind on the dance floor.

Jon leads me over to the far side of the room, by the stairs, where there's an expansive seating area overflowing with Rejects. Don't ask me how I know they're all Rejects members. Some of them have their tattoos clearly on display, but for the most part, I can just tell by the way they luxuriate in their seats, the subtle way their eyes roam around the room as if surveying their territory. They're at ease here.

Jon claps hands with a few of them, nodding his head at others as he passes. I get my fair share of questioning stares, but

I ignore all of them, keeping my head held high as I stride past them.

Like the king he is, Cain is lounging in the middle of his men, occupying a whole booth for just himself. A scantily clad woman is brushing herself up against him while he watches her tits bounce, and I have to grit my teeth as a flash of annoyance surges through me. Is that jealousy? Fuck, it better not be. He must sense us approaching as he lifts his head, the cocky grin from a moment ago morphing into a stern frown when his gaze meets mine.

He murmurs something I can't hear, and the woman stops rubbing herself all over him, getting to her feet and disappearing into the crowd. As we approach, he leans back in his booth, draping his arms over the back of the seat, smirking smugly like he thinks he's already won this round.

"I thought for sure you were going to make me send one of my men to get you."

Isn't that what he did with Jon anyway?

I don't react to his barb. "I came to tell you to stop having me followed."

That annoying fucking smirk doesn't falter as he slowly leans forward, placing his forearms on his knees. "Does that mean you're going to tell me the truth?"

I grit my teeth, forcing my expression to remain blank as I hiss out, "I am telling you the truth."

"Then no," he states casually, resuming his original position. His eyes move briefly to Jon. "Looks like you and Bones are getting along. Maybe I'll sic him on you permanently."

"What the fuck is your problem?" I snap, and I instantly know I've crossed a line. But of course, even as his face hardens and his eyes narrow on me in warning, I continue to run my

206

stupid mouth. "I was just some girl in the wrong place, at the wrong time. Stop fucking harassing me!"

Fuck. That is not at all what I came here to say. Well, that's not *how* I meant to say it. I thought by showing up here instead of hiding from him and reiterating for the millionth time that I didn't see the Reaper, that he'd finally believe me. Although the second the heated words leave my mouth, I can see I've crossed a line. He just makes me so angry when I'm around him. The second I look at his stupidly handsome face, that itch of annoyance flares to life inside me, making me do and say reckless things.

He's on his feet so quickly, I barely register the movement until his hand wraps around my upper arm and pulls me into him. I'm so close, I can see the anger burning in his emerald irises, feel it radiating off of him, and searing my skin where he's touching it.

"Listen here," he snarls. The deep timbre of his voice is dark and threatening. "I've given you plenty of leeway, but I won't tolerate you disrespectin' me in front of my men." His face is so close to mine, I can feel the waft of his breath against my cheek. He glares at me for a long moment, rendering me speechless in the face of his wrath. His grip on my upper arm is bruising, and I know I should be scared right now. I should be absolutely shitting myself, but I'm not. I'm angry, no, I'm fucking furious. But what's most disturbing is that I think I'm a little turned on. Okay, like a lot turned on. Which only pisses me off further. Men like him infuriate me. They're domineering, entitled assholes who think they can control everyone around them and get anything they want without putting in the work themselves. Men like him are the reason I am who I am, why Black Creek is falling apart and heading toward wreck and ruin, why people run scared when they enter a room. Men like him are the Devil.

"What's going on here?"

That voice behind me has my muscles tensing. Why is he here? Why is he inserting himself into the middle of this hostile situation? Because of me?

I try to turn to look at him, to tell him to leave, but Cain's tight grip on my arm holds me hostage, and his next words blow my freaking mind.

"Oliver," he snarls, looking over my head, to my mystery man standing behind me. I swear I can feel the heat from his body burning into my back. "Get *her*"—he spits out the word, his lip curling in disdain—"out of here before I do something she regrets."

Despite his threat being delivered in a glacial tone that is intended to have me pissing myself, it instead sends a shiver of desire down my spine, making me glower defiantly back at him. He uses his hold on my arm to shove me toward my mystery man—Oliver?—as if handing me off to him, like I'm some sort of fucking possession.

I tear my gaze away from the snarling beast of a man in front of me to look into the pale blue eyes that only moments ago I could have drowned in. Now, they're closed off, just like the rest of his expression as he frowns down at me.

O... I remember Cain saying that on the phone. O for Oliver.

This is O.

My mystery man is a fucking Reject.

# Chapter 13

Fucking. Christ. I leave for five fucking minutes to answer a call, and everything goes to shit. I was disappointed when I returned to the dance floor to find the enigmatic woman from before was gone. Of course, she was. She has a habit of slipping away before I'm finished with her. I didn't even get to ask her her name or get her number.

      I never, for one fucking second, thought I'd find Cain's hand wrapped around her arm while he glared at her with such disdain and loathing. The dark shadows dancing across his face, showcasing him as the formidable leader he is, have made lesser men sob like babies. Yet, the alluring redhead held her ground, returning his dark expression with a furious one of her own. Seeing her go toe-to-toe with a man that has built himself an empire, gathered himself an army, and established such an imposing reputation, well, if I wasn't a tad scared for her life, I'd have been rock-hard in my jeans. Although the semi I was sporting was uncomfortable enough against the restricting fabric.

The pieces all slotted together as soon as I saw them scowling at one another. She's the girl he's had a tail on all week. The one who saw the Reaper kill Python. The one he's been obsessing over.

Why was she even at a Satan party? And in Python's room? The thought that she was there to fuck him, that she'd forgotten all about me when she's occupied my every thought since that night, has my own anger spiking as I step up behind her.

"What's going on here?" I keep my voice carefully neutral, along with my impassive expression.

"Oliver, get her out of here before I do something she regrets." I can hear how close Cain is to losing his shit. He'd never hurt a woman, that's not how he works, nonetheless he doesn't tolerate disrespect. He has spent years carefully crafting an indomitable reputation and amassing a loyal army understanding of his cause, and the fiery spitfire in front of him is testing his last nerve.

Before the situation can escalate, I tug her away from him, noting the surprise in her eyes when she turns to look at me, quickly squashed by a flare of anger and suspicion. Thankfully she doesn't resist as I maneuver her past the watching Rejects members and through the sea of party-goers in the club. Neither of us says anything until we're out on the street, the loud thud of the music nothing but background noise as the cool night air lifts her hair, blowing it in my direction and sending a whiff of lavender and something else flowery that I can't quite place. It's refreshing and surprisingly feminine given her barbed attitude and take-no-shit persona.

The second we're outside, she yanks her arm out of my grip, spinning in her boots to pin me with as deadly a glare as she gave Cain. It's the first real chance I've had to look into her eyes, and even though they're spitting fire at me, the electrifying blue color renders me speechless for a moment. Together with her fiery hair, it strikes an impressive image. One that's likely to feature in all of my dreams for the proceeding future.

"You're a Reject?!" She spits out the words like they are poison on her tongue, and her gaze drops to linger on the tattoo sleeve of my right arm as she most likely tries to pinpoint the Reaper Reject tattoo. Not that she will find it there. Both of my Reject tattoos are on my chest. The original one I got when I was thirteen covers my left pec, right over my heart. I had it drawn freehand by a girl I was in love with, the girl I thought I'd marry someday. *Child-like love. Child-like fantasies. Child-like notions.*

The other Reject tattoo, the one that symbolizes what the Rejects are today, is painted on my other pec, the two sitting side by side, in contrast to one another. The past and the present. The life that could have been, and the life that is.

Her steely gaze meets mine, brimming with anger, but underneath it all, she seems almost... disappointed. I'm just not sure why. I don't know why it matters to her if I'm a Reject or not, but based on the hostility in her tone, it clearly does.

I open my mouth, but I'm not entirely sure what I'm going to say. Her question is obviously rhetorical.

"Were you going to have sex with Python that night?"

The question catches us both by surprise. *Dammit,* that sure as fuck isn't what I should be asking her. I *should* be finding

213

out what she saw and trying to determine why Cain thinks she's lying. Yet the answer to those questions is far down my list. I want to know about *her*. I want to know who she is, her name, if she feels this attraction as intensely as I do, if she's gotten herself off to that quick alley fuck as often as I have.

"That's none of your business," she snaps irritably, her refusal to answer my question only serving to annoy me. She's right, it isn't any of my business, but that doesn't mean the thought of her going off and screwing some other guy, moving on as if I was just another fuck, doesn't piss me off. It's irrational and out of character for me, even so, that doesn't make it any less real.

I take a threatening step toward her. "You've been stirring up a whole heap of trouble since that night. Cain knows you're lying about something."

"So?" she bites back angrily. "My secrets are exactly that—*mine*. He hasn't earned any right to know them. And neither have you."

I force away the scowl on my lips, attempting to soften my expression as I relax my stance, attempting to appear less intimidating. My fingers twitch at my side, desperate to touch her. "I'm sorry," I begin in a gentle tone. "Why don't we—"

The shaking of her head cuts me off, and she steps back, immediately reopening the gap I just attempted to close between us. With a straight spine, she lifts her chin to meet my gaze, and her closed-off expression halts me in place.

"Just leave me the fuck alone."

She turns on her heel and strides down the street while I reluctantly watch her go until the darkness swallows her up. When I'm standing alone in the street, I pull my phone out and text Bones, telling him to follow her home. I convince myself it's because Cain wants eyes on her at all times. He doesn't trust her. He thinks she knows more than she's letting on, and maybe she does, but I can tell myself I'm putting Bones on her under Cain's orders until I'm blue in the face. The truth is, I want to make sure she gets home okay. And I refuse to dig into what exactly that means.

When Bones confirms he's on it, I head back into Toxic, letting the loud music drown out my churning thoughts about her. Cain said her name was Red. I'm guessing it's a stage name or nickname of some sort. It's fitting, giving the glossy, copper-red strands of her hair, but I want to know her real name. I need to feel it on my lips and hear it in my ears like I need my next breath.

I grab a glass of whiskey off a passing waitress, barely sparing her more than a passing glance as I move to join Cain in his booth. Tonight is the first night we've opened Toxic and run our fight nights here since we took over the Satan's territory, and so far, it's been a success. Cain seems to think so, too, based on the slight uplift of his lip. You wouldn't know from looking at him that he's happy. In fact, to most people, he probably appears irritated, but if you've seen Cain furious like I have, you know when he's not. His frustration at Red earlier seems to have disappeared, and he surveys the club with a proud look. And so he should. He's thriving. He's creating an environment where men can come and release their anger without shoving guns in one another's faces. Sure, we're all thugs, and the shit we do is far from legal, but there are viable alternatives to selling firearms and drugs, sex and people. He doesn't talk about his future plans, other than getting vengeance for Evie, but I know he wants to change things here, to make the town safer for the people that live in it. I'm just not sure if it's a pipedream that none of us will live long enough to see come true or if it's a viable future for us all.

215

I slide into the opposite end of the booth and lean my head back against it. I let my eyes drift shut, but when her face flashes behind my eyelids, I snap them open again, finding Cain watching me with a questioning expression.

"What's wrong with you?"

I sigh, sipping on my whiskey. *Mmm, the good stuff.*

"Remember that girl I told you about?"

"The one you fucked here a few weeks ago? Yeah."

I jerk my head toward the entrance. "That was her."

His eyes widen, and he huffs out a deep chuckle. "No shit, are you serious?" His laugh turns into a caustic bark. "Well, did you make her come? Maybe she'll be more inclined to open up to you if she knows you can satisfy her needs." There's a wicked gleam in his eye, and I know he's only half-joking.

He wants to find the Reaper. Badly. Ever since he found Red in the Satan's clubhouse, he hasn't been able to think about anything except uncovering the Reaper's identity. He's no longer happy settling for the long game approach we have planned out. Instead, he's hellbent on doing whatever it takes to get her to talk—a plan I was all on board with, until right now. Now, I'm not sure what to think. Plus, if Red does actually know the Reaper, then we don't want to go pissing him off. He hasn't come for a single Reject yet, but without knowing the motives behind his kills, we're in the dark as to why.

We're not like the other gangs laying claim to Black Creek. We're not in this for the money, or the power, or the territory. We don't want to sell guns or distribute drugs, but no one outside of the Rejects knows that. If you were on the outside, looking in, I imagine we look like every other asshole vying for control. But at the heart of it all, we're nothing like them. Our objective is more significant than that. Our fight is one of vengeance, fueled by long-buried pain and a longing for a life

216

that should have been. Every single member of the Rejects feels that way. Whether that came about because of the Antonellis, like it did for Cain and me, or at the hands of some other asshole who thought they could do whatever the fuck they wanted at our expense, it doesn't matter, because that need for justice, that hunger for revenge, it burns inside all of us, pushing us forward.

I ignore Cain's question, asking one of my own. "Why do you think she's lying?"

There's always the hope that she genuinely didn't see anything, and Cain has allowed his desire to find the guy and get him to help us take down the Antonellis, cloud his judgment.

He thinks about it for a moment before responding. "I can't put my finger on it. Her story doesn't quite add up, but it's more than that. It was the look in her eye that night. It was as if none of it fazed her... the guns, the violence, the blood."

I shrug my shoulders. "She probably grew up here. She'll have seen her fair share of shit like that."

He's shaking his head, though. "Nah, it was more than that." I can see the frustration on his face as he struggles to make sense of something. "I just can't figure out *what*."

We lapse into silence as I mull over what he's said. I honestly don't know what to believe, but Cain is a good judge of character, so chances are she's lying about something, but what?

"Maybe she's protecting the Reaper's real identity?" I muse.

"Yeah, that's what I'm thinking, but why?... He could be threatening her to stay silent?"

I nod my head in agreement, having thought the same thing. "Or she knows him."

My gaze meets Cain's, and I can see it in his eyes. That's exactly what he thinks—or at least hopes—is the case.

"If so, we need to find out from her who he is."

217

"Are you sure we're wise to pursue this?" I ask. "We can continue with what we've been doing."

He gives me a wry look, and I can see in his eyes how badly he needs this. Even more than I do, and until I ran into Red, it was the only thing getting me out of bed in the morning.

"Fine," I relent. "I'll talk to her this week."

I ignore the way my heart rate picks up at the thought of running into her again. Based on the way she looked at me after finding out who I am, not to mention her parting words for me to leave her alone, I'm pretty sure she's not going to be all that excited to see me. But I have to say, the thought of getting to see her, of possibly even getting to know her better, has a smirk lifting one side of my lips.

***

Three days later, I'm sitting in a private booth at the back of Strip Tease, mesmerized as Red swirls around the pole on stage like a pro, swaying her hips seductively.

She's dressed up as some sort of dominatrix, and it is doing all sorts of fucked up shit to my dick. I can't seem to tear my eyes away from the large swell of her breasts, pushed up and accentuated by her leather bra, or the way her ass looks in the thong and suspenders she's wearing. The tattoo along her upper arm and shoulder only adds to the whole dominating vibe she's got going.

Based on the hoots and hollers from the men gathered around the stage, throwing money her way and tucking dollar bills into her thong and bra when she's within touching distance, I'm not the only one affected by her beauty. She just stands out from everyone else. From her unique shade of copper hair to

218

her wide-set hips, she's the complete opposite of every other woman working here.

When I first sat down and saw the attention she was drawing, I nearly flew out of my chair, intent on dragging her off that stage and away from the hungry eyes of the men surrounding her. Some primal voice at the back of my mind was whispering *mine*, but of course, that's so fucking far from the truth. She's not mine, and despite my draw to her, I'm not even sure if I want her to be. I came back to Black Creek with a purpose in mind, one I'm not even close to achieving yet. I don't have time to get distracted. Especially not by succulent curves and feisty eyes, plump, pink lips and soft, dirty moans.

I have to keep reminding myself why I'm here—to find out about the Reaper. Cain's been going about it all wrong, treating her like the enemy and having one of the kids follow her around. But that's Cain's way. He's always one to go on the offensive first. I'm hoping a gentler approach will help encourage her to help us. Obviously, I can't divulge anything to her, but I'm hoping she'll be open to at least talking to me.

When her time on the stage comes to an end and she walks off, the manager meets her at the bottom of the steps. I see the moment he tells her I'm waiting to talk to her. Her back stiffens, and she follows his gaze to where I'm sitting.

I keep my face impassive while her eyes burn into mine, her lips flattening in annoyance. Huh, maybe this is why Cain always takes the aggressive route. I get a kick out of knowing I've annoyed her. Sure, it would be better if she was happy to see me, like she was the other night at Toxic before she knew who I was, before I found out what she could mean to the Rejects. But, this is a close second.

She strides across the room toward me, every step emanating confidence and seduction. She screams sex, but not

219

like cheap, motel sex. The kind of sex that's like a drug, that gets you hooked and keeps you coming back for more. The kind of sex you'll never get out of your system.

"Didn't I tell you to leave me alone?"

I don't know if it's because we met before she knew who I was or if she's just got ovaries of steel, but the fact she doesn't cower before me the way most people do is even more of a turn-on than her delectable body.

She perches on the far end of the booth, deliberately keeping as much distance between us as possible. I don't fucking like it. My fingers itch to reach out and touch her, to pull her in against me, and I have to dig them into the upholstery to stop myself from doing exactly that.

Meanwhile, she crosses her arms on the table and stares me down. Even though Strip Tease is officially under Reject control, she behaves as though we're in her territory, like I'm the one who should be withering beneath her ire and not the other way around.

"You know I can't do that." My voice is even, neutral, so she has no idea of the double meaning to my words. No doubt, even if I weren't here to press her for information, I would still be sitting in this exact spot. This pull I feel toward her is magnetic. It makes me wonder how I walked around this city for so many years and never found myself in this part of town, in this club, watching her from afar.

I shuffle across the booth toward her, hating how she tenses at my close proximity. I know it's not out of fear. She's never once demonstrated that emotion, and I'm sure it would take a hell of a lot more to actually scare her.

"I just wanted to talk."

"Well, I'm working." Her words are sharp, dismissive, but she's not getting rid of me that easily.

"I'm more than happy to wait until you're done." I lean in closer toward her, and despite her rigid posture, she swallows roughly, and I don't miss the hitch in her breath. "We can go grab a drink when you're finished. Maybe even finish up that dance." My leg brushes against hers, and I can feel the heat of her skin, even through the fabric of my jeans. The second our bodies connect, she jerks away, breaking the contact.

"No," she grits out. "We can't."

I've gotten a little off track here, I know that. How the fuck can I not, when all I want is to have more time with her, to see the sparkle in her eye that I saw the other night when she turned around and realized it was me standing behind her on the dance floor. Is it really asking too much to want to see that again, knowing I was the cause of that moment of happiness?

"Why not?" I snap, the words coming like a whip in my irritation. "Because of Cain?" I let out a long exhale, trying to calm myself down. We're not going to get anywhere if we both let our tempers get the better of us. "He—we—" I trail off on a sigh, struggling to find my words. "We just want to talk to him... If you know who he is, we just want to talk."

She scrutinizes me with such a sharp look. It's like she's slicing me open with her eyes, digging into my soul, and rummaging around until she finds whatever she's looking for. She doesn't find it because her expression shutters, falling into this blank mask that gives me zero insight into what she's thinking. I don't fucking like it.

"Why? What do you want with him?" Even her voice sounds more monotone than it did before, lacking the raw, husky tone that I love hearing.

"I can't tell you." It's the truth. We can't have word getting out that we're gunning for the Antonellis. It would be suicide. Even if we do manage to find this Reaper guy and decide to use

221

him—assuming, of course, that he even agrees to help us, which is a big *if*—we will be taking a considerable risk.

She doesn't like that response, and I don't blame her. Sliding out of her seat, she gets to her feet. "Then I can't help you."

*Fuck sake.* My lips flatten as I bite my tongue, and with a final dismissive glance, she turns and walks away, getting back to work.

I sit back, flagging down a waitress and ordering a whiskey neat, all without ever taking my eyes off of Red. She works the room, dropping off drinks and collecting orders, laughing flirtily with customers, and pausing every now and again for lap dances.

She purposely avoids looking my way, but I know she can feel my eyes on her. It's in the tense way she holds her shoulders, in the way she deliberately angles herself so I'm never directly in her line of sight. She did give me one piece of critical information, though—she knows more than she's letting on, and if I were to hazard a guess, I'd say Cain's right. She does know who the Reaper is. But she's not going to say anything more without good reason. Cain can harass and threaten her all he wants, but I can already tell... she's a vault. I don't think anything he could do to her would be enough to make her crack. Which only leaves one option... we tell her our plans.

The question is, can she be trusted?

## Chapter 14

*Unknown: 2 pm, Radiant Park. O.*

What the fuck is this shit? I grit my teeth in frustration as I glare at my phone. I'd ask how the fuck this asshole got my phone number, but of course, he either asked Drew for it, or he helped himself to the employee files.

I'm about to reply with a middle finger emoji when another message comes through.

*Unknown: Please.*

Just that one word. I still want to tell him where he can shove it, but curiosity makes me hesitate over the send button, and after a moment's debate, I backspace, deleting the emoji.

*God, Sawyer, didn't you ever hear curiosity killed the cat.*

The last thing I need to do is be walking onto Reject property. And yet, that's exactly what I'm thinking of doing. I mean, if they start badgering me about the Reaper, I can just walk out... unless they're planning on holding me hostage and torturing me for information. No, they wouldn't do that, right? Ha, what the fuck am I saying? They're gang members, of course, they'd fucking do that if it got them what they wanted.

I glance back down at my phone, re-reading the word *please*. My teeth sink into my lower lip, chewing on it as I try to decide what to do. I might be annoyed that Oliver is a Reject— it's so fucking typical, but not altogether surprising given where we live—but I don't fuck gang members. A principle I live by.

The problem is, I can't stop thinking about the way he tasted on my lips, of whiskey and wicked intentions. Or the way it felt to be cradled in his arms, pushed up against that wall. He was passionate, with an edge of danger that spoke to the wildness inside me, but there's also a stability about him that I find myself drawn to. It makes no sense because I don't even know the guy. He could be as flighty as they come, yet I get the impression he's someone who stays—who fights through the crappy times, who stands up to challenges, and doesn't shy away from conflict.

I shouldn't. I know I shouldn't go, but I'm already talking myself into it. They want the Reaper, and they think I know who he is. They're also going to be wary of him—because any gang member with half a brain cell would be. So they're not going to do anything to me and risk potentially pissing him off. The last thing they'll want is him coming after them. Besides, it couldn't

226

hurt to find out what they want with the Reaper. What could they be after so badly that they're willing to negotiate with someone who is basically their enemy? It definitely has me curious.

*Ah fuck it, I'm going.*

Checking the time, I have an hour before I have to be there. I pull up my maps on the phone, realizing it will take at least that long to get across town on public transport. I guess I'll be taking Raven. Could be for the best. With assholes like this, it's always good to make a strong impression. I'm not some weak woman they can manipulate into doing what they want. I'm the fucking *Reaper* of all things wicked and evil. I dare them to mess with me. I'd relish in carving my name into their bodies.

Donning my leather pants, a tight black corset top that curves along the top of my wide hips and pushes the girls together—sexy, but not slutty—I lace up my chunky heeled boots and snatch up my leather jacket on my way out of the bedroom. I scrawl a quick note for Luc, letting him know there's left-over lasagna in the fridge for dinner before I grab my keys off the kitchen counter and head out the door. It's been a while since I've had a chance to get Raven out on the road—I couldn't risk going anywhere near her when that asshole, *Cain*, was having me followed. Bringing her to the meeting today will most definitely raise some questions, but fuck it. They're already suspicious.

I make the short walk over to the garage where I keep Raven safely hidden away, and goosebumps pebble along my arms when I start the engine and roll her out onto the street. I leave her running while I pull down the roller door and lock it. When I jog back to the bike, I pull on my helmet and connect my phone to the Bluetooth headset so that I can listen to the directions. As the woman's voice comes through the earpiece,

227

telling me to turn left onto the street, I twist the accelerator, and with a rev of the engine, I'm off.

The whole city flies past in a blur of gray. Gray buildings. Gray roads. Gray sky. Everything in Black Creek is gray. Even the people are gray, with their miserable, trudging demeanors and lack of hope and ambition. It's like this city has sucked the color out of everything. Was it always this way? It has been for as long as I can remember, but surely Black Creek must have once been a thriving town before the gangs dug their claws into it—before The Feral Beasts destroyed any optimism the townspeople had and the Antonellis squashed us under their boots. We've been beaten down and pulverized for so long, none of us know any better. This life of scrounging for scraps and surviving one day to the next, without ever giving any thought to the future, is all we've ever known. But is simply surviving enough? What happens if we dare to dream of more? If not for ourselves, then for those we love. I don't want this bleak city to be all Luc sees and knows. There's an entire world out there, and most of it is a hell of a lot better than Black Creek. Doesn't he deserve to see it? To do better for himself than end up in a dead-end job or running for some gang just to make ends meet?

I think so. I just don't know how to make that happen for him. An education at a Black Creek school is worth jack shit, and I sure as hell don't have the money to send him to some fancy school or college. It wouldn't matter how many clubs I worked at or rich-scumbag-killing jobs I took, it would take years to earn that sort of cash. So for now, I have to settle for making Black Creek somewhere he can live safely, where one day he can carve out a small but promising existence for himself, and not one where he ends up dead on some street corner, caught up in a gang war he had no business being a part of.

The problem is, I'm not sure how to achieve that. Sure, I'm living the nice little secret vigilante life, killing abusive men, but that does nothing to stop the frequent gang wars that break out on the street or the overarching rule of the likes of the Antonellis, Grim Bastards, or even the Reaper Rejects. Luc deserves to leave the apartment every day and not wonder if this is the last time he'll walk out that door. He should never have to worry if he's going to accidentally get caught up in a shooting or if some asshole is going to come around and tear his life apart just because he can. And the only way for that to happen is if there are no more gangs in Black Creek. Ha, it's a laughable thought. An unrealistic and impossible one, but it's a wish all the same.

I'm barely paying attention as I zip through the streets, listening to the woman from my phone spouting directions in my ear. I'm going to be early. A journey that takes over an hour by public transport, took half that time on my bike. Once I'm near Radiant Park, I veer off course. I work my way down the gears, slowing the bike as I take in the part of the city that's been under Reject control for the better part of a year now.

I don't know much about them before then, but I remember when the whispers started on the street of this group of thugs who were collecting territory like it was pocket change. This part of the city was divided up amongst several small street gangs until the Rejects came along and quickly conquered all of it, claiming it as their own. By all accounts, it was a bloodbath. Six gangs demolished in six days, or something insane like that. That is, if the rumors can be believed. Once they had firmly seated themselves as the overlords of most of the southern part of the city, they seemed to slow down, and they have been taking their time picking off the last of their rivals. Apparently, the Satan's were next on their list of targets, but no doubt the other

229

smaller gangs will soon fall too, which will leave only the Grim Bastards and Antonellis as the Rejects' rivals.

I'm not sure if it's because I've slowed the bike down or if the sun has popped out from behind a cloud, but there seems to be more color here than there was back on my street. I take my time, slowly winding along various avenues, and don't get me wrong, most of it is the same—homeless people crowded in doorways and hookers on street corners. But there are also glaringly apparent differences. I nearly stall my bike when I come across a flower shop. A motherfucking flower shop. In Black Creek. I don't ever remember seeing a flower shop here. People in Black Creek don't buy flowers. We don't have the time or energy to even stop and sniff the flowers, never mind the money to actually buy them. Yet here I am, looking at a fucking flower shop.

A woman who looks to be in her mid-to-late fifties steps out onto the sidewalk, sniffing at a large bunch of Tulips before she props them up in an oversized plant pot, displaying them just so.

A horn blares behind me, making me jump and jolting me out of my state of shock. It's only then that I realize I came to a dead stop in the middle of the road. The asshole blares his horn again, and giving him a middle finger, I roll the throttle and speed off. This time, I go straight to the address on my maps, having seen enough of this weird twilight zone.

When the map on my phone tells me I've reached my destination, I slow down and pull up to the curb. Turning off the engine, I take off my helmet and cast my eyes over the run-down apartment complex. I glance at the sign sporting the name of the complex—Radiant Park—before looking back over the shabby exterior. Yeah, I don't think that name fits. Maybe 'Rundown Park' or simply call it 'Pigsty'. Both are more fitting.

I'm pretty sure this complex was intended as high-end apartments when it was first built, but now it's as dilapidated as the rest of the city. Graffiti covers most of the brick wall, and paint is peeling off the wooden door. I think it was maybe a red color once upon a time, but now it just looks like it's covered in rust. Or dried blood. Actually, it's most likely blood on the door.

What I imagine was once a luscious lawn surrounding the building is now overgrown with weeds that come up to my knees. The lines marking out parking spaces in the lot have long since faded, and cracks have formed in the concrete path up to the lobby door.

A tall, iron fence, topped with wire, is all that separates the complex from the sidewalk and looking around, there isn't a soul in sight. Shouldn't they at least have someone manning the gate? I'm not entirely sure what I expected, but the lackluster veneer and absence of security are definitely not it.

Not hanging around, I push open the pedestrian gate and step warily onto the property. I'm still expecting someone to jump out from the bushes and attack me for setting foot on Reject property, but nothing happens, and after a few more cautious steps toward the building, my confidence builds. As I stride across the cracked concrete, I push back my shoulders and lift my chin, donning my typical *don't fucking mess with me, bitch* expression.

Just as I ascend the steps up to the main entrance, which I'm assuming leads into a lobby, the door is pulled open, and Oliver's tall frame blocks the doorway. He looks like fucking sin in his combat boots and jeans, with a tight t-shirt that clings to his muscular abs and chiseled biceps. In the light of day, his features are even more breathtaking, and I have to swallow roughly, my mouth suddenly feeling dry as I drink him in.

"I wasn't sure you'd come." His gaze sweeps over me before glancing over my shoulder. He quirks a brow when he sees the bike but doesn't comment on it.

"Well, you said please," I grumble, forcing my face into a frown in an attempt to hide the physical effect he has on me. One side of his lip lifts slightly. *Goddammit*, if fucking butterflies don't take flight in my chest at that simple movement.

"Come on in." He pushes the door open wider and steps aside for me to move past him into the dark interior of the building. The place is a hive of activity, men stocking shelves behind the bar with alcohol, arranging furniture, and cleaning the place up.

"Did you just move in or something?" I ask absently, taking in the heinous, flowery wallpaper currently being stripped from the walls and the light fixtures that look like they're from the seventies.

"A few months ago, but we haven't had much of a chance to get it all redone. We wanted to get the fighting pit across the way set up first."

"Red," someone calls out, and when I turn to locate the source of the voice, Jon is bounding toward me, carrying a box in his arms. I give him a tight smile. I like the kid, but I'm feeling uncomfortably on edge surrounded by all these men, even if most of them are giving me cordial smiles or nothing more than passing glances. I'm on enemy territory right now, and regardless of how friendly they may appear, I don't trust any of them. "How ya been?"

It's a struggle to keep the surprise off my face. It was one thing for him to talk to me so freely when we were alone, but in front of all his gang buddies? I've spent very little time in gang clubhouses, but I don't need to, to know women are rarely

232

treated with the respect they deserve—especially not virtual strangers. In gang life, anyone who isn't affiliated with the gang in some form is treated as an outsider, someone not to be trusted or befriended until they've proven themselves.

"Ehh, I've been good."

His smile broadens. "Well, I'll catch ya later, can't let the boss man here see me slacking." He juts his head toward Oliver, laughing freely, so it's obviously a joke.

As he wanders off, I turn to Oliver. "Exactly how high up in the Rejects are you?"

I'd just assumed he was a low-level player. I don't know why exactly. He just doesn't strike me as the domineering, overly aggressive, compensating-for-his-small-dick type. The sort of bullshit posturing every other leader exudes. Now, Cain is absolutely that typical, thuggish asshole of a kingpin.

He rubs awkwardly at the back of his neck, ducking his head, almost as though he's embarrassed, but I can't figure out why. "I'm Cain's second in command." *Huh, wasn't expecting that.* "It's not what you think, though."

I don't know what he means by that, and I deliberately don't ask. I do not need to be getting myself embroiled in their club shit any further than I already am. I get the uneasy feeling that if I dig too deep into Oliver's life, I'll only end up liking him more, and I can't afford to let that happen. No gangbangers. That's my rule, and I need to remember that around him.

He looks at me for a moment, and when I don't ask the question he's expecting, he changes the conversation. "We're in the process of converting this into a bar area for everyone. Got the bar bit set up a while ago but haven't had a chance to get the rest of it done."

I take all of it in silently as he escorts me across the room toward a hallway that leads down the back of the building. We pass several closed doors before he knocks on one, not waiting for a response before he opens the door. I follow him into a relatively large office that somehow manages to feel suffocating with Cain's emanating presence. Even though he's tucked behind a desk, his essence seems to envelop the entire room, sucking all the oxygen out of it.

Even seated behind a desk, he looks fucking ruthless. It's written in the tight lines of his face, in the narrowing of his eyes and his sharp jaw, which is hidden beneath a thick layer of dark stubble. His bulging biceps and broad shoulders make it clear he takes pride in his appearance. In his line of work, your body says a hell of a lot about you. Cain's body says he could tear you limb from limb and not even break a sweat. He's pure muscle, every inch of him built to destroy whoever crosses him.

He doesn't move from behind his desk as he silently observes me. I watch him right back, trying to get a read on him after our last interaction, but it's impossible. His face is a blank slate. Only the weariness in his eyes gives away his uneasy feelings regarding this meeting. *Interesting.* So this wasn't his idea then. Guess I have Oliver to thank for whatever the fuck this is about.

"Red," he eventually acknowledges, sounding more like he's going to the execution block than greeting someone in his home. "Have a seat." He nods his head toward one of the two chairs sitting opposite his desk.

I'm hyper-aware of the door clicking closed behind me and Oliver moving to lean against the room's back wall. At the same time, I make myself comfortable in front of Cain's desk, crossing my legs and quirking a brow in expectation. He's the one who called me here, so he's damn well going to be the one to get the ball rolling.

His lips flatten, and he glances behind me to Oliver before returning his intense gaze to mine again. He takes a long moment to look me over, noting my leather gear. I felt comfortable leaving my helmet on my bike. No one would be stupid enough to try and steal from right outside Reject property, and if one of the Reject assholes themselves dares to touch my bike, well then, I won't have any qualms about chopping off their hands.

I've unzipped my leather jacket, and I notice his perusal falter on the swell of my tits before he returns his wandering gaze to my face. My skin burns everywhere his eyes roam. It's like his intense green irises are lasers. He grits his teeth, and I can tell, whatever he's going to say, he doesn't like it. Not one fucking bit. Cain might be the leader of the Rejects, but right now, he's doing as Oliver has advised him, not what he himself wants to do.

"We want to negotiate a deal with the Reaper."

Silence sits heavy in the air at his statement, and I can feel the tension radiating off the two of them as they wait to hear my response.

"What sort of deal?" I counter in a flat tone, giving nothing away of my feelings. They are no longer asking me if I know him or saw him that night. They *know* I have some sort of relationship with him—I'm just betting it's not what they think—so there's no point in pretending any longer. Besides, I can't deny I'm curious.

Cain shakes his head. "That's between us and him."

"Why?" I ask instead. "Why do you need the Reaper? Surely, whatever problem you have, the mighty Rejects can handle it themselves."

235

My voice drips with sarcasm, which doesn't go unnoticed—or appreciated—as Cain's eyes narrow on me in warning. One I disregard. I can see the muscle at the back of his jaw tick, and I have to bite back my snort. This guy has got the shortest fucking fuse I've ever seen.

It's Oliver who speaks up, directing my attention his way. "We're having difficulties achieving this particular job on our own. It's really best if we just talk directly to the Reaper. For all we know, he won't even be able to help us."

What he's saying makes sense, and I tap my fingernails against the wooden arm of my chair as I mull it over. I choose each word carefully before I say, "I need to tell him something about the job you want him to do. He's not going to agree to a meeting otherwise."

"Not happening." Cain's sharp voice isn't altogether unexpected. Given how cryptic they've been, I didn't think they'd just volunteer the information. But just like they don't trust me, I don't trust them. Without knowing what they want, I'm unwilling to reveal my own cards.

I get to my feet, pinning Cain in place with a pointed look. "Then I think we're done here." This isn't a ploy or a tactic. I'm serious.

I move toward the office door, sparing Oliver a passing glance and ignoring his stern frown as I pull open the door and step out into the hall. I've made it back to the main bar area, where guys are still tearing down wallpaper and setting up various tables by the time Oliver catches up to me. His hand reaches out to touch my wrist, and I jolt, breaking his contact with my skin as I spin to face him. He's still wearing that same frown, and he glances nervously around the room, obviously not wanting to be overheard.

He's careful not to touch me when he leans in, but he may as well be rubbing himself all over me for the way his titillating scent invades my space, sending my brain on the fritz and rendering me speechless.

I feel the soft puff of his warm breath against my ear, and it makes me shiver. I swallow roughly, painfully aware of the damp patch forming in my panties. He's got a five o'clock shadow that I desperately want to run my fingers along as I wonder what it would feel like grazing against my inner thigh. I'm losing all common sense, quickly melting into a puddle of sex-addled hormones when his next words penetrate through the fog, registering with me.

"We're going after the Antonellis."

*They're what?!* It takes a second for me to wrap my head around what he's saying, and not only because my mind already drifted to far dirtier thoughts. What he's suggesting is complete fucking suicide. The Rejects might be formidable and ruthless, and yeah, they've proven themselves to be calculating and determined, but they are no match for the Antonellis. They're in a league all on their own. One of those long-established families who can be traced back to the dawn of the goddamn country. They have more money than any of us will see in a lifetime, and that money can buy them whatever the fuck they want. It would certainly be enough to squash this little rebellion without even putting a fucking dent in their overall financial worth.

"Are you insane?!" I hiss. "You're going to get yourselves fucking killed."

I can see it in his eyes. It only lasts a second, but it's there, shining clearly for me to see. He doesn't care. Going after the Antonellis is something he's prepared to die for. What in the ever-loving fuck could they have done to brew such loathing?

237

I slowly take a step back, and when he doesn't try to stop me, I take another, shaking my head. "I can tell you now, what you're doing is suicide, and the Reaper will want no part in it."

Oliver's face pinches, resulting in this aching sort of pain that sends a spike of sorrow through my chest. When he next speaks, his words sound broken, voice low and deflated. "Ask him anyway. He might be our only option."

Fuck. Me.

With a final nod, I turn on my heel, striding past the other members and out the door, squinting in the bright light of the afternoon sun. My bike and helmet are exactly where I left them and I hastily shove the helmet over my head, revving the engine so loud there's no doubt in my mind every person residing in Radiant Park heard it before taking off down the street.

*CAIN*

*Chapter 15*

I've got two glasses of whiskey sitting on the desk by the time Oliver returns, his withdrawn expression telling me all I need to know about how his conversation with Red went.

"Told you it wouldn't work."

He sears me with a scathing look, dropping into the chair Red just vacated with a sigh and staring absently at the floor.

I sip on my own drink, needing the sharp burn as it slides down my throat to distract me from the flaming anger and raging disappointment fighting for dominance within me. I knew it was a long shot, going after the Reaper, but when I realized he'd been in Python's room that night, that Red might have seen him—I just had to give it a shot. We're making next to no progress on our own and the Reaper has an uncanny ability to sneak on and off gang property unnoticed. I thought he might be able to help us find a way to get close to Giovanni and his family.

I hadn't quite worked out the specifics. It's not like I was going to let the Reaper claim Giovanni's death for himself. As the head of his Family, Giovanni is the one who ordered his men to come to *my* house that day to kidnap *my* sister, so the least he deserves is a death at *my* hands. And my men are more than capable of taking on his underlings. All I really need the Reaper for is to gather intel—something, *anything* that can give us an advantage and enable us to sneak up on Antonelli and his men unawares. He's so good at stalking around this city unseen, that he must know or be able to find out the Antonellis' dark and hidden family secrets.

I'm so lost in my own thoughts as I stare down at the amber liquid in my tumbler that I'd forgotten Oliver was even in the room until he leans forward, the movement catching my eye as he places his elbows on his knees, folding his hands under his chin. His lips are pressed tightly together, and it's clear he's deep in thought as he mulls something over.

After a moment, he speaks up. "Get Mac or Ian to tell us whenever Giovanni or one of his higher-ups next go into the casino or the club."

My eyes narrow as I frown at him, trying to figure out where he's going with this. Mac and Ian are the two men we have planted in the Antonellis' organization, and they've been able to pass along some scraps of information, but nothing actionable.

"I'll take a small team of men and trail whoever it is."

242

"What good will that do?" I ask, dubious.

He shrugs. "We might find something useful. Hell, we could uncover where Giovanni and his top men live and maybe take them all out in one, quick, surprise attack."

My ears perk up at that idea, liking the sound of it. No one knows for sure where any of the Antonelli Family live. There are plenty of rumors, of course, but only those at the top of the Antonelli hierarchy are privy to that information.

"If we can find out where they live, we can place twenty-four-hour surveillance on them while we come up with a plan," Oliver presses, incentivized.

Evie was as much a sister to him as she was to me. The two of them were as thick as thieves when we were growing up. Sometimes, I wondered if he even had a crush on her. I'd thought about asking him, but then that day happened, and what was the point? Nothing mattered anymore.

Regardless of the feelings he has—had—for my sister, he's just as driven as I am, and I know the lack of progress we've been making infuriates him as much as it does me.

This plan makes sense. We have to be stealthy when it comes to the Antonellis. Being unable to match their manpower, we can't afford to start an all-out war with them. If they suspected for one second that we were gunning for them, they'd come for us, and we'd be slaughtered like animals, our bodies thrown into the docks and forgotten about.

No, we have to be clever and cunning with the Antonellis. We need to slip under their radar and catch them off guard. It's a complete contrast to the brute force with which we have overthrown every other group of thugs so far, but the Famiglia is no disorganized street gang. They're a fucking dynasty, the crux of the Italian Mafia, and the Tideside Docks is their impenetrable fortress.

243

I down the last of my whiskey before I meet Oliver's eye. I can see the determination flickering in his gaze. He wants to do this. Needs to. "You're right," I agree, a malicious smirk curling at my lips, and hope swells in my chest, quickly displacing the suffocating disappointment that was beginning to brew. "I'll message Mac and Ian."

Oliver grins, this dark, vitriolic slice across his face that's so out of character it would concern me if I didn't fully understand the pain behind it.

Changing the subject, I ask, "What about the stripper? You told her our plans, didn't you?"

As soon as he chased after her, I knew damn well he'd give her more than I wanted her to know. He frowns at my name-calling, but doesn't say anything about it.

"She won't talk."

He sounds so confident, but how the fuck can he be so sure? He doesn't even know this girl. I lean back in my chair and scrutinize him for a second. "I thought it was just sex."

He shakes his head, running a hand through his short, dark hair as a frown mars his features. "I don't know what the fuck it is, but I can't stop thinking about her."

It's my turn to shake my head as I snort. "That's because you haven't had pussy in like, three years. I told you to fuck one of those hangarounds, man. You should have listened to me and gotten it out of your system. That girl is trouble."

She's already caused us such a headache, and we don't even fucking know her. Now she knows information that could annihilate us if it fell into the wrong hands. Even if the Reaper isn't willing to meet with us, we can't let Red walk around with the information she has. Not without keeping tabs on her. She's not loyal to us and has absolutely no reason to keep that information to herself. Not to mention the fact she's fucking

244

messing with Oliver's head. I can't afford to have him distracted by some cheap ass pussy.

I tap my fingers against the glass as I contemplate what to do about this new problem. I'll have to put Jon back on the job of tailing her ass to make sure she's not talking to anyone she shouldn't be. But something tells me that isn't enough. I'll give it a couple of days, see if the Reaper reaches out to us, and go from there.

***

It's been a week. One long, slow week, and we haven't heard anything from either Red or the Reaper. Nor have Mac or Ian been in touch with any updates. I feel like I'm constantly on edge, waiting for the phone to ring with an update of some sort. It's driving me fucking nuts. I've turned into a growling bear. Even my men avoid me when they see me coming their way. The only thing that helps is fighting and drinking. I've been in the pit every night this week and followed up each victory with enough alcohol to leave me unconscious.

Tonight's looking much the same as I throw back my third—or is it my fourth?—shot of whiskey. Whatever number it is, it goes down smoothly, warming the pit of my stomach. Oliver and I got in a fight earlier—only one of many that have broken out this week as shit has spiraled further out of control—and he's fucked off to god knows where. His absence only adds fuel to the fire of anger and hatred burning brightly in my chest.

I hate how optimistic I got about this Reaper guy. It was foolish of me, but I seriously thought he could be the key to it all. Our secret weapon that would enable us to best the Antonellis.

245

Lifting the bottle to my lips, I take another long gulp of whiskey, hissing as it burns my throat. This is all that fucking stripper's fault. I bet she didn't even talk to the Reaper. Just decided on her own that she didn't want him helping us. She decided from the very beginning that she didn't like us—why? Because we overthrew her precious Satan's? I get that her first impression of us wasn't exactly favorable, but Razor said she was in shock when he found her in that room, so I *know* he will have treated her with kid gloves. Although, I'm beginning to wonder if she even was in shock or if all of it was an act designed to throw us off.

I can feel the heat from the alcohol fanning the flames of my anger and pushing it to new heights, and before I've really thought through the decision, I'm out of my chair, following the sounds of loud music. The guys have done a great job transforming the lobby into a bar for all of them to hang out in during their downtime.

As I walk in, I spot Bones at the bar with a few other guys. He's holding a beer, and as he lifts it to his lips, I call out, "Nope, put that down. I need you to drive me somewhere." I'm far too drunk to drive myself. I fish my keys out of my pocket and toss them to him.

"Sure thing, boss." He sets down his beer and follows me outside. The parking lot is full of the various vehicles belonging to Reject members. I bought a few cars from Arnie for club purposes, and a few of the guys have bought themselves bikes or cars.

I make my way to a black Cadillac Escalade at the far end of the lot. "Where are we going?" Bones asks as he hops in behind the wheel, and I climb in the passenger side.

"Strip Tease."

With a nod of his head, he starts the engine and pulls out of the lot, and it doesn't take us long to make it across town to the club.

Alcohol is still coursing through my system, driving my actions as I storm into the club. Not that anyone is any the wiser. The loud bang of the door is drowned out by the heavy beat of some song through the speakers; the customers too caught up in watching and whistling over the dancers on stage or ordering drinks at the bar to notice my presence. That's fine, I'm here for one person, and one person only. I cast my eyes around the crowded room until I spot her delivering drinks to a table at the back of the room. My gaze stays fixed on her as I close the distance between us, skirting around anyone in my way and nearly bowling some guy over. My mission is single-minded— to get to the bane of my existence. I'm not entirely sure what happens then. My drunk mind hasn't quite figured that part out yet.

She turns to face me just before I crash into her, snatching the empty tray from her hand and dropping it on the floor as I use my superior strength to barrel her backward through the staff entrance door that I know leads into the back hallway, where the manager's office and dressing rooms are located.

"What—" Her words catch on a gasp as I wrap my fingers around her narrow wrist, pushing down on the door handle, so we tumble through it into the empty hallway beyond. We stumble backward, my weight pressing her against the opposite wall, so she's forced to look up at me.

Her eyes, wide with surprise, narrow in annoyance when she realizes who's disrupted her otherwise regular shift. I momentarily get distracted by the unique azure blue of her irises, churning with tumultuous clouds that speak to the complex nature of the alluring enigma glowering at me as if she'd like to slit my throat.

"Did you even talk to him?" I bark.

Confusion flashes across her face before a sharpness enters her eyes. "You're drunk. I can smell it on you." She pushes against my chest, but I'm still pinning her to the wall, and she doesn't stand a chance of moving me unless I want to be moved—which I sure as hell don't.

"Did you?"

Her nostrils flare. "Surprisingly, he's uninterested in getting involved in your suicide mission."

I eliminate the slither of space between us, caging her in more tightly against the wall. So tight, I can feel her soft curves pressing against me, feel the heat of her body warming my skin. I didn't have a chance to take in what she was wearing before— or more importantly, the lack of what she was wearing—but now that I feel her breasts pushing against my chest, I can't help the way my gaze dips, taking in the rapid rise of her chest, matching her short, sharp pants.

"Why would you even risk everything you've built just to go after them? Are you seriously that power-hungry that you'll jeopardize the lives of your men?"

My eyes snap up to meet her tumultuous blue gaze, narrowing to a glare as I slam my hand into the wall beside her head, making her jump. My lip curls back on a snarl. "My men know what they're risking. They know what they're fighting for."

"Half of your *men* are nothing more than children. They have no idea what they want."

I bark out a cold, caustic laugh. "You have no idea what my men have been through, the lives they've led. Like me, they're tired of letting someone else dictate their lives, walk all over them, and tell them what to do. Where you see children and a

248

gang fighting for territory, I see men that deserve the chance to fight for something they believe in, and a gang that wants to do right by the people of Black Creek."

By the time I'm finished, she stares up at me with wide eyes, speechless for once. Her lips are slightly parted, drawing my gaze to her plump lower lip. I find myself captivated by the way it glistens in the light of the hallway, and whether it's the alcohol or this vixen is some kind of witch, I find myself murmuring, "Have you ever had your life upturned in a single moment? One second everything was going along as normal, and in the next, all you've ever known has gone up in flames and been burnt to ashes?"

A heavy silence falls between us, the air thick with the weight of my words. I dare not look her in the eye. I'm not used to moments of vulnerability—I'm not used to vulnerability at all. I shut down any soft emotions the day Evie was taken. That softness is for boys. For children. It's a weakness that can be exploited. Yet, here I am, sharing the most broken part of myself with a girl I know nothing about. One I don't trust.

I push off the wall and move to turn my back on her, intent on leaving. I have no idea what I was thinking coming here; what I thought it would achieve. Chalk it up to drunken intentions and desperation.

The last thing I expect is the one-syllable word that she whispers so quietly, for a second, I think I imagined it.

"Yes."

That one word pauses me in my tracks, and I slowly lift my gaze to meet her eyes, seeing the honesty reflected in them. For the first time since I laid eyes on her in the Satans' clubhouse, I see what she never allowed me to glimpse before. Her own vulnerability. The pain she carries every day that's incredibly similar to my own.

I lose myself in her eyes for a moment, taking some comfort in the fact someone else feels that same aching loss gnawing away on their insides that I do. Eventually, I find the strength to look away, and without a backward glance, I turn on my heel, leaving Red and the club behind.

## Chapter 16

I'm still playing Cain's words on repeat the next day as I let myself into the apartment. Combined with what Oliver told me about how they plan on taking down the Antonellis, I can only assume they did something to Cain—and possibly Oliver?

I empathize with him. I really do. I know what it's like to have your entire life torn to shreds—ripped into so many fragments that you don't even know where to begin with picking up the pieces. I got my revenge on the man who destroyed my life. He was my very first kill; the reason behind what I do—the driving force of the Reaper. So I understand the need for retribution more than anyone, but there's a massive difference between going after some gangster low-life and the entire Antonelli empire. If he was even going after one person within their organization, I could maybe get behind that. Yes, it would be challenging, but it wouldn't be fucking impossible.

Despite how much he grates on my fucking nerves, I actually do wish I could help him. While I spend most of my time around Cain wanting to gouge his eyes out—and ignoring my damp panties—no one deserves to feel that clawing need to right the wrong against you. I understand that feeling... how it starts off as a small seed of anger, warming the pit of your stomach, but over time it grows. It takes root in your insides, twining around your heart and embedding itself in your soul. It digs itself so deep that vengeance becomes all you know. Everything you think about. You exist solely for that one purpose, and you just can't stop until you've achieved it—irrespective of the risks and potential casualties.

So I know nothing I say or do will stop them from starting a war with the Antonellis. But I don't have to insert myself in the middle of it. The intelligent thing to do is keep my head down and hope the Antonellis destroy them swiftly, without inflicting too much damage on the rest of us caught in the crosshairs. Now that I know what's coming, I can prepare myself and focus on keeping Luc and me alive.

"Luc," I call out as I walk through the door, kicking off my boots and hanging my leather jacket up. "You here?"

My question is met with silence, and setting my keys on the kitchen counter, I move over to his bedroom door and knock on it. When I don't get a response, I crack it open, looking around the empty space with a wrinkled nose. His clothes are scattered everywhere, and it fucking stinks in here. Moving deeper into the room, I crack open a window to air the place out and head back to the kitchen to get started on dinner.

After staring into the half-empty fridge for a good ten minutes, debating between leftover Thai or pizza, I eventually grab the box of pizza and close the door. As I'm setting the box down on the kitchen table, I spot a scrap of paper with Luc's sloppy writing on it.

*Gone to hang out with Jon and his friends. Be back later.*

Ehh, what the hell? I have to read the page twice before the words finally sink in. Luc is with Jon? How the fuck did that happen? I know Cain had some asshole following me all week— and now I'm guessing that asshole was Jon—but I've deliberately stayed out of trouble. I've even ignored every fucking message in my inbox with a potential new job. Now more than ever, I could do with watching the life drain out of an abusing asshole, but nope.

I haven't even realized I'd crumpled the note in my palm, my anger getting the better of me until I look down to find out where Luc is so I can go hunt him down. Unfurling my hand, I flatten the piece of paper on the table and read it once again. *Are you fucking serious, Luc?* He doesn't even say where he is, and I can only assume these *friends* of his are fellow Rejects.

My hunger forgotten, I put the pizza back in the fridge, and feeling absolutely fucking furious, I snatch up my keys and put on my boots, storming out the door intent on dragging my little brother back by his goddamn ear if I have to.

I repeatedly call Luc's number the whole way to the garage, but he ignores every damn one of my calls. When the fifth one goes unanswered, I hang up with an angry snarl and stomp the remaining few feet to my bike.

Grabbing Raven from the garage, the city passes by in an angry, red blur, the blood in my veins heating with every mile

255

I get closer to Radiant Park. I told Jon to stay away from Luc, and I gave Luc the same warning. *How could he be so stupid?*

I'm so angry with him by the time I pull up outside the Rejects clubhouse that I can hardly see straight as I turn off the engine and climb off. I'm still clutching my helmet in my hands as I shove open the gate to Radiant Park and step through. The second I do though, a blaring alarm goes off, and before I've even figured out what's going on, I'm surrounded by men, all of whom are pointing various-sized guns at me.

*Fuck.*

"Don't take another step," some guy I don't recognize orders. *Like I was about to.* You're pointing a fucking gun in my face. Why the hell would I move right now?! God forbid you misinterpret so much as an inhale as a sign of attack and shoot my fucking brains out.

"I'm looking for Jon," I call out, roaming my gaze around the various Rejects. The one speaking to me has dirty blond hair styled in a short buzz cut, making him look ex-military, and as I swing my attention back his way, he speaks up again.

"What business do you have with the Rejects?"

Ha, fuck, just today or in general?

Despite the sweat gathering along my spine, I can feel myself getting irritated. I just want to find my brother so I can ream him out. Is that too much to ask? Before I can snap something back at him that would definitely guarantee me a lovely little bullet wound, a voice calls out, "Drop your weapons. She's not a threat."

I really want to contradict Oliver's statement, but now probably isn't the time, and I have to admit, I breathe out a sigh of relief when the men surrounding me all do as they're told. Where the fuck did they all come from anyway? I didn't get such a warm welcome the last time I was here.

I glance around for Oliver, frowning when I don't immediately see him. I do, however, spot what I missed before—security cameras placed along the fencing surrounding the property, with what looks like motion detectors around the sidewalk gate and the entrance into the parking lot.

Huh, more high-tech than I expected, or that I've seen before. Usually, gang security amounts to some half-baked idiot sitting on a chair, passed out on the job. I know the Grim Bastards have a more reliable system, but it's still men just manning the entrance to their once-fire-station-now-kingpin-kingdom and reporting who enters and leaves.

The clubhouse door opens and out strolls Oliver. The afternoon sunlight reflects off the tawny strands of his hair and makes the tattoo sleeve of his right arm stand out in contrast to his pale skin.

I forget myself for a minute, momentarily drawn back to the mystery man from that first night in Toxic as his gaze meets mine. Gone is that flirty glint and devilish smirk, and in its place is a steady gaze and a closed-off expression that, frustratingly, only annoys me further. I know I told myself to forget him and move on. That he was a distraction I couldn't afford, but fuck me, fate—you cruel bitch—couldn't you have at least made him someone I could have been allies with? So long as he's a Reject and they plan on going after the Antonellis, we're always going to be in opposition. I'm never going to be able to offer him what he wants—the Reaper—and he will never be able to provide me what I want—for him not to be a gang member, or be starting a war he can't possibly win.

He gives a silent signal to his men, and without question they break apart, moving back to their posts and returning to whatever they were doing before I showed up. He waits until we're alone before approaching me, stopping a respectable distance away. It infuriates me that I want him to close the gap between us so I can feel the brush of his skin against mine.

"Did you talk to the Reaper?" he asks in a hushed voice.

Of course, that's why he thinks I'm here. Why would that asshole Cain tell him anything about our conversation the other night?

"Actually, I'm looking for Jon."

His brows knit together in confusion. "Bones? Ehh, I think he and the others are over at the sports complex." He juts his chin forward, gesturing toward the building behind me on the opposite side of the road.

Now that I no longer have guns shoved in my face, I'm back on my mission of tearing Jon a new one and dragging my brother back home. If anything, the welcome I received is just more proof that Luc shouldn't be here. It's not safe. What if they'd done the same to him. He's a guy, so he would have been treated as even more of a threat than I was. What the hell was he even thinking by coming here?

Pissed off again, I turn on my heel and move to storm across the street.

"Wow, hold on," Oliver calls out, reaching out to grab my arm. "What's going on?"

I glower at him. "What's going on," I snap, yanking my arm out of his hold and ignoring the tingling sensation his touch leaves on my skin, "is that your men have been following me all week. I can't go to the fucking bathroom without them knowing, and today I arrive home to find a note from my brother informing me that he's hanging out with the fucking kids you call gang members."

The fury I've been bottling up inside spills over, and I take a threatening step toward Oliver, ignoring his wide eyes as I throw him my deadliest glare. "Your men have no right to be

258

anywhere near my little brother. He's got nothing to do with any of this, and the last place he should be hanging out is a gang clubhouse filled with guns and whores."

A frown forms on Oliver's face. "I thought Jon said he was like fifteen or something?"

"What does that have to do with anything? He's got no business being here." I gesture with my hand toward the apartment complex. "Look what just happened. He doesn't deserve to have guns shoved in his face, and I sure as hell don't want him getting hurt or killed because of your *gang*."

"He's just playing ball with the guys. Nothing's going to happen to him."

I shake my head. He just doesn't get it. Not wanting to waste time engaging in a pointless argument with him, I take off across the street toward the gym. I can still hear him behind me, his heavy boots slapping against the asphalt as he follows me.

"They're around back," he states as I approach the gym. At his words, I veer away from the front entrance, following a path that leads around the side of the building. As I get closer, I can hear voices and the sounds of laughter along with the thump-thump-thump of a ball bouncing against the hard ground.

Turning the corner at the back of the building, I find a bunch of guys—Jon and Luc included—running around a makeshift basketball court that's been spray-painted onto the asphalt.

"See, he's perfectly fine," Oliver states, earning himself a glare before I focus back on the guys on the court, noticing that they must all be only a few years older than Luc.

"Why are they all so young?" I ask Oliver. It's not surprising to see teenage boys hanging around clubhouses. They're at an impressionable age that makes it easy for assholes to manipulate them into doing shady shit for them. However, I've never seen so many who are already affiliated with a gang and seem to have a good relationship with the rest of the members. Usually, they are nothing more than grunts—bottom of the food chain, expendable members that do the jobs no one else wants to do.

Oliver's shoulder brushes against mine as he steps up beside me, the two of us watching the game unfold before us. "They were all being held captive in this compound in Cali where they were being trained to become killers."

At his words, I tear my gaze away from the game to gape at him in shock.

"They don't talk about it much, but they were street kids that were taken and were being molded into soldiers when Cain rescued them."

"So he could use their skills for himself." My dislike for Cain only grows. He's as bad as the people that initially kidnapped these kids. He just wants to use them for his own gain.

Oliver barks out a laugh and shakes his head before looking at me. "You've got Cain all wrong. Yeah, he's an asshole, but he's not the person you think he is." He focuses his attention back on the game when a round of hollers goes up as someone scores a basket. "He found homes for as many as he could, but these guys here had nowhere to go. They want to be here. For the first time in their lives, they have somewhere they belong, where they can be themselves and build a life they want." He looks back at me, pinning me in place with a serious expression. "If they decided tomorrow they wanted to leave, Cain would let them. Hell, he'd probably buy them a bus ticket to wherever they wanted to go and give them money to get themselves started."

I don't know what to make of that. Have I really misjudged Cain? Is his dickish exterior just that? Somehow, I doubt he's a fluffy little bunny rabbit that saves desperate children on the inside. I think Oliver is a little blinded by Cain, but I'm not here to interject myself into their gang politics. Hell, I'm supposed to be staying as far away from them as possible.

"Well, it's really none of my business," I state in a hard voice, refusing to let what he just told me to soften me toward Cain or the Rejects. "I'm only here to get Luc." Before he can say anything further that might break the tenuous hold I have on my tough exterior, I stride toward the guys running around the court.

When I'm close enough, I call out Luc's name. The interruption has all of them stopping mid-game as they turn to look in my direction. Luc's eyes widen when he spots me, and although I can't hear what he says, I'm pretty sure he mumbles *fuck* under his breath.

I quirk a brow and pinch my lips, letting him see how pissed I am at him. He starts to move toward me, but Jon comes jogging over, and I shift my glare from Luc to him.

He grimaces. "Look, I can see you're angry. I'm sorry. I just thought he'd wanna hang out with kids his own age."

"That's what he goes to school for," I snap. "He doesn't need to be hanging out with teenage gang-wannabes right outside a fucking clubhouse where any number of dangerous things could happen. Do you have any idea the risk you've put him at by bringing him here?"

I can see the guilt swimming in Jon's eyes, and written into the hard press of his lips as I rip into him, the anger that's been simmering in me sparking to life the more I talk.

"It was reckless. This might be the life you've chosen for yourself, but it's not Luc's." I shake my head in disappointment. "I don't want to see you anywhere near him. You're not to

261

message or call him, and I definitely don't want you in our apartment."

I almost feel bad as his head drops, and he looks properly chastised, but Luc's safety is my number one priority, and I'll do whatever it takes to protect him.

"Hey," Luc snaps at me, looking furious himself. "I'm old enough to be making my own decisions. You think the kids I go to school with aren't already deep in gang life? Do you have any idea the number of times someone tried to get me to sign up for the Satan's? I can't hang out with anyone at school without someone thinking I'm associated with one gang or another. I just wanted to have some fun for once."

"Well, fun time is over. We're leaving."

"We're not finished."

I glower at Luc. "I don't give a shit. *You're* finished."

"No," he snaps. "I'm not leaving. What are you going to do? Drag me out of here?"

I take a threatening step toward him, planning on doing just that when Oliver interjects. He steps between us, putting himself in the line of my wrath. "Why don't we let them finish up their game, then I'll take him straight home?" I open my mouth to argue when he cuts me off, leaning in to whisper in a quiet voice that's meant only for us to hear. "It's not like you can take him on the back of your bike anyway."

I snap my mouth closed because, well *fuck*, he's right. Why the hell did I get a goddamn bike?!

Seeing that he's got me there, Oliver catches my gaze with his capturing sky-blue eyes. "I'll have him back in an hour." I can see the sincerity in his gaze, and despite the fact I don't want to leave Luc here alone, I get the impression Oliver won't let anything happen to him.

262

I grit my teeth for a long moment, mulling it over, but I know I have no other choice. I don't have a spare helmet for him to ride my bike, nor am I actually capable of dragging his ass out of here if he's going to fight me on it.

"Fine," I reluctantly snap. "One hour."

When Oliver nods in understanding, I pin Luc with a serious look. "You and I are going to have a serious talk when you get home."

He still looks pissed off, but Jon drags him back to their game, and not wanting to hang around or have to talk to Oliver, I storm off back to my bike, and start the engine. Swinging my leg over the seat, I tug on my helmet and take off, blinking back tears the entire way back to the garage.

The second I pull up in the garage and take off my helmet, I fall apart, letting the tears fall. Luc is the only person in this entire world that means anything to me, and the fear I felt today was overwhelming. I just want to keep him safe, but he's reaching that age where he wants to do these things. Where he wants to hang out with his friends and make his own decisions, and honestly, it scares me. I'm terrified he'll make the wrong choices in life. That he'll end up running for a gang. I don't want him to throw his life away, and I couldn't live with myself if he ended up dead before he had a chance to grow up and really live.

I have to start letting him live his own life, but I have no idea how to do that, how to just sit back and let him be. I know he's smart, and he will make good decisions for the most part. The fact he's made it to fifteen without falling into gang life is a testament to that. He's surrounded by that shit in school— something I was already aware of. It's more of a recruitment center for lowlifes than it is an educational establishment. And I know if any of the kids in school asked him to hang out, it wouldn't be to play ball. It would be to party, drink and do drugs, and try to entice him into that life. I do think Jon was just trying to be friendly and include him... and I blew a fucking fuse at him—god, I'm such a bitch.

I let myself have a pity party for one on the floor of my garage for a few minutes before sniffling back the last of my tears and wiping under my eyes. Getting to my feet, I lock up and head toward my apartment, careful to keep my head down so no one can see my red, puffy eyes. If I can make it back before Luc gets home, then I can get a cold compress on them. The last thing I want is for him to see me upset over this.

"Red," a voice I recognize calls out just as I step into the doorway of my apartment building. *Fuck.*

Straightening my shoulders, I spin to face Oliver. I didn't think it had been an hour already. Was I really having an emotional breakdown for that long? Dammit, I need to pull my shit together.

No doubt he can see the red rim around my eyes, but I make sure the rest of my face is set in its usual resting bitch face as I meet his eyes. He's leaning against a black Escalade and squinting through the front windshield. I don't see any signs of Luc inside, so he must already be in the apartment. Why is Oliver still hanging around out here then?

When he sees my no doubt blotchy face, his lips flatten as though he's annoyed, although I don't know what about it could be angering him. "Can we talk?"

I cross my arms over my chest, needing the extra layer of defense between us right now. "I don't see how we have anything to talk about. I think it's best if you just go your way, and I'll go mine, and we can pretend we never met."

The muscles in the back of his jaw tighten—an indicator that he didn't like what I said—and he pushes off the side of the

264

car, moving toward me. "Is that what you genuinely want? To just ignore this *thing* between us?"

I have to swallow around the lump in my throat. His proximity makes it impossible to think straight, and suddenly the hard-bitch exterior I had erected is starting to crack and crumble.

After a moment's silence, he jerks his head to the right. "Let's go grab some food—"

"I can't," I interject, cutting him off. "Luc... "

"Luc's upstairs. Let him calm down for a bit before you confront him." With the way his gaze hovers over my puffy eyes, I can tell what he's really saying is *I'm sure you don't want him to see you crying.* Knowing he's right, I huff out a long exhale before reluctantly agreeing.

He tosses me a small, warm smile, and we walk side-by-side down the street to a small twenty-four-hour diner. The bell above the door tinkles as we walk in, and I lead us over to an empty booth along the window.

The inside is designed in a shabby, retro vibe, which could be cool if it wasn't for the fact I'm pretty sure the only reason for the decor is because the owner can't afford to update it. There are holes in the faux-leather upholstery of my chair, and the linoleum table is chipped, the top layer peeling away.

An older woman with graying hair—who stinks of cigarettes—wearing a uniform and an apron approaches, barely sparing us a glance as she hands us menus and takes our drink orders.

Neither of us says anything as we peruse the menu and wait for the waitress to return with our coffees.

"Anything to eat?" she asks as she sets a chipped mug down in front of me and fills it.

"Ham and cheese panini for me," I tell her, handing back the menu.

265

"Yeah, I'll take the same," Oliver supplies before the waitress leaves us alone. An awkward silence settles over us as I take a sip of my coffee, grimacing before I drop a couple of lumps of sugar in the cup and stir it, pointedly looking out the window as I do. I refuse to allow myself to ask him any personal questions, even if I am curious to know more about him. It won't do me any good to get further invested with him or the Rejects. My involvement with them over the whole Reaper thing has already resulted in Luc being dragged into their life. I can't afford for the lines to become even more blurred.

"Is Luc the only family you have?" Oliver eventually asks, drawing my attention away from the old couple walking arm in arm down the street.

"He is."

"He's lucky to have a sister like you. One who cares enough to walk onto gang-owned territory and yell at one of them for him." His lip quirks up to let me know he's joking.

I chuckle out a weak laugh. "I'd do a lot more than that for him."

The waitress returns, setting our food down on the table, and another moment of silence falls over us when she's disappeared.

"So, how long have you worked at Strip Tease?" he asks. It would seem, he's all about the personal questions today.

"Five years."

His eyebrows lift. "That's a long time. Do you enjoy it?"

I snort, giving him a quizzical look. "Do I enjoy giving lap dances to overweight, middle-aged men and assholes with bigger guns than they have dicks?"

He simply shrugs, and I can tell his question was a genuine one. He wasn't trying to take a dig at what I do for a living, he was genuinely curious to know if I enjoyed what I did.

266

"I enjoy when I'm dancing on stage," I admit. "It's impossible to make anyone out with the bright stage lights, so it feels like I'm in my own little world. It makes it easy to get lost in the music."

"That sounds nice. I rarely get a moment to myself anymore. It's quite an adjustment. In prison, I had hours every day where I wouldn't see or talk to another person, and now I'm lucky if I can get two minutes to piss in private."

My eyebrows climb up my forehead at his easy admission that he was in prison, and I have to bite my tongue to hold back the burning questions. *I am not getting personally involved,* I remind myself.

I force back the questions threatening to spill past my lips, biting off a considerable chunk of my panini and munching on it for as long as I can. I feel Oliver's eyes on me, though; I can feel his puzzling stare as he tries to figure me out.

"You're good at it," he says after a long moment of silence. "Dancing."

I make decent tips, and the hoots and hollers I receive when I'm on stage certainly imply the customers are enjoying the show I'm putting on for them. Still, no one has ever said it quite like that—as if it's about the actual movements, and not just the shaking of my tits and circling of my hips. The strange compliment makes me blush, and I duck my head, mumbling a weak thanks as I lift my panini to my mouth, unsure how to respond to that sentiment.

Oliver doesn't try to engage me in conversation again, and we end up eating the rest of our meal in silence. Surprisingly, it doesn't feel awkward. It's actually kinda nice. Something I can see myself doing on a regular basis. I refuse to let myself ruminate on that for too long, so I steer my focus

267

instead on the mechanical process of chewing and swallowing until my plate is cleared.

When I look up, there's a playful smirk on Oliver's face. He's holding one half of his panini in his hands, halfway to his mouth as though he was about to take a bite but got distracted. "Hungry?" he jokes with a chuckle.

I glimpse at his plate, which still has the other half of his panini to my own one, which looks like it's been licked clean, and let out my own small laugh.

"Maybe a little," I confess, unwilling to admit nerves and an uncanny urge to actually open up and talk to him had me practically wolfing down the food.

He finishes off the half of the panini in his hand before asking, "So did you grow up in Black Creek?"

"Yeah, I did," I answer, starting to feel uncomfortable about all the one-way questions. "Did, uh, you?"

A small smile graces his lips like he knows what it cost me to ask that question. "Yeah, I did. Cain and I grew up on the same street."

A pained expression crosses his features but it disappears so quickly, I have to wonder if I imagined it.

"So you've known him your whole life?"

"More or less." He doesn't expand further than that, and I don't pry.

"And now you're a member of the Rejects."

I don't mean for the words to sound disdainful, but they do all the same. It's just difficult for me to view any of the Black Creek gangs in anything other than a negative light.

Oliver's eyes jump back and forth between mine for a moment, as if he's trying to discern my thoughts before he speaks up. "Is it just the Rejects you have an issue with or all gang members?"

"Don't go thinking you're special. I truly hate all of you equally."

My whole life, gangs have laid down the law and forced us to comply with their whims. My mom paid so much of her earnings to the gang that ran the territory we lived in, that she barely had enough left to clothe and feed us. They insisted she pay *rent* on the street corner she stood on, plus a nominal fee for protection, and I'm sure there were other bullshit charges thrown in there. Not to mention the way they abused her and got her hooked on drugs so she'd be under their control. The final straw was when one of them—her fucking *boyfriend,* if you can even call him that—beat the shit out of her and murdered her in front of Luc, leaving her body for me to find when I got home.

I saw the same shit day in and day out on the street. Gang members throwing their weight around, using their position, their size, their weapons to demand whatever the fuck they wanted. They'd hang around outside shelters and try to lure desperate people into gang life by offering them drugs and money. Flirting with women and promising them safety and security, but those same women would be right back in the shelter a month or two later, covered in bruises. So, yeah, it's safe to say I have a fucking reason to hate gang members.

"What have they ever done for me or the people of Black Creek? All they are interested in is themselves. So long as they have drugs, alcohol, territory and can wave their big ass guns in people's faces, none of them give a shit about the problems they cause for the rest of us."

Oliver just sits and watches as I get myself riled up. I can feel the color in my cheeks as my anger takes over, and I have to take a deep, calming breath to rein myself in. I don't need to

269

be spilling my guts to Oliver. What the hell does he know or care about it, he's one of those fucking gang members.

"And yet, you were there to fuck Python the night he died."

He's watching me intently, searching my face for any reaction to his prying statement.

I keep my expression carefully shuttered as I state in a dry tone, "I don't see how that's any of your business. If I want to get off by rubbing myself against a tree trunk, then that's my prerogative, and it's got fuck all to do with you."

He wipes a hand over his mouth, hiding the half-smile threatening to make an appearance, before leaning across the table toward me. "I just don't see that someone like Python would be your type."

There's a playful twinkle in his eye at that statement, and what the fuck can I say to that? He knows exactly what my type is—him.

Unable to think of a half-decent comeback, I simply shrug my shoulders, refusing to say anything more on the subject, and after a moment, he switches lanes, getting us back on track. "I don't know if you've noticed, but the Rejects aren't like the Satan's or any of the other gangs."

I frown, pinching my lips together. I have noticed—how could I not? And it only confuses me more. It's practically ingrained into my blood to hate any and all things gang-related, but the Rejects aren't like any gang I've come across before. They don't appear to be the lowlife scum I'm used to, but that doesn't make it any easier for me to just discard my hatred for their kind. Besides, if I stopped viewing the Rejects as *the bad guys*, then that would open the door for me to see them as something more, which terrifies me. My feelings for Oliver are confusing enough. Then, if you throw in whatever electrified chemistry I have with

270

Cain... If I can't tell myself that they're off-limits because of who they are, then where does that leave me?

"I had—noticed. I'm just not sure if that changes anything."

I lose myself in the depths of his gaze for a moment, the two of us falling into a world where only we exist. I can't even begin to describe this pull I feel toward him. I've felt it ever since I sidled up beside him at the bar. I hardly know the guy—I've made a point of not getting to know him—but that doesn't lessen this attraction between us. If anything, every time we cross paths, my resolve to stay away from him weakens.

Coughing, he clears his throat before asking, "You ready to go?"

With a nod of my head, I agree, "Sure."

I go to grab a few dollar bills from my pocket but he beats me to it, dropping enough on the table to cover both of our meals.

"I don't need you to pay for me," I state with a frown of annoyance.

"Never said you did. I might be a Reject, but I do have some manners, and I know to settle the bill when you ask a girl out for a meal."

I hesitate for a moment before relenting. Fair enough. So long as he realizes this isn't a date, who am I to argue with a free meal.

His palm rests on my lower back, the light touch and chivalrous act making my stomach flip as a horde of butterflies take flight as he escorts me across the diner and out the door. I'm aware of his every movement as we walk down the street, and when the back of his hand brushes against mine, I get literal goosebumps. It doesn't matter how many times I tell myself he's

271

a Reject and that he's on a suicide mission, my body still craves him.

When we approach my apartment building, he pushes me against the wall, crowding me with his broad chest as he leans an arm against the brick above my head. "Go out with me."

It's not really a question. More of a demand. One my slutty side responds to. I stare into his pale blue eyes for a long moment, allowing myself for just a second to imagine a world where he isn't a gang member, and I'm not just trying to keep my brother and me alive. I could definitely picture myself dating him. I imagine he would be easy to fall for, with his boyish charm and casual demeanor, not to mention he's easy on the eyes. Yup, I could definitely lose myself in Oliver... in another life.

"I can't," I begin, watching as tight lines form around his eyes and his shoulders tense. "Maybe if you weren't who you are... " I trail off, unsure how to bluntly say if he wasn't associated with a gang, then *maybe* things could have been different between us.

"That just sounds like an excuse to me," he states, unperturbed.

I shrug my shoulders. "Maybe so, but Luc needs me. As much as I couldn't live without him, he couldn't live without me. And going out with someone like you, well, that's just asking for trouble."

He stares intently back at me for a second. "I think you're just so used to doing all of it alone that you don't know how to rely on anyone else. You think I'd bring more trouble to your door, and maybe I would, but I'd also bring more protection and better support. If trouble did come knocking, you wouldn't be facing it alone."

He paints a pretty picture, one I could easily fall for, but I know it's not that black and white. If we were to break up, there would be a target on my back from rival gangs thinking they could maybe get information about the Rejects out of me. Not to mention the fucking war they're about to start with the Antonellis. Anyone associated with them will be skinned alive.

"I'm sorry," I breathe out, watching as his face shutters and he closes himself off from me. I fucking hate it, but I've made my decision. He gives a sharp jerk of his head before pushing off the wall and stepping backward.

"Yeah, me too." With one last lingering look, he moves around to the driver's side of the car, glancing over at me before he gets in. "Take care of yourself, Red."

He's already in the car with the door closed and the engine started by the time I find my voice, feeling strangely emotional as I watch him drive away. "You too, Oliver."

## Chapter 17

Luc is waiting for me when I let myself into the apartment. His anger from earlier is gone, as is my own, and when I step into the living room, he meets my apologetic gaze with a regretful one of his own.

"I'm sorry," he blurts out before I can say anything. "I knew you'd be mad—"

"I was, but only because I care about you."

He's already nodding his head. "I know."

We stand and look at each other for a moment before I let out a long exhale and close the distance between us, wrapping my arms around him. "I'm sorry. I just don't know what I'd do if something happened to you."

"Nothing happened, though. I was fine. They're good people."

God, I'm getting sick of everyone telling me Cain and the Rejects are *good people*. They're fucking gang members. They're inherently designed to be gun-toting, dick-wielding assholes who can't see past their own ego long enough to give a shit about anyone but themselves.

"They're thugs," I snarl more sharply than I intended. The last thing I want to do is get into another argument with Luc over them. "They might be better than the Satan's, but that doesn't mean they're *good.*"

Luc's lips pinch, but he thankfully doesn't argue with me. "I still need my own friends, though. Guys to hang out with. I deliberately stay away from the kids in school 'cause I know they're affiliated with one crew or the other, and I don't want to get caught up in that shit, but Sawyer, I need more than just you in my life."

There's no denying the sting of pain at that comment, and I have to carefully hide my hurt feelings from him. I know he doesn't mean it that way. What bothers me the most is that he's everything to me. I don't really have anyone else. No one I can rely on or call up to chat with after a crappy day. There's Sheryl, sure, but she's a mess. I can't dump any of my shit onto her. So I guess it hurts a little that Luc needs more than just me, but that's a seriously selfish thought. He's a teenage boy, of course, he needs people other than his sister-mom.

I have to swallow around the lump of emotion in my throat before I can respond. "I get that. I'm just not sure that Jon and his friends are who you want to spend your time with."

He quirks a brow, and his words are coated in sarcasm when he says, "Would you prefer I hang out in a drug den, surrounded by coke and hookers, with one of the kids from school?"

I grimace, hating the harsh reality he's painting.

"Jon just asked me to play ball with him," he continues. "They didn't try to get me to go into their clubhouse, and they didn't offer me drugs or alcohol or wave a firearm in my face. Honestly, if it weren't for their tattoos, you wouldn't have known they were associated with a gang at all."

Groaning, I press the heel of my hands against my closed eyes, staving off the headache forming behind them.

"Fine," I relent. "I get it." Lifting my head, I pierce him with a reluctantly acquiescent look. "Just, promise me you'll be careful."

His shoulders drop, and he gives me a soft smile as he nods his head. "I promise."

We chat for a bit longer before he moves to lounge on the sofa, channel surfing while I help myself to a large glass of wine and grab my bathrobe before heading into the bathroom and running the taps for the bath.

Once the water is warm enough, I sit on the edge of the tub, drop a citrusy-smelling bath bomb into the water, and wait for it to disperse while sipping on my wine. When the room smells like a vineyard, with the zesty, flowery scent, I shed my leather clothing and sink into the blissfully hot water, letting the bubbles melt away all my stress from today.

I've got no idea what I'm going to do about Luc. Okay, I know what I need to do, I just don't know how I'm going to actually manage to do it. I have to stop smothering him and let him branch out on his own, but how the fuck am I meant to do that? How does any mother stand back and watch their child go out into the world, knowing they'll make mistakes and fuck up along the way? It's even worse when that world is Black Creek, and a simple mistake can result in your brain matter being sprayed all over the sidewalk.

Still, I risk losing Luc for good if I continue to smother him the way I have been, and that's the absolute last thing I want. So, despite my overbearing nature, I need to find a way to take a step back and let him just be himself; to grow up, and ultimately learn to stand on his own two feet. Even though I still see him as an eight-year-old boy, he's a teenager now; practically a man.

Regardless of my de-stressing bath, I toss and turn all night. Recurring nightmares of Luc getting shot or something terrible happening to him play on repeat in my head, driving me insane, and by the time the gray light of dawn peers through my window, I'm in a pissed-off mood and in need of a serious caffeine fix.

My day only goes from bad to worse when, once I've filled the coffee pot and poured myself a steaming hot mug, I pull out my burner phone—the one I use specifically for Enzo. Rather than finding the usual text confirming this afternoon's meeting, he's demanding a last-minute time change.

*Enzo: Can't do this afternoon. Meet me at 9:30 am instead.*

I see no please or thank you, and with it already being after nine o'clock, I don't see myself making it on time. Not that I'm going to even bother trying. That's what he gets for being so bossy and trying to mess with my schedule at the last minute. I hate when he reschedules on me. Admittedly, he rarely does. I can probably count on one hand the number of times he's had to cancel or change our plans in the last seven years. Still, it's as much about the *way* he said it, as it is about the actual inconvenience of messing up my plans—besides, I'm not in a mood to cater to his bullshit today, and I always feel like I need time to psych myself up for my meetings with him. Almost as though I have to put on mental armor to protect myself from him. Not that he's ever done anything to hurt me. Hell, on paper, he's a hell of a lot more decent than most of the people I come into contact with every day. But there's something about him that just irks me. I can't put my finger on it, but it makes the hairs on the back of my neck stand on end and gives me this feeling like I need to put up boundaries between us—which is why I usually spend the morning before our meetings putting on my war paint and emptying my mind of everything so I can come across as an impenetrable fortress to him. Basically, I let him see the deadly side to the Reaper while keeping the crazy part of myself that craves the bloodshed locked up tight.

I deliberately wait until after nine-thirty to message him back. *No can do. Will meet you at the usual place and time.*

Pressing send, I stare at the screen, expecting an immediate response. After several moments, I give up when one still hasn't come through, assuming his silence means he's fine with that. Just as I get up to refill my mug, the phone vibrates with an incoming message. *Tomorrow then.*

Frowning, I type out a quick response. *Nope. Today. Usual place and time.* As soon as it's sent, I power the phone off. The screen flashes with an incoming call, Enzo's number at the bottom, less than a second before it goes black.

I smirk at the screen, knowing I won that argument. I move to get another cup of coffee. I've got a feeling I'm going to need it today.

\*\*\*

279

With my long hair flowing freely down my back and a full face of makeup, including darker than usual eyes and bright red lips, I feel fucking fierce as I step into G&T in my chunky heeled boots, black skinny jeans, and a faded band t-shirt that I've knotted around my midriff. My leather jacket provides the finishing touches to the badass bitch persona I'm rocking.

I'm momentarily blinded as I move from the sunshine into the dark interior of the pub, and I have to blink a few times before my eyes finally adjust to the light. Before I can look around to see if Enzo is here, the man himself practically pounces on me. I hadn't even noticed he was sitting at a table right by the door, and he must have stood up as soon as he saw me enter.

"I told you not to come," he snaps, staring down at me with narrowed eyes. There's a wild look in his blue-green gaze, and between his weird behavior and attempt to reschedule today's meeting, he's acting suspicious as fuck.

I scrutinize him closely, taking in the tight lines of his face that give away whatever strain he's been under recently. "What the fuck crawled up your ass and died?" I snark with a raised brow, not appreciating his attitude. "*I* told you I couldn't reschedule. Besides, you were clearly able to make it just fine."

I can see the muscle in his jaw working and his nostrils flaring before he lets out a long exhale. "Fine. Here's your cash, now give me my info." He holds his hand out with my envelope in it. Another red flag. He's never gotten straight down to business.

I glance from his outstretched hand up to his face. "What, no drink and you asking me inappropriate questions first?"

He grinds his teeth, getting more and more frustrated with me with each passing second. My snark has always grated on his nerves. I think he's the kind of guy who likes to think of himself as a straight shooter, and my constant deflections piss him off. But the thing is, he's as tight-lipped as they come. I don't know a goddamn thing about him. Not that I've let myself ask him any personal questions. Our relationship is strictly business. I don't need to know every little thing about him to work with him. And honestly, I get the impression if I go digging too deep into his life, I won't like what I find, and I do like the money he gives me every month, so I choose not to go snooping.

"I've got other shit to do today," he snaps irritably. His gaze bounces around the room like he's expecting something to happen, and I focus my attention on his pupils, trying to work out if he's on drugs or something. It would definitely explain his weird behavior.

*Nope, his pupils are a normal size.*

"Shame." I pout and slip past him, sliding onto an empty barstool. "I'm in the mood to talk and drink today."

"Not here, you're not." He grabs hold of my upper arm, and as I go to yank my arm out of his grip, everything goes sideways. The blistering heat of a blast knocks me backward as a whooshing sound threatens to burst my eardrums, and I hit the ground with a painful thud that vibrates through my bones. My head smacks against the floor with what I imagine is a deafening crack, seconds before a heavy weight lands on top of me, knocking the last of the air out of my lungs.

My ears ring, and time loses all meaning as I lie there, struggling to breathe. I choke on nothing as I try to force air into my lungs for a terrifyingly long moment before the weight lifts off my chest, and I finally manage to suck down some oxygen.

I'm faintly aware of someone rolling me onto my back and shaking my shoulders, but my eyes feel too heavy to open.

My whole body feels numb. Is that a good thing? I feel like that can't be good. Some asshole pulls back my eyelid, and I jerk away from the harsh glare of light with a groan. Whoever is harassing me continues, and I eventually find the strength to peel open my eyes, finding Enzo's face hovering above mine.

His lips are moving, but I can't make out the words. Blood drips from a cut along his brow, and a layer of dust coats his face. I focus on the movement of his lips, not in any attempt to understand what he's saying, since they just look so... pink. Have they always been that pink?

The ringing in my ears dulls, the odd word making it through the buzzing. "Red. Red!"

I close my eyes, focusing on the noises around me. People screaming. Tires spinning against asphalt. Gunfire. Something is burning. The acrid, pungent smell singes my nostrils, the scent of burning flesh making my stomach revolt.

"Sawyer!"

My eyes snap open, once again finding Enzo hovering over me with a look of concern instead of his usual expression of stoicism. The left side of my head is still throbbing from where I hit it off the ground, and when I lift my hand to my temple, my fingers come away coated in blood. I stare at the bright red substance for an inordinately long time until Enzo's voice penetrates through my psyche. "Come on, we have to get out of here."

I barely register his words before he's lifting me off the ground. The sudden movement has me gritting my teeth against the sharp pain in my side, and I stand on shaky legs while he supports most of my weight until I gain my bearings. Once I'm confident I'm not going to collapse to the floor, I pull out of his hold and pat myself down, checking everything is intact. *All good—well, as good as can be expected.* The whole left side of my body, where I hit the floor, hurts, but I don't think anything is broken.

"What happened?" I croak, looking at the carnage surrounding me. The explosion upturned tables and windows were blown in, littering the ground with tiny shards of glass. The shelves of booze behind the bar have smashed, coating the floor in sticky liquid, and amongst the rubble, bodies are strewn everywhere. Some are groaning and struggling to move, while others are clearly dead. *Jesus.* Except for the front exterior wall, the rest of G&T is nothing more than a bombed ruin. There's hardly anything left of it. All around me, people are screaming, crying, running away, and I can hear the loud echo of gunshots from somewhere outside.

With my head spinning, I step toward the front of the building, figuring that's the quickest way out of here. God knows, what's left of the foundations can't be enough to prevent the roof from falling down on top of us at any second.

"No," Enzo barks, his hand snapping out to grab a hold of my arm and tugging me backward. "They're gunning down everyone that goes out that way." He pulls me across the room, in the direction of the bar, and I step over dead bodies, trying not to look into their glassy, sightless eyes as I pass. It's difficult, though, since I have to keep looking down to ensure I don't trip over any debris. One particular man catches my attention. He's just lying there, and at first, I think he's dead, but after a second, he blinks, and I realize he's in shock. I don't fucking blame him. Blood coats the ground around him, and he's missing half an arm. I look around his immediate vicinity, unable to locate where it was thrown in the blast. *Holy fuck, what is this day?*

I'm distinctly aware that *I'm* in shock, and I once again cast my gaze over my arms, suddenly fearful that I may not even realize I'm missing a vital organ. *Nope, definitely all intact. Thank fuck.*

Dust hangs heavy in the air, catching in my throat, and I stumble as a cough wracks my body. My hand goes out to lean against a dark wooden pillar for balance until my coughing fit passes, and when I push off the beam, my hand is covered in a red substance. It takes me longer than it should, to realize it's blood, and I gape at the wooden pillar in shock. The entire thing is covered in a red, blood mist.

"Come on," Enzo urges when I've been frozen in place for too long. "We need to go."

He resumes tugging me behind what remains of the bar, and glass cracks beneath my boots as I hurry across it. A thought niggles at the back of my mind, but I push it away, focusing on following him as we reach a storage room. There's a fire exit on the far side of the room, most likely where deliveries are made, and Enzo wastes no time moving toward it. He cracks open the door and peers out before pushing it open further, and we stumble onto a back alleyway. The sky seems darker than it did when I first arrived, and when I look upward, a thick layer of smoke is blocking my view of the sun. Despite the smoke, the air is clearer out here than it was inside, and I suck it down, bending over to place my hands on my knees. My ribs ache with every inhale, and I can feel something sticky running down the side of my face. All in all, I'm feeling like fucking shit right now.

For the first time since the explosion, I really take myself in, noticing the rips in my leather jacket and jeans. Thankfully they seem to have protected me from the worst of the blast, and I've only got a few superficial scrapes on my arms and legs. I lift my hand to touch the wound on my head, wincing when my fingers touch the tender skin. It's still bleeding, although I think it's slowed. It definitely feels like the worst injury I've sustained.

284

"You have to go," Enzo rushes out, drawing my attention his way. As I lift my head to look at him, ignoring the continued rattle of gunfire coming from the other side of the building, a moment of clarity hits me, and I look at him—covered in dust and blood—in a new light. It dawns on me that I truly know nothing about this man, and while an hour ago I didn't care to change that, I suddenly realize that not knowing is a weakness.

"You knew this was going to happen." I cough, but I don't dare look away from his face, searching it for any confirmation I'm right. He doesn't give anything away, his expression pinched and unreadable. "How?"

For a split second, he drops his guard, and a multitude of emotions flash across his face, too quick for me to pinpoint any individual one. As promptly as his barriers fall, he reconstructs them, his expression turning to stone. It's not one I've seen before, and it catches me off guard.

My eyes narrow on him, and I bark out, "Who are you?"

He doesn't answer me, instead pointing toward the far end of the alley, away from the ongoing sounds of an attack. "Go. Now." His words are snapped off the end of his tongue in an acerbic tone, and I don't immediately react to them, continuing to stare at him as I wonder just who the hell he is.

"Not until you tell me who you are," I argue, vaguely aware that the man standing in front of me isn't the same one I normally meet once a month for our exchange. He's currently emanating an aura of authority and danger. One he's kept carefully under wraps in all of our previous meetings.

His lips pinch and his eyes narrow, but after a second, he says, "I work for the Antonellis."

I blink owlishly at him, almost certain I've heard him wrong. The Antonellis? Are you kidding me with this shit? It's entirely possible I hit my head harder than I realized and I

285

misheard him... right? *Goddammit*, somehow, I don't think I did. His expression certainly doesn't look like he's joking. The question is, what the fuck has he wanted from me all these years? My stomach churns precariously as I think about all the information I handed over to him.

Before I can fully process what he's said, never mind form any sort of response, he barks out in an authoritative demand, "No more questions. Get the fuck out of here."

Realizing I'm not going to get any more answers from him—at least, not today—I take one last look at the man I know nothing about and take off down the alley.

## Chapter 18

I stumble down the alley and practically run with blinders on until I reach the garage where I park my bike. My hands are shaking as I search my pockets for the key to the roller door and pull it open just enough to slip inside.

Finally safe and alone, I sag to the ground, unable to believe today's turn of events. They play repeatedly in my head, and I still can't wrap my head around the fact that Enzo works for the Antonellis. I don't understand what he's wanted from me all these years. Surely the intel I handed over could easily have been obtained elsewhere? Do the Antonellis even care about the mundane on-goings of street gangs?

More importantly, how had I never connected those dots before? It never even crossed my mind that he could be in the Antonellis' pocket. The small behaviors that never quite made sense to me, slot into place like the final pieces of a jigsaw. The way his face scrunched at cheap whiskey; how he was always more smartly dressed than most people that live in Black Creek; the fact he never seemed to quite fit in here like the rest of us do. They were all little tells, pointing to his true identity, and like a fucking idiot, I ignored every single one, not wanting anything beyond the cash in his hands.

Putting two and two together then, that only leaves one possible explanation for today... the Antonellis attacked G&T. The only question is why? What issue could they possibly have with a small, barely afloat bar in the middle of Black Creek?

The nameless faces of the dead flash across my brain like a bad memory, and I suddenly feel sick to my stomach. My head swims, and anger sparks to life in my veins as I think about all those innocent people caught in the crosshairs of their attack today. People like me who just so happened to be in the wrong place at the wrong time. Whatever their gripe was with G&T, there was no need for such a senseless loss of life today; absolutely no fucking need to blow a building to smithereens with people inside it.

My anger only grows, providing me with a much-needed surge of adrenaline that enables me to push to my knees. Rage clouds my thoughts, most likely affecting my judgment as I rummage in my pocket for my keys and find my helmet, and before I can second guess my decision, I'm racing my bike out onto the street, heading in the direction of Radiant Park.

I'm all fire and pent-up rage as I pull up at the curb outside the Reject's clubhouse. I run my eyes over the darkened exterior while I pull off my helmet, wincing as the interior rubs against the gash on my temple. The sound of loud music from across the street draws my attention. Several people, clearly drunk, are loitering outside the old gym where Luc was playing ball just yesterday... fucking hell was that only twenty-four hours ago?!

Flashing colored lights shine through the windows, and it looks like there's some sort of party underway. I swing my leg over the bike and place the helmet on the seat before crossing the street, hazarding a guess that this is where the Rejects usually hang out.

Reaching the entrance, I ignore the flashing strobe lights as I stomp through the gathered crowd. I'm still wearing my outfit from earlier, covered in dust, blood, and god only knows what else. I probably look like death right now, but thankfully, none of those details are discernable in the darkened club.

I barge past people until they learn to get out of my way, opening a path before me that leads straight to a three-person-deep throng that I have to elbow and snarl my way through until I'm balanced precariously on the edge of an empty swimming pool.

I stutter to a stop, staring in surprise at the two men battling it out amongst the ceramic tiles. There is a splattering of smeared, bright-red blood on the floor beneath their feet, intermixed with an older, rusted color that is reminiscent of fights long forgotten. As I watch, more blood joins it when Cain's fist slams into his opponent's face with such force, it must send his brain rattling around inside his head. The crowd screams its satisfaction as he goes in for another punishing blow, and I swear I see one of his opponent's teeth fly loose.

His opponent falls to his knees, but Cain doesn't stop there. His hands meet the back of the guy's head, pushing him down as he lifts his knee, and I don't need to hear the noise of bone shattering to know his nose is broken. The guy cries out as he collapses to the floor, and with a heaving chest and an altogether feral look in his eye, Cain lifts his hands in the air and rotates in a full circle to the sound of the crowd's cheers and applause. Once he's had enough, he hauls himself out of the far side of the pool, and the crowd quickly parts to let him through, closing in behind him. Only his tall frame prevents me from losing sight of him as I blatantly ignore the cussing I get every time I dig my elbow into some asshole's side, pushing my way through the crowd, circling around the pool as I attempt to chase after him.

When I reach the far side of the pool where he climbed out, I lose sight of him for a second, turning my head left and right as I stand on my toes, attempting to pick him out of the dense crowd. In the poor lighting, it takes me a moment, but I spot him just as he disappears behind a door with a male changing room sign on it, and with renewed energy, I surge forward.

My lack of height and brick-wall exterior means I'm several minutes behind him, and by the time I push open the door, I hear the sound of a shower running. The door clicks shut behind me, and I press my back against it as I glance around the otherwise empty room, noting how dark it is. There's a switch on the wall beside me, but when I flick it, nothing happens. The lights don't seem to be working back here. There are windows, set high along one wall, which provide some light from a street lamp outside, bathing everything in a yellow-orange glow. There's a row of lockers lining one wall, and a long, wooden bench in the middle of the room, containing a pile of clothing that must belong to Cain.

In the sudden quiet, as I listen to the steady stream of running water from the shower and the faint screaming of the crowd behind me, I suddenly find myself unsure as to why I'm here. Why did I come here out of all the places I could have gone after today? Why am I chasing after Cain?

The anger from earlier is still burning a path through my system, and I know my initial thinking was that I couldn't let the Antonellis get away with what they did today. However, as I stand alone in the changing room, with adrenaline pumping through me after watching that fight, I sense the reason I'm here is about more than just that. Underneath the simmering anger, there's a dark, heady sensation that only Cain's close proximity can bring about. It makes me feel light-headed... or maybe that's the head injury I sustained earlier.

I'm still trying to make sense of what I'm feeling—or whether I require medical attention—when I hear the water switch off, and a moment later, Cain's broad-shouldered frame fills the entranceway to the showers. He's wearing only a towel, wrapped loosely around his waist, showing off his broad chest and chiseled abs. Every single inch of skin is covered in tattoos, too many for me to focus on any individual one, not that I can make out any of the detail in the low light.

"What the hell are you doing here?" he bites out, not the slightest bit happy to see me. "I thought we were done with you."

"Charming as ever," I retort with a scowl, falling back on my usual defense tactics with him. "Can't you ever just be fucking nice?" I've been through more than enough for one day, and my reasons for coming here are beginning to escape me. Amid my anger toward the Antonellis, I stupidly thought coming here would help. I just wanted to do something, to fight back against them in some way, and the only people I could think of to help were the Rejects. But as I look up into Cain's shadowed face, I can't help but wonder if offering to assist them is wise.

What would happen if he actually won? I could end up trading one monster for another.

My sharp tone sparks something within him, and his already ridiculously short fuse must burn out because his features darken. As he storms my way, quickly closing the distance between us, all I can think about is that he's wearing the same foreboding expression he wore in the ring when he was obliterating his opponent. Everything about him screams, *I can destroy you with a single touch*, and hot damn, does it not speak to the fucked up psycho within me.

"*Nice?*" Cain sneers, spitting out the word. "Why the fuck would I be *nice* to you?"

From his snarling tone and towering presence, my anger skyrockets to never before reached heights. How dare he try to fucking intimidate me. Does he think I'm that easily cowered? I came here to offer my fucking help to this asshole. After what he confided in me the other day and what I witnessed today, I realize what I've been doing—ridding the town of cheating scumbags—is nowhere near enough. I talk about wanting a better life for Luc, wanting to make Black Creek a town that he can live in safely, yet I don't do anything to help make that a reality. If I want Luc to be able to walk the streets of Black Creek without worry, then I need to do my part to make that a reality. And that starts by getting rid of the Antonellis.

He looms over me, pressing one hand flat against the wood beside my head, and the other one wraps around my neck, pinning me firmly to the door. With his face barely an inch from my own, I can see the fire burning in his eyes, the angry set to his jaw, but simmering beneath all that hate, I spot something else... puzzlement. Uncertainty. Distrust.

Or maybe I'm just seeing everything I'm feeling reflected back at me.

"You're trouble, and if I don't stop you, you'll ruin everything."

I have no idea what he means, and I part my lips to say what exactly, I'm not sure. The slight movement catches his gaze, and his eyes zero in on my mouth seconds before he dips his head, using his hold on my throat to drag me forward until our mouths clash in a scorching heat that threatens to incinerate me.

Every swipe of his tongue is controlled and dominant, intended to put me in my place and remind me who's in charge here. I try to fight him, battling my tongue with his, but he's relentless, plundering into my mouth like a one-man army on the warpath. Needing to make him realize I'm not some floozy who's going to let him do whatever he wants, I bite down on his lower lip, hard enough that I feel blood coating my teeth, and when I run my tongue over them, there's the tangy taste of copper. *Well, if I'm covered in blood, it's only fair that he's bleeding too.*

He pulls back, and a resulting snarl is the only warning I get before he smashes his lips to mine again, assaulting me with a bruising force. I lose myself to wild abandon, blaming today's events for the crazy way I'm behaving as I attack him with equal enthusiasm. He practically tears my leather jacket from my body, nearly breaking the zip of my pants as he tries to rip them open.

He manages to push my jeans and panties down over my ass, but the tight material clings to my thighs, and he quickly gives up, deciding he's got them low enough. He spins me, so my chest is crushed against the door. I barely register the flare of pain in my ribs as he scrapes his teeth and bites his way down the side of my neck, the stings of pain only heightening the pleasure coursing through me as I groan aloud. The rushing of blood in my ears is so loud that I hardly hear the soft thud as his towel hits the floor. A throaty moan that sounds nothing like me escapes my lips as he pushes his hand between my legs, checking I'm ready before lining himself up behind me and slamming all the way in. The force sends me smacking into the door until I can plant my palms and adjust to his length. Not that he gives me much time to do any of that as he pulls back.

"Fuck," I hiss as my nails claw against the door.

Cain chuckles darkly from behind me, his warm breath tickling my neck. Moving more slowly, he thrusts into me, enabling me to properly feel what I couldn't before. A desperate cry escapes my lips as sensations wrack my body.

"It's called a magic cross," he growls low in my ear, "magic 'cause it can make women come in no time."

Fuck, if that isn't true. I'm already tipping over the edge. Now that he's demonstrated exactly how mindblowing the sex is going to be, he gets down to business, slipping his hands under my top and tugging down my bra so he can grab my tits. He squeezes them as he uses me for leverage to move harder and faster, his piercings only adding to the obvious talent he possesses.

I wish I could see his skin against mine, the contrast of his tattoos against my pale complexion, but he doesn't give me a chance to act on the thought as he slams back into me, causing me to cry out.

With my pants caught around my upper thighs, my movements are restricted. In this position, I'm dancing along a pain-pleasure tightrope as Cain's thick cock stretches my walls. All I can do is stand there and take every punishing thrust he delivers. I cry out at the delicious ache every time he hits that spot deep inside me, and as my pussy clenches down on him, he grabs the back of my head, fisting his hand in my hair and using the tight hold to turn my head to face him. He captures my lips with his as I go careening over the edge, screaming out my release into his mouth. A second later, I feel his seed hit my inner walls, scarcely comprehending the quiet voice of reason at the back of my head reminding me we just fucked without a condom. Nothing I can do about that now. That is future Sawyer's problem to deal with.

I'm still struggling to catch my breath when he pulls out of me, and I turn to sag against the door. The dull aches of my injuries begin to make themselves known as I watch him grab his trousers off the bench and pull them on, forgoing any underwear—*damn, something about knowing he's going commando is super hot*—and I catch a glint of one of the steel bars piercing the head of his cock before he tucks himself away and zips up his pants. The anger emanating from him seems to have abated somewhat, but I can still see the confusion and distrust in his eyes.

My inner thighs are damp with our combined releases, and I grimace both in disgust and pain as I pull up my panties, and they immediately dampen. *Ugh, gross. I need new panties, stat.* Once I've got my jeans buttoned again, I tuck the girls back into my bra and fix my top, and when I glance up, I notice him looking at me with an unreadable expression.

"What the fuck happened to you?" He gestures toward the tears in my clothes, apparently only now noticing the layer of dust and dirt covering my clothing.

"Nothing," I say dismissively, but he ignores me, taking a step toward me again. Now that he's not consumed by rage, he's picking up on all the small details he missed before, like the scrapes along my arms, and he's paying particular attention to the side of my head, where I hit the ground earlier. Self-consciously, I reach up to touch it, wincing at the sting of pain. I

297

can feel blood crusted around the wound, but my fingers come away dry, so it has obviously scabbed over.

"Doesn't look like nothing," the infuriating shithead notes. As I stand there, I can feel the adrenaline wearing off, my energy rapidly draining as my legs begin to feel shaky and unsupportive. Exhaustion hits me with the force of a wrecking ball, and I don't even have it in me to scowl at him. A pounding has started up behind my head, and all I want is to go home. I place my hand against the door, stabilizing myself as I bend to snatch my leather jacket off the floor, and without a backward glance, I pull open the door and step out onto the floor of the club.

The thudding bass of the music doesn't help, and nausea churns in my stomach as I push my way through the writhing mass of bodies, needing desperately to get outside for some fresh air before I puke all over some poor person. I ignore the curses and grumbles as I shove people out of my way, single-minded in my focus to get out of here. I'm not even sure what is wrong with me, but I know I've had enough of this day. I need to go home and sleep.

I stumble out into the night, placing my hands on my knees as I bend over and suck down lungfuls of cool, crisp air.

"Seriously, what the fuck is wrong with you?" His snarling tone grates on my nerves. I hadn't even realized he'd followed me outside. I spin to glower at him, but my stomach revolts at the sudden movement. *Oh, fuck no, shouldn't have done that.* I feel the rapid climb of vomit as it ascends my esophagus, and I end up bending over at the waist, pressing my hand against the brick wall of the gym as I puke my guts out.

"Jesus Christ," I hear Cain grumble, but I tune him out, swiping the back of my hand across my mouth, and feeling a little better, I throw on my leather jacket and fish my keys out of the pocket.

"Ehh, where the fuck do you think you're going?"

*Oh my god, can this asshole not take a fucking hint?!* "Go away," I gripe, not liking the feeble tone. There's no power behind those words, just weariness. Too tired to care, I go to move across the road toward my bike, but he reaches out to grab hold of my wrist, tugging me backward and spinning me to face him while his other hand steals the keys from my fingers before I can stop him.

"Hey," I snap irritably.

"There's no fucking way I'm letting you drive that beauty home and crash her." He gestures with his chin toward my bike. "Not when you're drunk, or high, or whatever the fuck you are. You can sleep it off here, and go home in the morning."

"It's a concussion," I mumble weakly.

It takes me far longer than it should to realize he's dragging me across the street toward the apartment complex. The spinning of my head makes it impossible to focus on anything around me, and the next thing I know, I'm standing in the doorway to a bedroom.

"I'm not sleeping in your bed," I huff. Although honestly, staring at the bed with its dark blue sheets, it looks so damn comfy. I just want to fall face-first onto it and pass the fuck out.

He snorts. "Like I'd fucking want you in my bed. Just 'cause we fucked, doesn't mean I don't still fucking hate you."

"Same," I agree with a shake of my head, but I quickly stop when the pounding starts up again. No longer giving a shit whose room this is, I stumble over to the bed and collapse onto it, spread eagle on my back as my eyes drift shut.

I listen out for the sound of the door clicking shut, knowing I won't be able to fully drop my shields until he's gone.

However, instead of the expected sound of the door closing as Cain fucks off, he moves further into the room. I crack open an eyelid, watching as he disappears into the bathroom, wondering what the fuck he's doing. A moment later he emerges with a box in his hands. He tosses it onto the bed beside me, and gives me a long, scrutinizing once over. "For your head."

Lifting my head, my gaze flicks down to the first aid kit before jumping back to his, surprised at the small act of kindness. With flat lips, and a furrow between his eyebrows, he stomps out of the room, finally leaving me alone, and I drop my head back to the sheets.

I don't even realize I've fallen asleep until I startle awake sometime later. Rubbing at the grit in my eyes, my head swims, and I still feel like shit as I push myself upright. Grabbing the first aid kid, I move to the bathroom. Rummaging through the vanity cabinet, I find a spare toothbrush, still in its packaging, and help myself to it and some toothpaste. I wash my face and inspect my injuries, noting the bruising forming along my ribs all down my left side, where I hit the ground.

Once I've cleaned myself up, I move back into the bedroom, spotting a chest of drawers and rifle through them in search of a t-shirt. Finding one that's suitable for sleeping in, I strip out of my clothes and climb in between the covers, moaning my pleasure as my eyes grow heavy once again.

SAWYER

*Strip Tease*

## *Chapter 19*

When I next awaken, light is streaming through the window. As I glance around the unfamiliar room, it takes me a second to remember how I ended up here, but as I clench my thighs, feeling the dull ache from the rough way Cain took me last night, the reality of what I did comes crashing down around me. *Fuck,* I can't believe I screwed that infuriating shithead. What the fuck was I thinking? Well, clearly, I wasn't right in the head last night. I definitely had a concussion, which is obviously to blame for my lack of judgment and reckless behavior.

I lie there for a second as I take stock of how I'm feeling. Definitely better than I did when I fell asleep. It crosses my mind that it was probably incredibly reckless of me to sleep at all if I had a head injury. Aren't you supposed to stay awake for like twenty-four hours or something? But fuck, I feel so much better for the rest.

I move to stretch out on the bed, but when I bump against a hard body, I freeze. *Eh, what the fuck? I know for a fact I fell asleep alone last night.* If that son of a bitch snuck in here while I was passed out, I'll fucking castrate him.

Slowly, I turn my head, only relaxing my posture when I find Oliver lying beside me, sound asleep. It takes a second for the penny to drop. *That asshole!* He put me in Oliver's room, knowing damn well he would be coming back here at some point during the night.

My eyes drift over the smooth lines of his face, noting the faint scruff of a five o'clock shadow dusting his jawline before I drop my gaze to his chest, tracing the hard edges of his pecs with my eyes. He's got two similar, yet obviously different tattoos on each one. Both of them have the initials RR in them— presumably for Reaper Rejects—but one is clearly old and poorly drawn, whereas the other is newer and more professional. I can't figure out why he would have two, though.

Storing the information away, I push the question to the back of my mind as my gaze drifts further south. He's not wearing a top, and with the sheet draped low over his hips, I have an unobstructed view of the carefully toned and built masterpiece that is Oliver's body. I spot another tattoo with scrawly writing that I can't make out, sitting low on his left hip, but other than that, the rest of his torso is soft, creamy skin.

Once I've looked my fill, I return my gaze to his face, wondering what I should do. I've never fallen asleep beside a guy before, so this is unchartered territory for me. Am I supposed to sneak out? Lie here awkwardly until he wakes up? Pretend to be asleep? It's made even more uncomfortable by the fact we didn't even have sex last night. It's one thing to fuck then fall asleep, but he just came home and found me lying in his bed. Like fucking Goldilocks. Considering how I turned him down when we last spoke, he might not even want me here, but he was just too polite to ask me to leave in the middle of the night.

Turning away from him, I go to slip out from beneath the covers when a hand clamps down on my hip, preventing me from getting up.

"Where do you think you're going?"

Oliver's voice is thick with sleep, giving it a deep, husky quality that does inappropriate things to my insides.

"Uhh, getting up?"

"Not yet," he mumbles sleepily. "Too early."

He tugs me back against him, burying his head in my hair and... sniffing me?

"I was hoping you'd change your mind."

I tense at his words, slowly turning my head to look over my shoulder at him.

"Change my mind about what?"

"Us," he answers, not lifting his head from where he's running his lips along my shoulder blade. "I mean, I thought you'd just send a text, but I like this much better."

His hand slips under my t-shirt, gliding up my side, making my brain glitch as I momentarily forget about what he's saying and get distracted by the goosebumps forming beneath his touch. I can feel his hard cock pressed between my ass cheeks, his morning wood making itself known, and oh man, would it be easy to melt against him.

"Oliver, I'm not here because I changed my mind," I tell him, struggling to keep my tone neutral so as not to give away how his soft caresses are doing naughty things to me.

I'm not even sure he heard me, as his fingers continue to trail over my hip and along the area across my ribs that I bruised yesterday. The skin is still tender and sore, and I tense beneath his touch, hissing out a pained exhale that stalls his movements.

He leans up on his elbow, a frown marring his features as he tugs the sheet down to expose my midriff, and he gently rolls me onto my back so he can push my top up further, giving him a perfect view of the mottled bruises. *Damn, they look even worse this morning.*

"What the—who did this to you?" His voice comes out harsh and demanding, and when I don't respond, he lifts his eyes from my abdomen to look at my face. He immediately spots the welt on the side of my head. I don't even need to touch it to know it's swollen. I can feel it pulsing with every movement of my left eye.

His fingers clasp my chin gently, turning my head so he can get a better look as dark storm clouds roll in across his face. His jaw ticks, his teeth clenched so tight I'm surprised he doesn't crack a tooth.

"It's nothing," I assure him. "I got caught up in that explosion yesterday at G&T."

His eyes are wide, his normally light blue irises clouded to a stormy gray. His expression is still set into a hard line, and it's the first time I've seen someone other than Luc look at me with such an intense level of concern.

"I'm fine," I assure him, sensing he needs to hear it. "Nothing that won't heal in a day or two."

I don't know what it is about Oliver, but this connection between us makes me want to behave in ways I normally wouldn't. Whenever he's around, my barriers begin to crumble, and I have to work at keeping them in place. As much as Cain seems to fortify my bitchy persona, Oliver manages to chip away at it, and the more time I spend with him, the more he's exposing the real me hidden underneath.

I'm not sure if it's the residual effects of the knock to my head, the physical exhaustion still wracking my body from yesterday, or if he's just finally wormed his way past my defenses, but I lower my armor, letting him see past the hardened exterior I carefully don before I leave my apartment every day.

He meets my gaze, the clouds parting in his eyes as he lowers his own walls. The air between us feels warm and sparked with electricity, making my breaths come in heaving pants. After an intense moment, he dips his head, his lips brushing over mine in a move that steals the last of my oxygen. My lips tingle at the brief contact, and I lift my head off the pillow, chasing after him when he pulls back. I think he meant for it to be a chaste kiss, but when our lips meet again, I slip my tongue into his mouth, sliding my hand into his hair and holding him to me. He hesitates for a second before deepening the kiss, meeting my exploration of his mouth with his own probing tongue.

He moves to settle between my thighs, careful to keep his weight off my side, and I hook my legs around his hips, grinding myself shamelessly against him. I couldn't bear the thought of sleeping in my damp panties all night, so I took them off when I got changed, and my bare pussy rubs over the soft cotton of his boxers, likely soaking the material as I use him to work myself into a frenzy.

"Fuck, Red," Oliver pants, tearing his lips away from mine. He plants kisses along my jaw until he reaches my ear, before tracing a scorching trail with his tongue down the column of my neck. "What is it about you? I can't get enough."

His hands push up my t-shirt, and I lift up enough for him to pull it off. Lowering his head, he runs his tongue around one peaked nipple before sucking it into his mouth, kneading my other breast with his hand. My back arches, and I moan as I grind harder against him, feeling the telltale tingles of an orgasm forming in my lower belly.

Releasing my nipple with a pop, he adorns my other breast with the same attention as his hand snakes between our bodies, effortlessly finding my clit and rubbing tight circles around it that have me crying out. Moving lower, he slides two fingers into my dripping cunt, moving them in sync to the way his thumb strokes across my over-sensitized bundle of nerves. The combination has me coming apart in no time, and I throw my head back as I come all over his fingers.

My pussy is still spasming when he pulls out, smirking cockily when I whimper at the loss of his fingers. Reaching into the bedside table, he retrieves a condom, quickly sheathing himself before he slides into me, filling me up.

"Fuck," he grunts out between gritted teeth. "I've thought about this tight little pussy every day. Feels even better than I remember." His words are strained, but so much passion burns in his eyes. They hold me captive as he starts to move, each thrust a pleasurable ache that pushes me higher. He never looks away from my face, and I'm not sure what's happening between us right now, but it feels big. Monumental and terrifying all at once.

"Fuck, Red. So. Fucking. Good." He penetrates each word with a thrust of his hips, and my fingers dig into his shoulders, leaving crescent moon indentations as I meet him thrust for thrust. Desperate, pleasure-filled moans tumble from between my lips as I descend into a world where nothing exists except Oliver and me, and whatever never-before reached pleasure he is quickly pushing me toward.

"Oliver," I gasp, right before my pussy spasms, and he swallows my cries with a blistering kiss as he reaches his own climax before collapsing onto the bed beside me and discarding his condom.

"Holy shit," he pants. "That was even better than last time."

A chuckle bursts out of me, even as my chest heaves, still trying to catch my breath. My ribs ache from the movement, but it's nowhere near enough to dampen the high I'm on right now because he's right, that was... something else.

After a moment, he gets up, moving to the bathroom to shower. When he's done, I jump in, and, having stolen a pair of Oliver's boxers as underwear for the day, I'm pulling on the last of my clothes from yesterday—ignoring the dirt and grime still covering them—when he approaches me. He's dressed in dark, distressed jeans, with combat boots and a tight, fitted top, and *holy fuck* does the ensemble look good on him. Tilting my head back so I can look up into his face, I catch the glimpses of a fire burning in his eyes. He watches me like a man possessed as he reaches out to slide a hand through my still damp hair, cupping the back of my head. His eyes bounce back and forth between mine, and I can't do anything but stand there and watch him.

"I meant what I said." His voice is a low growl, more reminiscent of Cain's. "I can't get enough of you. Whatever this is just feels *right*. You clearly feel it, too, if you sought me out."

I open my mouth to tell him otherwise, but the words stick in the back of my throat. Is that why I came here? Was I secretly seeking out Oliver in a moment of weakness? Fuck, I've got no idea.

My tongue darts out to wet my lower lip, and I swallow before saying in a strangled voice. "I need to talk to you and Cain." My words break the moment between us, and I watch as the fire of desire dies in Oliver's eyes, and he takes a step back, releasing me from his hold.

It takes him a second before he responds, and when he does, there's no hint of the emotion that was burning in his gaze a moment ago. "Sure. He's probably in his office."

I'm pretty sure I'm incapable of responding, not that I really have anything to say, so instead, I give him a sharp nod of my head and follow him out of the room. For the most part, Radiant Park is set up like a motel, with individual rooms accessible from the parking lot or walkways on the second floor. However, Oliver's room seems to be within the main building itself, and he leads me through hallways that I have no recollection of until we reach the main bar area at the front of the building. The smell of bacon hits me when we enter, and saliva floods my mouth as I bite back a groan.

I'm careful to maintain a respectable distance from Oliver as we slowly cross the room. He keeps getting stopped by men asking questions, but it allows me the opportunity to take in the other Reaper Reject members in their natural habitat. Many of them are young, younger than me, but just as many are older, with several sporting graying beards, making me think they must be in their fifties. I can see questions in their eyes as they watch me, their gazes bouncing between me and Oliver as they speculate.

I'm about to tell Oliver I'll meet him in Cain's office when he's done, but then Jon's voice cuts through the crowd. "Red!" he calls out as he enters the room carrying several plates. He sets them down at a table before making his way to me. "Come, sit. I'll get you breakfast."

He's acting like I didn't chew him out in front of his buddies the other day, and I decide if he wants to pretend it didn't happen, then that suits me.

"Oh no, that's not necessary—" I begin, but he ignores me, leading me toward the bar and looking at me expectantly until I sit on the barstool. The surprising thing is, I let him. I dunno what it is about the kid, but I kinda like him.

"Stay there," he orders with a friendly grin that has me chuckling as he races away through a set of double doors that I'm assuming leads to some sort of kitchen area.

He emerges a few seconds later with three plates, setting them all down on the bar. He places one in front of me, along with some cutlery, before sitting on the stool beside me and digging into his own plate.

After a moment, he catches me looking at him, grinning at me around a mouthful of sausage and egg. "It's good," he promises, pointing at my plate with his knife. Swallowing his mouthful, he continues, "Marcus is an awesome cook. He's been teaching most of us so that we can help out in the kitchen more."

I cut into my bacon, taking a small bite. *Damn, he's right. It's so friggin' good.* I shovel the rest of the food into me, absolutely starving, and as I'm finishing it off, I turn to him. "How did you"—I glance around the room at the other young members—"all of you, end up here?"

I know what Oliver said the other day about some compound training them to be killers, but it sounds like a far-fetched story, so I guess I want to hear it from Jon.

His face darkens over for a split second, then it's gone, and I almost wonder if I imagined it. "Cain saved us." That's all he says before he bites into his sausage, and I can tell he doesn't want to talk about it anymore. He definitely has me curious, though, as to how and why he thinks Cain saved them all. Is saving them so they can risk their lives fighting his war *truly* saving them? So many questions bounce around in my head, and I'm so distracted watching Jon that I jump when a hand touches my lower back.

I feel Oliver's breath along my neck as he chuckles softly, and Jon jumps to his feet, grabbing his now empty plate and cutlery and giving Oliver a nod as he rushes back to the kitchen. Taking the now vacant seat, Oliver pulls the third plate of food in front of him and starts eating. Once I've finished my own breakfast, I return to taking in the other members of his gang while I wait for him to finish.

"What conclusion have you come to?" he asks, drawing my attention back his way.

"What?"

"You've been eyeing up every guy in the room."

I turn in my chair to face him, scrutinizing him closely before I respond. "If you're not after territory and power, then I don't really understand what it is you want."

Oliver smiles softly, but there's pain behind it, telling of past suffering. With a tilt of his head toward the back corridor, he says, "Let's go to Cain's office. We can talk about it there."

Unsure but definitely curious, I follow him to Cain's office, finding the brooding asshat sitting behind the desk as he works away on a laptop. He looks up as we enter, his gaze zeroing straight in on me. I'm immediately assaulted with the memory of what it felt like to have him balls deep inside me last night, and even though it was some fucking fantastic sex, I should have never allowed it to happen. I can see it in the cruel curl of his lips, and I just *know* before he opens his mouth, that his words are going to cut.

He reaches across the desk for a small, brown paper bag and tosses it my way. "Take that. And I need to know if you have any diseases so I can get it taken care of."

My cheeks burn, and my teeth grate together as I open the bag, pulling out a medication box. My eyes scan the front of the packet, *Plan B*. That fucking asshole.

I snap my gaze to him, glowering. "Seriously?" I hiss. I chuck the damn thing at him. "I don't need that, I have an implant, you shithead."

"Ehh, what is going on right now?" Oliver asks, his gaze bouncing between Cain and me, his brows drawn together in confusion.

Cain latches onto the question, his grin broadening. It's bitter and cruel, and before he even opens his mouth, I know his words are intended to hurt. "Didn't she tell you? We fucked last night. Not sure I see what the fuss is about, though. She was just alright. Three stars at best."

*I'm going to fucking murder this bastard.*

I swear I see fucking red as I stare daggers into his skull. "What the fuck did you just say?" I snarl furiously, taking a menacing step toward him. "Seriously, fucking say that again."

"Whoa, hey," Oliver snaps, stepping between us. He pins me with an unreadable look, and I can't tell if he's pissed off at the revelation. Not that he would have any right to be—well, maybe he'd have a little justification since I slept with him this morning. *God, this is getting complicated.* "Is this what you needed to talk to us about?"

A half-hysterical laugh bursts out of me. "Hell no. I came to tell you both that the Reaper is willing to help you." I tap my finger against my lip and tilt my head to the side as if I'm thinking. "But now I'm not so sure getting caught up in whatever bullshit you're playing here is a wise idea."

You could hear a pin drop as both Oliver and Cain gape at me.

"He's going to help us?" Oliver asks.

I snort. "Not anymore."

I'm lying. Mostly. Maybe. I didn't even get to completely make up my mind, but the thought of dangling the possibility in front of Cain after the shit he just pulled was just too good to pass up. Although, now that I've said the words aloud, maybe it's not such a crazy idea.

Ha, no, it's definitely fucking insane. But maybe it's something that I need to be a part of. Perhaps it's time that I step out of the shadows and show the overlords of this city what I'm truly capable of. I really *really* don't want to work with Cain, but I also don't want to find my brother dead in the street because his death was a necessary casualty in whatever fucked up game the Antonellis are playing or any other fucking street gang who thinks they can do whatever the hell they want and get away with it. I'm fucking sick of it and, so help me god, if Cain can help change things around here, then I guess I'm willing to fucking work with him.

That doesn't mean I can't make him suffer first, though.

Oliver turns his head to sear Cain with a stern look, and I can see some wordless discussion going on between them. Cain's jaw gets tighter with every passing second, and I can only imagine the silent conversation is not going his way.

"She could be fucking lying," he eventually snaps out. "We don't even know if she knows the Reaper."

I throw my hands up in exasperation. It's like dealing with a bunch of children. "Are you kidding me?!" I snap. "I *am* the fucking Reaper."

There's another moment of stunned silence as that information sinks into their brains. A myriad of emotions

314

crosses their faces, each of them trying to put the puzzle pieces together.

After a minute, Cain snorts and shakes his head, quirking a brow at Oliver. "The bitch is fucking delusional!"

"Rude much," I snark, making his intense, green gaze snap to mine. "I'm standing right here, I can fucking hear you."

"Prove it," Cain dares me, his voice dripping with that haughty arrogance that tells me he's so fucking confident that I'm bullshitting them.

I return his arrogant stare with a confident one of my own. "You want me to carve a pretty little R in your abdomen? Or maybe you'd rather I slit your throat?"

His eyes narrow at that casual threat, and I can see the muscle working in the back of his jaw. "I'd love to see you fucking try," he hisses.

I move to take a menacing step toward him, although I've got no idea what I'm going to do. Despite my fingers itching to throw a blade at his fucking head, most of my skill set lies in catching my targets unaware. I rely heavily on my targets being high, inebriated, or horny when I make my move. I can hold my own in a fight, but I couldn't take on someone like Cain. I work best when I catch people by surprise. Besides, I don't actually have a blade on me. The gun I had underneath my jacket when I met Enzo must have gotten dislodged in the explosion yesterday. I hadn't even realized until this morning when I was looking for it—which shows just how fucked in the head I was last night.

Oliver moves between us again, preventing me from getting any closer to Cain. I don't know if he's acting to protect Cain or if he's just trying to stop us from gouging each other's eyes out, but whatever. I've had enough of this shit.

I came here to offer my help. The help they've been fucking hounding me for. If Cain doesn't want to accept that because I've got a vagina instead of a dick between my legs, then that's his loss.

"You know what." I hold my hands up in front of me. "I'm done with this shit." Ignoring Cain's hateful glare, I focus on Oliver. "You know where to find me if he ever pulls his head out of his ass."

Casting a quick glance across the desk, I notice the keys to my bike and hastily snatch them up, wanting to get the fuck out of here. Turning, I pull open the door and glance back over my shoulder, making sure to raise my voice loud enough to be heard all the way down the hall, "By the way, I hope I did give you an STD, and it makes your dick blister and blacken before it falls off." Grinning, I slam the door closed in Cain's furious face, and with a pep in my step, I saunter down the hall through the now-silent crowd of Reject members, and out the front door.

## Chapter 20

I bite my lip to hold back my snort as the door swings shut behind Red. *Pretty sure Cain won't find the same humor in her departing statement as I did.* He deserves it, though, for being such an ass to her. Cain does naturally have a barbed attitude, one that has gotten a lot sharper since we were kids. Understandably, he doesn't trust anyone outside of the family he's created in the Rejects, but he's being particularly dickish to Red, and I can't figure out why.

His words from when she walked in, about how they fucked, come to mind. Surprisingly, I don't feel any jealousy at that notion. Maybe it's because she slept in *my* bed, and we had our own intimate moment this morning. Or the fact that, even after whatever happened between them yesterday, they still glower at each other with such undisguised hatred.

"Fucking bitch," he grumbles under his breath, leaning down to open the bottom drawer of his desk and lifting out the bottle of whiskey he stores there, along with two tumblers. He pours a measure into them both and pushes one across the table toward me.

With a sigh, I sit down in a chair on the opposite side of his desk, but I don't reach out to touch the glass he poured me. Unlike the effect Red seems to have on him, which has him downing his drink in one go, she doesn't push me toward alcohol at ten o'clock in the morning.

"Do you think she really is the Reaper?" I ask, thinking aloud.

"Hell no," Cain scoffs, setting his now empty glass on the table. "There's no way. She's playing us."

"Why would she do that?"

His brows draw together, "How the fuck would I know? She's clearly not right in the head."

I manage to hold back the natural instinct to roll my eyes. He's letting his anger toward her cloud his thinking. As far as I can tell, she has no reason to lie. All this time, she's just wanted us to leave her alone, and now that she finally got what she wanted, she shows up here offering to help? Something must have changed her mind. I recall the scratches and bruises on her arms from yesterday. I'd heard G&T had been targeted by the Antonellis. News like that spreads quickly. They rarely leave their part of the city to bother us, but when they do, they like to leave carnage in their wake, ensuring we never forget just how powerful they are. They want us to know that, if they wanted, they could destroy us with a flick of their wrists. Of course, they don't just target us randomly. The owners of G&T must have done something to get on the Antonellis' radar. And the innocent patrons that just so happened to stop by at the exact time of the Antonellis' strike are just the necessary casualties of war. It seems Red was one of those casualties. She's seriously fucking lucky, and if she knew the Antonellis were behind the attack—which she apparently does—then it would explain her showing up here.

But hearing her say she's the Reaper? Holy crap, that's a shock. Not because she's a woman, it's just that we'd always assumed it was a man. Everyone does. Men are more likely to engage in violence than women, and it just seemed so much more likely that a man was going after gang members.

Although, now that I think about it, a woman makes sense too. It would explain how most of the men she's killed are found without defensive wounds. Most men wouldn't let someone they don't know or trust get that close to them... but a woman? Never mind a woman like Red, with all her feminine wiles. Those suckers wouldn't have stood a chance.

As Cain reaches across the desk to snatch up my abandoned drink for himself, I realize he's not in the mind frame to talk about it today. He won't be reciprocating anything I have to say in favor of Red. So instead, I ask, "So, what happened last night?"

He frowns into his glass, swirling the amber-colored liquid for a moment before he knocks his head back and downs it in one. "I did it for you," he bites out, his words catching me by surprise.

"You fucked her for my benefit?" I ask in a slow, disbelieving voice.

He scowls at me. "You said it yourself that you were getting too attached." He waves toward the now-closed office

321

door. "But she clearly doesn't give a shit about you if she so easily climbed aboard my dick last night."

I frown as I think over what he's saying. When I first found Red in my bed, I thought she'd come here for me, but now I'm beginning to realize that's not quite the case. Even so, there was something about her this morning that was different. She wasn't as hostile as she has been ever since she found out who I am. For the first time, she dropped her guard and let me just see *her*. I could see how hard it was for her to do that, and yet she did it... for me.

"Well, what a sacrifice you made, brother," I retort dryly. The smug smirk that plays along his lips before he smothers it is telling enough. He can tell himself he did it for me all he damn well wants, but he wanted to fuck her.

I snort out a laugh as realization dawns—Red's under his skin. "You're a fucking idiot." The smirk drops off his face as he glowers at me. "You're fooling yourself if you think you fucked her for my benefit."

"Seriously?" He gapes at me with wide eyes. "It doesn't bother you?"

"No," I admit in all honesty. "We're not in a relationship, she doesn't owe me anything. Hell, she'll barely talk to me. She's free to fuck whoever she wants." An uncomfortable weight shifts on my chest, not liking the sound of that. "Uh, well, you... she's free to fuck you." It bothered me a hell of a lot more when I thought she was at the Satan's clubhouse to fuck Python. I have to admit, knowing she was there to kill him instead sits much better with me.

Cain just looks at me like I've gone completely fucking insane, and maybe I have. But sharing a girl isn't a completely new concept to me. I have several friends involved in such relationships. Not that that's what I'm suggesting. Based on the confounded look on Cain's face, it's not something he would even consider—at least, not with Red. It just maybe explains why I'm so unbothered by the fact he slept with the girl I've been chasing after relentlessly.

"So, what happened last night?" I ask again. I can't deny I'm curious to know how he convinced himself fucking her would help me, but instead he surprises me. His shoulders drop at my question, and he leans back in his chair, tilting his head toward the ceiling as he lets out a frustrated groan.

Before he responds, he pours himself another hefty measure of whiskey, knocking it back before he focuses on me again.

"Fuck if I know," he grumbles, banging the bottom of the glass against the desktop. "She caught me off-guard, just after a fight. The adrenaline was still racing through my system... and suddenly she was just there, scowling at me with those blue eyes that seem to be glowing with fury." He shrugs casually, but the tight lines on his face give away how bothered he actually is by his actions. "She was the ideal outlet for the last of the energy buzzing under my skin. If she didn't wanna get fucked, she shouldn't have followed me back there."

His expression is pinched, and he hasn't lifted his gaze from the table as he most likely replays the events of last night in his head. I know Cain well enough to know that loss of control won't sit well with him. He can make out that it was deliberate all he wants, but I can see the truth in his eyes. The fact he had sex with her without a condom is telling enough of his lack of control.

Interesting. Not only might Red be the secret weapon we've been looking for, but she also might be Cain's kryptonite. God knows he could do with having his world shaken up a little. He's used to being the leader; the one calling all the shots, and ever since Evie was taken, he hasn't let himself give a shit about anyone else. His walls are higher than even Red's, and reinforced with steel and concrete. Evie was always the one who was able to get through to him when he withdrew into himself and pushed everyone else away. Without her around, there hasn't been anyone to pull him out of the darkness. Red might drive him nuts, but she also challenges him in a way that only Evie did. Who knows, perhaps she could be a good thing for him... or one of them will end up killing the other.

***

Cain may have written off Red and the Reaper, but I'm not giving up on her just yet. She came offering her help once, and I'm hopeful I can convince her to do so again. The only thing she truly cares about is Luc, and I can only imagine the anxiety it causes her, worrying about what might happen to him when he's out and about in Black Creek. But what if she didn't have to worry about that? We could offer him protection, ensuring a few of the kids are with him whenever he's out. But better than that, we might be able to offer him a future that's not rife with gang violence. Cain's ultimate aim is to seize control of the whole city once the Antonellis have been taken care of. If he doesn't, someone else will. Most likely the Grim Bastards, and other than the Antonellis, Grim is the last one we want taking control. He's a sadistic fuck in his own right. In fact, he's next on our list— after the Antonellis. Even so, let's deal with one megalomaniac at a time.

It's been a week since Red stormed out of Radiant Park, leaving Cain in a piss poor mood. A week of waiting for her to make her move. I knew she wasn't going to come back and offer her help again. She's got too much pride for that, but I've been waiting patiently for her to go after her next victim. I believe her when she says she's the Reaper, but the only way Cain will, is if I can provide proof. Besides, there's no point denying I'm dying to see her in action. The infamous Reaper. Just the thought of it has my foot pushing down on the accelerator as I follow the dot on my map across town.

I got Jon to put a tracking device on her bike for this very occasion, and I've been keeping an eye on it ever since, waiting for her to take it out for a spin. My phone went off with an alert that she was on the move fifteen minutes ago, and I immediately grabbed my keys and got in the car.

It's just past eleven at night, and even though it's late, I pass plenty of people on the street, walking down the sidewalk, ducking into bars, huddled in doorways, as I follow the blue dot on my map toward the city limits. Soon, the tall buildings fade away to suburban streets as I approach the outskirts of the city. Looking out the windshield at the ramshackle houses, I can't help but wonder what business Red has out here. Half of the homes look derelict and vacant, covered in graffiti with smashed in windows where vagrants have broken in, most likely to do drugs or to have a roof over their head for a night or two.

Checking the map app on my phone, I notice Red's bike has stopped in the clearing just up ahead and, slowing down, I pull up to the curb outside an abandoned house, squinting down the street to see if I can spot her through the darkness. Unable to make anything out, I grab my phone from the holder and make sure my gun is tucked in the waistband of my jeans before climbing out of the car.

The cool night air blows around me as I quietly close the car door, peering left and right down the street to make sure I'm alone. I've never been to this neighborhood before and honestly I'm not even sure whose territory I'm in right now. Probably some no-name gang who hasn't made enough noise to feature on the Reject's radar.

Satisfied that I'm alone, I head down the sidewalk at a brisk pace toward the clearing. Just as I'm passing the last house, the faint whisper of voices reaches my ears, and I slow down, lowering myself to a crouch so I can remain hidden as I peek around the side of the building.

Across the road, the avenue opens up into a reasonably sized lawn area that's overgrown with weeds and looking half dead. In the center is a children's playground, containing rusted equipment that most likely hasn't been used in years. I can just make out a swing set, with the seats missing, leaving dangling chains that jingle in the breeze, and standing in front of it is Red and some dude I don't recognize.

He tries to grab her, but she easily sidesteps him, kicking her leg out to connect with the back of his knee in a move that sends him to the ground with a cry of pain. He whips his head toward her and snarls something I can't make out from here.

Frowning, I keep low as I cross the street, ducking behind a burnt-out car. I don't want to alert Red to my presence and end up distracting her. Remaining in a crouch, I angle myself, so the action camera attached to my chest has a clear shot of what's going on. It would probably be enough for me to just tell Cain I saw her with my own eyes, but I want him to see it for himself. Red's not just any woman. She's fierce and defiant. She's not afraid to stand up for what she wants, and I'm pretty sure I've only scratched the surface of the intricate paradox that is this mystifying woman.

I watch as she barks out a laugh at whatever the dude said, sneering at him like he's dog shit on her boots. He climbs to his feet, a look of thunder on his face, but before he can turn to face her, she wraps one of the chains from the swing set

326

around his neck, yanking hard on it, so he's forced backward, his back arching to an uncomfortable point.

He claws at the chains around his throat as he struggles to remain on his feet, but Red easily keeps a hold of the other end, only pulling tighter on it the more he fights. She's saying something to him in a low voice that I can't hear, but as his lips start to turn blue, I'm pretty sure he's not listening to a word she's saying.

His clawing becomes more frantic as he reaches desperately for Red. His nails dig into her leather jacket, but she manages to shake him off, shifting to stand slightly behind him, so she's out of reach of his flailing hands. As he runs out of air, his legs give way beneath him, only resulting in the chains digging more painfully into his neck. A deathlike gurgle bubbles out of his mouth as his whole body starts to convulse, his hands falling to his sides as the last of his life drains out of him.

With a final, full-body jerk, he falls still, his body going slack. Red watches him closely for another long moment before finally loosening her hold on the chain. The links tap together, the metallic noise ringing out across the otherwise silent clearing as she unwraps it from around his throat, and with a soft thud, his body drops to the ground, lifeless.

Standing over it, she looks down at him with an impassive expression, like she isn't the reason he's dead. But then, she's done this countless times before, so why would she look bothered by what she just did.

"You can come out now."

She's still staring at the dead guy, but after a second, she turns to look in my direction. *Fucking hell, how did she know I was here?*

Not seeing any point in continuing to hide, I stand and step out from behind the car, striding toward her. She never takes her eyes off me, and her inscrutable expression makes it impossible to determine how she's feeling about my being here. As I get closer, I can make out the hard lines around her lips, the cold glint in her eye. She almost looks like a different person. Nothing like the seductive vixen I met that night in Toxic, or the fiery redhead who shows up at the clubhouse and goes toe-to-toe with Cain without blinking an eye.

It's almost like Red has stripped herself of everything that makes her *her*. Like she's an empty vessel, void of thoughts and feelings, focused solely on the task in front of her. It's disorienting, like she's here, but at the same time, she's not.

When I'm standing over the body, I tear my gaze away from her stony one to glance down at him, noting the mottled bruising around his neck.

"Who was he?"

"The result of spunk that should have died in a condom."

With a final sneer, she lifts a narrow, five-inch blade out of her jacket pocket and crouches down beside him. With professional movements, she flicks up his top and begins to cut through his skin in a clinical manner, slicing from the top right of his abdomen down to just above his pubic bone before she carves across the underside of his ribs until an *R* is inscribed into his blood-smeared skin.

"Why the Reaper?" I ask as she wipes the blood off his abdomen, as if checking her handiwork before she wipes the blade clean on his jeans and gets to her feet. She fixes me with an apathetic look.

"You're the ones that started calling me that."

My brows pull together as I glance back down at the guy's chest. "Then what's the R about?"

She shrugs, sheathing the blade before tucking it back in her pocket. "It can be whatever the fuck you want it to be.

Reaper, Red, Reprobate, Rapist, Repugnant shitstain. It really makes no difference to me." She waves her hand toward the dead man. "I use it on my gang-related kills, but they're all the same abusive assholes who deserve the end they get."

There's a lot to unpack in that one sentence, but before I can figure out what question I want to ask first, she speaks again.

"So, why did you follow me all the way out here?"

"I want you to reconsider."

Scoffing, she shakes her head and begins to walk away from me. I cast a final glance at the lifeless dude at my feet—*guess we're just leaving him here*—before I rush after her.

"Why should I?" she asks when I catch up. "I'll be putting not only myself but Luc at risk, so what's in it for me?"

"We can protect you both," I blurt out instantly.

"Yeah?" she taunts. "How the fuck are you going to do that when the Antonellis have killed you all?"

I'm beginning to get frustrated, and I pull on her arm, yanking her to a stop. "Well, maybe they won't slaughter us if we have your help."

Her lips purse as her brows knit together. A frown tugs at the corner of her plump lips as she glances down at the camera attached to my chest that's still recording. She gives it the middle finger before lifting her head to meet my gaze, quirking a brow. "I take it Cain isn't exactly on board with this plan."

"He will be... when I've spoken to him."

"You mean when you've shown him proof... because my word apparently means jack shit to that asshole."

"That's not it," I begin, but she waves off whatever excuse I was going to make on Cain's behalf. It's not like it's my fucking job to clean up his fuck-ups anyway.

329

"Why don't you go show Cain your little video before you try talking me into the job."

Sighing, I run my hand through my hair before reaching down to turn off the camera so the two of us can talk in private.

"Look," I begin, stepping in closer to her. I'm itching to reach out and touch her, but the hard lines on her face and the tense way she's holding herself say she wouldn't appreciate that right now. "I know now why you showed up at the complex after what happened at G&T. I know you're sick of being ground into the dirt beneath the heels of arrogant assholes; that you want more for yourself than being a stripper. But most of all, you want a better life for Luc."

Her lips pinch together, but I can see the hopeful sheen in her eyes. It only lasts a split second before she covers it with that tough exterior she wears like armor. "And you think you're the ones to change things in Black Creek?" Her question is dripping with cynicism, but I see it for what it truly is—a front. Something she clings to because the thought of letting herself hope for something only to be disappointed is too much.

Lifting my hand, I prop a finger under her chin, slowly lifting it until her gaze meets mine. "You know we are."

## Chapter 21

"That'll be Jon. Can you grab it?" Luc calls out when there's a knock on the apartment door.

Biting back my grumble of complaint, I move to open it. I'm
still not happy about the fact Luc is hanging out with the Reject kids again, but at least this time, he told me where he was going.

"Red!" Jon grins when I answer the door. Despite my
unease about letting Luc hang out with them, I have to admit

that I'm warming up to the kid, and in all honesty, if he wasn't a member of the Rejects, I'd think he was a great friend for Luc.

"How are ya doing, Jon?" I ask, moving aside so he can step into the apartment. I know I need to make more of an effort with him, not just for Luc's sake. If I am—and that's a big fucking if—going to take on this job with the Rejects, then I'm going to be spending more time than I'd like with them. The only way I'm going to feel comfortable with that is if I get to know them.

"I'm good. Real good. Cain just told me this morning I can get into the ring next week for my first fight."

He looks so goddamn happy about that, and I can't for the life of me understand why the thought of getting your face pummeled would be exciting.

"Congratulations?"

His grin brightens. "You'll come watch, yeah?"

"Ehh," I hesitate, not entirely sure I want to watch him get beat up on. I've been paying more attention to the whispers on the street, and apparently, Cain's men are unbeatable. More specifically, the kids are unbeatable—every single one of them. So I can only assume that applies to Jon too. "Pleaseeee," he begs, fluttering his lashes like an idiot.

I snort out a laugh and shove him lightly in the shoulder. "Fine," I relent. "I'll come to watch you. But if I put money on you, you better fucking win."

The grin on his face gains a cocky-as-fuck air. "You can bet your ass I'll win, baby."

I roll my eyes at his antics as Luc emerges from his room. His gaze darts anxiously between Jon and me, as if he was expecting me to have chewed Jon's head off by now.

"Hey, man," he greets Jon. "You good to go?"

Jon gives him a chin lift in greeting, saying, "Sure," before looking back at me. "Cain asked me to bring you, too."

Of course, the fucking asshole did. He couldn't have just asked me to come over himself. It's been over a week since Oliver followed me to the edge of the city and watched me murder one of Bedlam's men in cold blood. In all honesty, I've been expecting the summons for days now, although that doesn't mean hearing the actual demand doesn't grate on my fucking nerves.

"I'm in the middle of something, but I'll swing by this afternoon."

Jon grimaces, and before he even has to say it, I know that's not an option. "Sorry, Red. He gave me strict instructions."

I'm sure he did, and when the dipshit king gives a decree, it *must* be obeyed.

Pursing my lips, I huff out a breath before growling, "Fine, give me a sec."

I take my sweet time doing my make-up, ensuring I've got the whole smokey-eye effect just right and that my lips pop with the bright red lipstick before I change into dark skinny jeans and a band tee, and I finish the look off with my thigh-high boots. Reaching under my mattress to retrieve my blades, I tuck them into the slit along the top. Just before I leave the room, I grab my purse, ensuring my small Glock 43 is inside it. I don't expect to need either the knives or the gun, but as far as I'm concerned, Cain has called a meeting with the Reaper, so the Reaper is who he'll get.

I plaster a bright smile to my face as I step out into the living room, finding both boys glued to the TV.

"Ready."

Jon barely spares me a passing glance as he gets to his feet, but Luc gives me a quizzical look that makes my insides twist uneasily. I've been telling him I've been liaising with Cain and the Rejects regarding issues to do with Strip Tease, but I

335

think he's beginning to see through that bald-faced lie. Thankfully he doesn't say anything, though. Instead, he follows Jon to the door while I grab the house keys and lock up, and the three of us head down to the street.

There's a large SUV parked at the curb, similar to the one Oliver was driving when he dropped Luc home several weeks ago, and the lights flash as Jon taps the key fob, gesturing for us to get in.

Luc doesn't bat an eye as he slips into the front passenger seat, and I guess why should he, he's been in the car before, but I hesitate for a second before pulling on the handle and climbing into the back. I notice Jon glance up at me through the rearview mirror, like he half expected me to put up a fight before Luc engages him in conversation, and the two of them talk about some computer game I've never heard of as we peel down the street.

I drown out their conversation, instead focusing on steadying my breathing and getting into the headspace of the Reaper. It's difficult because, even though I hate Cain, he's not an abusive shitstain who deserves to die. It makes it hard to grasp that cold, detached part of me that revels in the blood and violence. Nevertheless this meeting I'm walking into with Cain is purely business. There's no room for anger. There's no space for emotions. The last time I approached them about this job, I was a fucking fountain of emotion, pissing anger and resentment everywhere. That led me to fucking Cain in a changing room and having sex with Oliver mere hours later. That can't happen again. If there's to be a business relationship between us, then there can't be a sexual one. It's as simple as that.

Not that I want to have sex with Cain again. That was a momentary lapse of judgment brought about by said leaking of emotions and a nasty concussion.

Now Oliver, well, that's an entirely different matter. The jolt of excitement shooting through me at the mere mention of his name is telling enough of how easily I'd climb back into bed with him. But if I'm going to team up with the Rejects to take down the entire Antonelli syndicate, then that needs to be the focus—the *entire* focus. Fuck knows it's a near-impossible job as it is, nevermind throwing some sort of sexual or emotional relationship into the mix. That would be a guaranteed recipe for failure.

I'm startled out of my thoughts as the car comes to a stop, and I blink as I look out the passenger window at the front entrance to Radiant Park. *Damn, I hadn't even noticed we'd made it across town already.* I follow Luc and Jon out of the car, but as they move toward the building rather than the gym across the street, I call out, "Uh, where are you two going?" It hadn't crossed my mind that they would be going into the complex—the heart of the Rejects, where no doubt shady shit is going down. They were setting the front lobby up as a goddamn bar last time I was here. There could be hookers or anything right behind that door.

Luc rolls his eyes, frowning at me as he grits out, "Sawyer," in a low voice.

My own eyes narrow on him, as I see Jon physically perk up. His lips part in a silent O, and I shift my gaze to him, pinning him with a grave glare—a silent threat that he should casually ignore what he just heard. Very few people know my real name. Not because of any particular reason, it just kinda happened that way. When Mom died, and we started living on the streets, I had to become a different person—someone tougher—but I didn't want to lose *me*. The person I had to pretend to be when I was pickpocketing, fighting over scraps of food, or giving blow jobs for cash, wasn't the person I wanted to be when I was with Luc. I didn't want him to see me as all sharp edges and emotionally unavailable, so I found it easier to develop a different persona when dealing with people on the street while at the same time keeping the softer parts of myself just for Luc. It was like our little secret. Sheryl and Grace are the only other people who know my actual name. To everyone else, I'm Red. The red-haired bitch who'll slice you in half with a death glare and won't hesitate to put you on your knees if you dare go near what's hers.

"Relax, *Red*," Jon says with a smirk, earning himself another glare. "We're just going to play some video games. We have a room down the back. There won't be any drugs or alcohol, or guns, or hookers."

I purse my lips, still not liking any of this. "Fine, you can go."

"It's not like I was asking for your permission, but thanks," Luc drawls, his attitude making my eyebrows climb up my forehead. *The fucking nerve of him!*

Before I can say something that will no doubt only escalate things, Jon drags him off across the parking lot, and with a resigned sigh, I follow after them.

I follow them through the front bar area, which is surprisingly empty—although it is only early afternoon—and into the hallway leading toward the rear of the building. When I pause outside Cain's office, I watch them for a second until they disappear around a corner at the end of the hall before putting all thoughts of Luc to the back of my mind. I take a moment to empty my head of all thoughts and feelings, descending into the cool calm of the Reaper. When I'm confident my expression says, *you don't want to mess with me*, I turn the door handle and step into the office.

I hesitate with my hand still on the handle as I glance around the room, surprised not to sense Cain's suffocating presence immediately. Instead, Oliver is reclining in the chair behind the desk, with his fingers hovering over a laptop in front of him as he looks right at me, a small smile lifting his lips.

"He's in the gym," he explains before I can ask. "Figured it was in everyone's best interest if he burnt off some of that anger he constantly has."

I give a slow nod of my head. "Good to know it's not just me he can't stand."

Oliver barks out a soft chuckle. "Oh, you definitely have a way of getting under his skin."

I still haven't moved from the doorway, and honestly, I'm not sure how to behave around him. He's made it clear he wants something more with me, but I'm not sure I can offer him that.

"Did you show him the recording?" I ask, wanting to understand the situation better before getting any closer to him, and my rising hormones start messing with my logic.

Oliver's gaze drops to take in my outfit before returning to my face, lingering there as he grows serious. "I did." He lifts his hands off the laptop, interlocking them and resting them on his lap as he relaxes back in his chair. "What do you know about the Antonellis?"

It's a fair question, but one that surprises me all the same. "Ehh, not much. Our paths haven't really crossed."

He nods and ponders over something for a moment before he leans forward, placing his forearms on the desk as he sears me with an intense look. "When we were thirteen, the four of us—Cain and I, our friend, Beck, and Cain's sister—were hanging out on the front porch when they tore down our street, firing off bullets. They stormed their way onto Cain's property and kidnapped his sister." My eyes widen in surprise. I figured they had to have done something to invoke Cain's wrath, but *Jesus*, I wasn't expecting that. "He never saw her again."

I swallow around the emotion clogging my throat. "Why are you telling me this?" I ask in a quiet voice. I highly doubt Cain wants me knowing such personal shit about him.

"Because you need to understand what this is all about. We're not after Antonelli territory; we don't want their money. This is cold, hard vengeance. Cain has dedicated his entire life to this war, and nothing will stand in his way."

All the words he's not saying rattle around in my head— this is why Cain acts the way he does, why he was so hellbent on finding the Reaper. It certainly explains the weird moment we shared at Strip Tease that night he was drunk. Most importantly, Oliver's telling me that, whether or not I help them, Cain's going to avenge his sister. Nothing will stop his crusade. Whether I like it or not, there's a war coming, and I can either sit on the sidelines and watch, or I can finally stand up and fight for this town.

"What about you?" I ask. "Why are you here?"

His lips flatten, and I can tell he doesn't want to share that personal detail with me. "Because that's what family does for one another."

It's a non-answer at best, but Oliver's reasons for being here are none of my business.

Before either of us can say anything else, I hear heavy footsteps behind me in the hall and turn as Cain's ominous presence fills the doorway.

"Oh goodie, you came," he drawls, his voice dripping with sarcasm.

I have to bite back my retort, mentally reminding myself of what Oliver just disclosed, so I don't chew the asshole's head off. Glowering at him, I step aside so he can move into the room, and he pushes the door shut behind him. With the three of us packed into the small space, I begin to feel uncomfortably

340

claustrophobic—not that I'd let on to either of them how on edge I am. I'm the goddamn motherfucking Reaper. I'm a badass bitch. I'm not going to let some moody manchild get the better of me.

"Is that really how you want to speak to someone whose help you need?" I retort snidely.

"Will the two of you just park it for five minutes so we can all get on the same page?" Oliver interrupts before Cain can follow through on whatever violent thoughts I'm sure are flashing through his head right about now.

With a shrug, I turn away from Cain, dismissing him. "Sure. I know *I'm* capable of acting like an adult."

A low growl comes from behind me, but Oliver throws him a warning look before he can voice whatever scathing reply he had in mind. Instead, I hear him grumble something incoherent under his breath as I focus my attention on Oliver.

He rolls his eyes as he stands up from behind the desk and moves around it. Crossing his arms over his chest, he looks between Cain and me. "There's no reason we can't work together," he begins, acting as mediator. "Overthrowing the Antonellis would benefit us all."

"What happens when the Antonellis are destroyed? Who gets their territory?" I question.

"We do," Cain says with all the arrogance of someone who's used to being in charge.

Before I can snark back that I'm not entirely sure that's better than the Antonellis—although I don't know if I really believe that any more—Oliver huffs out a frustrated breath.

"The plan is that, eventually, no one will be in charge of Black Creek."

His words gain my attention, and I lift my head to meet his gaze. "You mean no gangs?"

"Yup."

341

I stand there shocked for a moment as I try to picture that reality before my eyes narrow and a crease lines my forehead. "Is that even possible?"

Lifting his arm, Oliver runs his hand along the back of his head. "Honestly, I'm not sure, but it's worth a try, right? The people of Black Creek deserve to live their lives without the fear of retribution if they step even a toe out of line."

*Huh, their plan is so much grander than just a vendetta.* It's actually a noble goal, there's just one problem... "What about the Grim Bastards?"

"Uhh, yeah," Oliver starts with a grimace. "We're going to take them down, too."

I'm completely fucking stunned, unable to do anything but blink at him for a moment as I process that information. Eventually, though, a scoff bursts free and I shake my head in disbelief.

"Of course, you are because why go after one criminal conglomerate when you can go after two."

"So you're in?" Cain's voice is unnaturally soft, almost as though he's nervous to hear my answer. I meet Oliver's gaze, seeing the determination burning within his eyes before I turn to face Cain. He's wearing his usual stoic expression, but that same resolve is smoldering in his green depths.

With a roll of my eyes, I sigh. "Fuck it, yeah, I'm in. Black Creek is our city, and it's about time they realized that." I let the resolute energy wafting off them soak into my skin, bolstering me as I lift my chin. "Let's rain down absolute fucking mayhem."

## Epilogue

I rewind the tape again, watching for the millionth time as the brunette runs across the room before she crashes into me. No matter how many times I watch it, though, I can't put my finger on what it is about her. There's just this flicker of *something* at the back of my mind. This niggle that I know her from somewhere... but where? I definitely don't recognize her from the club. That night I'd just assumed she was new. I rarely have anything to do with our sex clubs, but I'd stopped by to look into the accounts. Someone's been skimming off the top of our profits, and it's my job to find out who, and then deal with them... permanently.

Of course, when I returned the next day, no one seemed to know who she was. Is it a coincidence that she just so happened to be in the club the same night one of our most popular clients dies? I think not, and it only adds to the intrigue surrounding her

If anyone suspected her of having killed one of our top clients, she'd already be added to my hit list, but no one but me suspects foul play. As far as everyone else is concerned, Chad died of natural causes.

I focus back on the recording just as I take off down the hall toward the dead man, and after a moment's hesitation, where the brunette watches me, she rushes out of the club and into the night. I've already checked the outdoor security cameras, and none of them picked her up. It's like she just disappeared. Blown away by the wind as soon as she stepped outside the club.

Once I reach the end of the tape, I skip it back to the beginning and play it again. Every time I get a moment alone, I watch this damn recording, trying to figure out what it is about her. Maybe my fascination is just from the fact she managed to sneak into Belle Donne and kill someone right under our noses—it speaks volumes to the holes in our security—but I feel like it's more than that.

I hear the door to my home office open behind me, and I don't even need to look over my shoulder to know it's Lor. He's the only one who has access to my house. The only one in this whole organization that I trust.

"Still haven't figured out who she is?" he asks, watching the tape over my shoulder. Her face is pixelated and impossible to make out, but it doesn't stop me from watching as though if I can just stare hard enough at the screen, the pixels will all slot into place and give me the answers I seek.

I slam the lid of the laptop closed with a thud. "No," I growl.

His eyebrow lifts at my sudden outburst of anger. I never get emotional. It's not that I don't ever let people *see* me emotional, but that I never actually *feel* emotions. Something my father takes great pride in—as if he engineered me to be this way. He says I'm broken in the best possible way. That it's a gift that will make me the most feared and powerful Don the Antonellis have ever seen. When I was a kid, I used to believe him. I'd shine under the glow of his praise, but as time went on, I started to see my inability to feel for what it really was—a curse.

I can count on one hand the number of times I've felt that spark that I think resembles feelings. Having never actually felt it for longer than a split-second, it's difficult to identify.

The first time was when I was five, and my father beat Lor to within an inch of his life when he caught the two of us playing together. We spent a lot of time together growing up, but even at a young age, he was being trained as my bodyguard, which meant our relationship should be nothing but professional. Even back then, I knew Lor mattered more to me than anyone else did, but it wasn't until that day, when I first felt that heat of anger and the sickening crush of fear, that I realized just how much he meant to me. The feeling was gone as quickly as it appeared, although it was there nonetheless.

The second time I felt it was in a dark, dingy alley. I'd just killed some traitor—I don't even remember his name or what he looked like. All I remember is looking into the bluest eyes I'd ever seen. That day I went against my instincts, against everything I'd been taught, and I let a witness go with nothing but a measly warning.

I still dream of those eyes at night. They worm their way unbidden into my subconscious and stare at me, so bright and open. They feel so real that sometimes I wake up thinking she must be in the room with me. I never let myself dwell on thoughts of her during the day. I can't afford for my father to see me distracted or to think I'm anything less than focused on the job, on our family, at all times. After all, the Antonellis are all that matter. Blood in, blood out. Not even in death can you separate yourself from the ties that bind you to the Family. As the only heir to the Antonelli empire, that is especially true of me.

Instead of stepping back from my anger like most people would, Lor moves toward me, a flicker of lust flaring to life in his eyes. "Well, I can think of one way to make you forget about her."

I quirk one of my own eyebrows in a challenge. One he readily rises to as he closes the distance between us with another large step. The move has his body brushing against me as his lips meet mine in a rough kiss. He pushes his tongue into my mouth, fighting for dominance, and I'm quick to bite his lower lip in chastisement. His hiss of pain goes straight to my dick, the increased blood flow making it swell in my pants.

As I lose myself to pleasure, the weight of my responsibilities falls away. I forget about my father's empire, soon to become mine. I forget about the list of names in my black book, marking a person's death. But most importantly, for half an hour, I can forget about the blue-eyed girl and the brunette vixen that haunt my dreams.

THE END

348

# Acknowledgements

A massive thank you to the amazing team I have around me for this series. Firstly to my PA/alpha reader/friend Nikki for everything she does keeping me on track, supporting me and building hype for every book. Not to mention the amazing covers and teasers she's created!

Another thank you to my other alpha, UK Nikki, and to the fantastic beta team I have for this series. I already know we're going to have a blast.

I have to thank Angie, my editor for her awesome editing and proofreading!

Lastly, thank you to all of you, the readers, for picking up this book and reading it. Without you none of this would be possible!!

# Also by R.A. Smyth

## Crescentwood Series

#1 Three Divisions

#2 Two Forces

#3 One Family

\*\*\*

## Pacific Prep

#1 Broken Trust

#2 Brutal Lies

#3 Beyond Vengeance

#4 Break Free

#4.5 Blurred Lines

\*\*\*

## Black Creek Series

#1 Rebels & Rejects

#2 Murder & Mayhem

#3 Damaged & Deadly

#4 Chaos & Carnage

# About the Author

R.A. Smyth is an author of dark romance. She lives in the UK with her husband, although they frequently talk about moving to live abroad (so who knows).

She has always been an avid reader, starting from the Harry Potter books as a kid. It's an interest that has grown into an obsession over the years and becoming an author has been a secret lifelong dream of hers.

When she's not writing, Rachel enjoys spending time with her family, drinking cups of tea (or glasses of wine or gin) with a good book and exploring the small island of Ireland with her family.